THE JAGUAR DANCES

*For Scoop & Leslie,
good friends and
Scoop is a great
carver.
Love,
Barbara Winther
Oct 10, 2013*

BARBARA WINTHER

BOOKS BY BARBARA WINTHER

Plays from Folktales of Africa and Asia
Plays from African Tales
Plays from Hispanic Tales
Plays from Asian Tales
They Like Noble Causes
Let It Go, Louie–Croatian Immigrants on Puget Sound

Copyright © 2010 Barbara Winther
All rights reserved.

ISBN: 1453710272
ISBN-13: 9781453710272

Cover design and maps by Richard Kinsman

*For Juan and Sonia,
Peruvian friends*

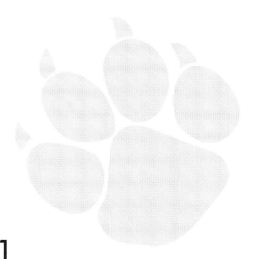

CHAPTER 1

They landed at Lima's airport under a gray-brown sky that turned late afternoon into night. When Jan stepped out onto the portable stairs, she felt the weight of hot, moist air. Beside the runway crouched a dark building, dots of lights shining from it like cats' eyes. She took a deep breath and pushed back her uneasiness. "Didn't expect such a gloomy sky," she called below to her friend.

"It'll get worse in a few months," Carrie replied over her shoulder. She jerked her suitcase down one step at a time, her collapsed luggage cart in the other hand, the yellow daypack bouncing on her back. "That's when the *garua* sets in."

"*Garua?*"

"Coastal fog, sometimes the color of gravy."

"Yuck."

At the bottom of the stairs, Carrie struggled to set up her cart. Jan reached down to help. She worried about her friend's exhausted appearance: shoulders slumped, deep circles under her eyes, face so pale it looked translucent. Had it been a mistake to take this flight from San Francisco only five days after Carrie's abortion? Carrie's father had insisted they go ahead as planned. *It will help with the healing process*, he had said. *Besides, I've already purchased the tickets.*

"Feeling okay?" Jan asked her.

"I'm fine," Carrie murmured. "Just lousy with mechanics." She yanked her cart towards the terminal as if it were a reluctant child.

Immigration was easy. In a small, stuffy room, the official stamped their passports with barely a look. Then he indicated the arrows on the floor that led to Customs. They entered an even warmer room and stood in a long line to process non-residents.

Five minutes later a door marked *Prohibida la Entrada* burst open. Through the doorway squeezed a heavy, middle-aged man with bulging jowls. From the breast pocket of his white linen suit, he pulled a red silk handkerchief, mopped his face and surveyed the crowd, his eyes darting from face to face. A sudden smile made his cheeks protrude into shiny balls. He wobbled forward and stopped in front of Carrie. "I do believe...you must be...*Señorita* Ross." His words shot out in breathless clusters, his English perfect. "You have your father's... golden hair." He stuffed the handkerchief back in his pocket and threw his arms apart. "Greetings!"

"Mr. Acosta?"

"*Sí, sí*. Call me Ignacio. Here I am...at your service."

"I appreciate your meeting us. This is my friend, Janet Fielding." To Jan she said, "Ignacio's an important man in Peru—owns fish fertilizer plants along the coast and a silver mine in the Andes. My father represents him in the U.S."

Ignacio bowed. "Welcome to Peru, both of you." He eyed Carrie's suitcase and Jan's duffel bag. "Any more luggage?"

"No," Carrie said, "this is it."

"Ah, light travelers. Wise. Follow me."

He edged forward with a polite nod for each person he passed. Smiling broadly, he spoke to the customs official who waved them through a vacant aisle on the other side of his desk.

"Don't we have to go through customs?" Jan asked.

"No, everyone here knows me," Ignacio replied, "and I vouched for your honesty." His breathing was more regular now, the smile imbedded on his face. "Come along," he commanded and led them through an empty neon-lighted passageway as if he were a mother duck guiding a brood across the freeway.

A guard stood at the far end. When Ignacio greeted him, he stepped aside. Beyond the doorway waited a group of black-haired men, holding up tour messages: *Rafael en Trujillo; AeroPeru; Coltour; Tengo reservado Señor Chavez.* Seeing Ignacio, they lowered their signs.

The main terminal was cooler, spacious and vacant except for an old woman with wispy hair who swept the floor. Remembering the packed San Francisco airport, Jan called out to Ignacio, "How come no travelers? Not even a ticket agent."

Ignacio kept on walking as if he hadn't heard her.

They exited the terminal through its main entry doors. Once again oppressive air hit them. Ignacio aimed for a black Toyota parked by the curb. Old and dented, the car was not the kind Jan had expected a wealthy tycoon to own. The rear doors and trunk were open, and a man in his late twenties, wearing a long-sleeved white shirt unbuttoned to the waist, smoked a cigarette and lounged against the rear fender.

Suddenly, Carrie grabbed Jan's arm.

Jan tore her eyes away from the man. "What's wrong?"

Carrie nodded at a group of soldiers. They held machine guns and continually panned their barrels across the sparsely filled parking lot, lingering on anyone in sight.

"My God!" breathed Jan. "Something terrible must have happened." She hadn't heard of problems in Peru. *Terrorists are in the past*, Carrie's father had assured them. A soldier caught her stare. With an icy look, he pointed the muzzle at her. She looked away, her skin prickling.

"Excuse me," she said to Ignacio, standing in front of him, making eye contact so he would have to answer. "How come the machine guns?"

His smile disappeared. With a dismissive wave of his arms, he said, "Nothing to worry about."

"Soldiers don't point weapons without a reason," she persisted.

As if bothered by a fly, he shook his head and then reinstituted his wide smile. "Ah, *Señoritas* Ross and Fielding, let me introduce my dear son, Luis."

Luis tossed his cigarette into the gutter and scrutinized each woman as if appraising her market value. A macho jerk, Jan concluded. She saw little resemblance between Luis and his father. All they had in common was straight, black hair. Ignacio looked Spanish, skin fair, body rotund, manner unduly polite, while Luis looked Indian, skin dark, body slim, cheekbones high and nose sharply angled. Arrogance showed in the tilt of his head and the way he wore his shirt pulled apart like a victory sign, revealing chest muscles that shone like polished koa wood. She watched him stow their luggage in the trunk, his movements surprisingly graceful, almost feline. A moment before climbing into the driver's seat, he glanced over the top of the car and smiled at her, an intimate smile that nearly stopped her breathing. She fumbled in her pocket for a tissue and dabbed the perspiration on the back of her neck.

"Come, come," Ignacio cried impatiently, ushering her into the back after Carrie. With a grunt, he squeezed into the front seat beside Luis. In a few minutes they were clear of the parking lot and driving swiftly along the wide road toward Lima.

In heavily accented English, Luis said to his father, "It is late. Tonight is my meeting. We may not get home in time."

"Then you must leave your meeting early." Ignacio turned his head to explain. "My dear *Señoritas*, at the moment, Lima has a curfew. You cannot travel on the streets after 10:00. Last week the curfew was 1:00 AM, but, well, that was not"—he briefly closed his eyes as if to find the correct words—"effective. It is earlier now."

Jan leaned forward. "Why a curfew?"

"Government regulations," Ignacio replied.

"Guerrilla activity," added Luis.

Ignacio glanced at Luis. "Explanations are not necessary."

Luis raised his chin and continued anyway, "A week ago rebels bombed a bank. Two days ago, a power station. Government troops, they now guard the streets."

Ignacio laughed, a series of wheezy sounds that ended with a blast on his handkerchief.

"Who are these rebels?" Jan pressed.

"*Campesinos*," Luis answered, "peasants from mountain areas, they want a better life. Educated *mestizos,* sons of *campesinos*, they try to—"

Ignacio interrupted in a loud voice, "Soon we reach the city's outskirts. *Señoritas*, please close your windows. At this time of year, children love to throw buckets of water and waste matter, a practice related to *Carnaval* which precedes Lent." He glanced back at them. "However, there will be no difficulty around your hotel. Downtown is well policed."

Luis shrugged and concentrated on the road.

A musky odor drifted back to Jan. It came from Luis. She guessed it was his hair oil or aftershave. Unusual smell, not unpleasant. Did Logan use stuff like that? She never had been close enough to her boss to know. He didn't seem the kind who would, though.

On the left side of the road loomed a hill covered with geometric designs. At first she believed it to be an art display, a giant mosaic. Then she noticed lights, flickering like glowworms in dark holes. As they drove closer, she realized the hill was covered with buildings made of tin and cardboard. Vague shapes moved about. People? "On that hill," she called to the front seat, "are those houses?"

Luis started to answer but Ignacio touched his arm and cleared his throat.

Carrie said, "When I lived with my parents in Lima, I don't think anything was up there. But then that was ten years ago."

"Even if all was there," Luis burst out, "your family, they would not see it. The rich do not see how the poor live."

Ignacio blew his nose hard.

Carrie blinked at the hill and rubbed her eyes. "Must be awful to live that way."

"*Sí*, awful," Luis forged on. "Always, they search for their next meal."

Again Ignacio touched his arm.

With a sigh, Luis turned on the radio. Jazz blared from two overhead speakers, the bass thumping like a giant heartbeat. Ignacio turned the level down. Luis speeded up and passed a truck loaded with cages of squawking chickens.

Jan tried to still a quiver in her stomach, tried to ignore her unsettled thoughts: bombings, curfews, uprisings, soldiers pointing guns, people living in hovels. She smoothed her long dark hair behind her ears and sat bolt upright. Everything seemed foreboding.

CHAPTER 2

The gray-suited hotel clerk studied Jan's passport. "*Buenas noches, Señorita Fielding.* A fax is here for you." He pulled an envelope from one of the many boxes lining the back wall, at the same time signaling a porter, who hurried outside to retrieve their luggage from the car.

Perplexed, Jan tore open the envelope and read the message.

"Bad news?" inquired Ignacio.

She shook her head. To Carrie she said, "Logan settled the Dowsky case. I don't remember mentioning this hotel to him. Must have." She slid the message back into the envelope. Running a finger gently over the torn edge, she felt a sudden longing to see Logan, to sit at her computer in the law office of McCloskey, Warner and Jarvis and push reliable keys.

"Is this Logan fellow your boyfriend?" inquired Ignacio.

"No, my boss," she answered quickly. "I'm Mr. McCloskey's secretary." She slipped the fax into a pocket of her denim vest and then extended her right hand. "*Gracias,* Mr. Acosta. Nice meeting you."

He clasped her hand between both of his. "You are most welcome, but I am not leaving."

Jan pulled away.

Ignacio gestured toward the glass doors. "See, my son has driven off to his meeting. I must wait for his return." His fat cheeks rose to punctuate his smile, and his eyes flickered about the empty lobby. With birdlike twists of his neck he checked the desk clerk, the porter who waited with the two suitcases and the switchboard operator before focusing on Jan.

"At night," he continued, "Luis is my chauffeur. It is our time to be together." He turned to the desk clerk. "Take good care of these lovely *señoritas*. The hotel owner is my good friend. If there are problems, he would be most unhappy."

"*Sí, Señor.*" The clerk pulled a yellow-tagged key from the maze of wall boxes and slid forward two registration cards and two pens. "*Por favor, señoritas.*"

Jan filled out the form, aware of Ignacio hovering over her. "Am I doing it correctly?" she asked in a cool voice.

"*Sí, sí.*" He stepped back and gazed up at the line of silver-rimmed ceiling lights as if they needed counting.

The switchboard buzzed like an angry wasp. A tall, blonde gentleman with a goatee sauntered into the hotel and sat down on one of the red velveteen couches. Jan returned to her writing. She was glad the form didn't ask for the name of a relative to contact. She preferred to forget about her parents, especially her mother. Hard to do whenever she looked in the mirror.

She turned to Ignacio. "Does Luis look like your wife?"

His smile disappeared. "Why do you ask?"

She realized she couldn't say, *Because I look like my mother*; it would make no sense to him. "Well, he doesn't look like you," she answered and handed her completed form to the desk clerk.

Ignacio continued to inspect the lobby. "This is not the time to discuss heritage." His voice was overly polite, his smile so wide that crinkles nearly hid his eyes. Abruptly he said to Carrie, "*Señorita Ross*, please, complete your registration." He gestured at the glass door entrance. "A German tour group is arriving. Soon their leader will take over the desk."

"Sorry," murmured Carrie, concentrating again on the form.

Ignacio whipped out his handkerchief and wiped his face. To the porter he said, "Deposit the *señoritas* luggage in room 927. *Ahora, en seguida.*" To Jan and Carrie, "Tip no one at the hotel. I took care of it all."

Ten tour members surged into the lobby, all talking at once. Their leader commandeered the front desk. The clerk shot keys to him in rapid succession. Through the entry doors another porter appeared, nearly hidden by a mountain of luggage on the cart.

Ignacio drew Jan and Carrie away from the turmoil. "Put away your room key," he insisted. "Never display it. No telling who might grab it and run away."

Jan shoved the key into a vest pocket and zipped it up.

"While I wait for Luis," Ignacio continued, "I shall buy you *señoritas* a nightcap." As if about to perform a magic trick, he waved his handkerchief toward an inner doorway. "The lounge is over there." Stuffing his handkerchief into his breast pocket, he grasped Carrie's elbow and moved her forward.

Jan wasn't interested in a drink but didn't think Carrie should be alone in a bar with this weirdo. The way he peered around, nosy on her registration card, phony with his smiles, waving his arms about. His whole demeanor made her nervous. Just because he was a business associate of Carrie's father didn't mean he could be trusted. In fact, that relationship was a minus. Only once, at Carrie's insistence, had she gone to dinner at the Ross mansion in Pacific Heights, enough to realize Carrie's father ruled over everything and everyone within his grasp.

Jan followed Ignacio and Carrie through the doorway. The dimly lit lounge reminded her of an overgrown forest: walls padded with moss-green leather that matched velvet chairs, the same green on the ceiling and carpet. Recessed lighting gleamed on crossed swords, old Spanish helmets and body armor that decorated the walls. Shadowy couples deep in conversation huddled around small tables. Jan surmised most were lovers, hands intertwined, faces close. One pair cast furtive glances at the doorway as if afraid of being discovered.

Ignacio located an empty table and sank heavily into a chair. "I recommend a Pisco Sour," he said as Jan and Carrie sat opposite him. "It is a popular drink in Peru, made of white grape brandy with egg white. They make a fine one here. Of course, if you ladies would rather have another kind of drink...."

"Whatever you recommend," Jan said and Carrie nodded.

Ignacio snapped his fingers at the waiter and ordered three Pisco Sours.

"Now," Ignacio said, "tomorrow morning Luis picks you up at 10:00. First he takes you to the *Museo de Oro* to view the gold artifacts. Then, on to Pizarro's monument and other sights in Lima. The following day, Sunday, you should rest around the hotel pool and read guidebooks. The Sky Room on the 21st floor has an excellent buffet. Should you wish to see more of Lima, leave word at my villa. I will be out of town, but Luis is on call at all times to assist you." He swept his hands outward as if concluding the movement of a symphony.

Inwardly, Jan groaned at his agenda, but said nothing.

"Monday," Ignacio plunged on, "Luis will drive you down the southern coast to Paracas. From there, he takes you inland to Ica, where the resort of *Las Dunas* is located. I understand you contacted a travel agent and made reservations there for two nights."

Jan wondered how he knew that.

Three whitish drinks appeared on the table. Ignacio signed the tab.

"After *Las Dunas*," he continued, "Luis drives you back to Lima Airport. Then, he flies with you to Arequipa, where you stay at that hotel you booked by the river. Luis also travels with you by train to Lake Titicaca and onward to Cuzco. When the three of you return to Lima, I shall meet your plane and bring you to my villa for a farewell feast with my wife and two daughters."

Jan had to speak up. "Surely Luis has more important things to do then shepherd two women around the country. We hadn't counted on traveling as a threesome. Another thing, although Mr. Ross reserved this Lima hotel, how did you learn about the reservations I made?"

Ignacio's chuckle sounded more like a wheeze. "Oh, come, come, *Señorita Fielding*, two women alone in a strange country should be cared for properly. Mr. Ross knows this. He felt it necessary to discover your itinerary. In his business he must know what people around him will do. And his business is my business."

"But, we might want to go other places. Our itinerary isn't etched in—"

Ignacio raised his arms to stop her. "*Señorita Fielding*, Luis works for me in various capacities. His job now is to guide you everywhere. At this time it is prudent for foreigners to be accompanied by a Peruvian. Traveling in recent days has become, well, a bit difficult."

Jan raised her chin. "You don't seem to want to talk about that. Carrie and I came to Peru to enjoy a peaceful vacation. Perhaps we've come at the wrong time."

Ignacio's shoulders tensed, his eyes widened. "Not at all. Peru is no more dangerous than any foreign country. Thievery is common the world over." His smile slowly returned. His shoulders relaxed, and he sipped his drink. "Naturally," he continued, "you must be careful in crowded streets and markets. Especially keep an eye out in train stations. However, with Luis along"—he tossed his hands as if clearing the way for them—"you will have no problem. No problem at all."

He eyed them over the rim of the glass. Setting his drink down, he patted his fat lips with a cocktail napkin. "Our country contains marvelous sights." His eyes flitted from Carrie to Jan and back again. "*Señoritas*, you have not tasted your drinks. Come, now, is this any way to greet Peru?"

CHAPTER 3

The elevator stopped on the ninth floor. Crown-shaped chandeliers lit the wide, deserted hallway. Against the wall stood a gilt table that held a basket of red flowers, and above it a large painting of a Spanish explorer—Cortez, Jan thought. According to a placard, their room was to the right.

A door marked *Salida* shot open. Thoughts of terrorists leapt into her mind. She flattened against the wall, pulling Carrie back with her. In the doorway stood a thin man in a dark suit, a stairway behind him. He entered the hallway and closed the door. As he strode past, she noticed *Seguridad* embroidered on his pocket. He nodded curtly and then disappeared around the corner.

Relieved, Jan hurried down the hall, checking room numbers. "It appears we'll be surrounded by guards and soldiers everyplace," she whispered. "Our travel agent didn't mention problems in Peru. Maybe she didn't know."

Carrie shrugged. "Apparently my father didn't know either. A good thing Luis'll be with us."

"Well, I don't think it's a good thing. He's…he's arrogant."

"Arrogant? Ah, come on. He's fascinating. Sexy. Magnetic."

Jan rolled her eyes. "Haven't you had enough of that?"

"He isn't at all like Paul."

"I bet he's just as harmful."

Jan located room 927, unlocked the door and pushed it open. Carrie walked in while Jan glanced around the hall to make certain nobody watched them enter.

A crash. A muffled scream. The sounds came from inside the room. Jan fumbled for the wall light switch. Carrie lay sprawled on the floor.

"Are you hurt?" Jan asked, helping her up.

"No, no. The porter left my cart in the middle...." Carrie's voice faded out as she glanced around the room. Her open suitcase lay on the end of one of the two beds, her clothes strewn about the carpet.

"My God!" exclaimed Jan. "We've been robbed, don't touch a thing." She scrutinized Carrie's suitcase. "Look"—she pointed—"somebody slit the lining."

"It's a brand new case," Carrie said. "My father bought it for me."

Jan examined the room. Her duffel bag rested on a wrought iron bench by the bathroom, the closed padlock still attached to the zipper. "Only your suitcase was torn apart, nothing else disturbed." She hurried to check the bedroom window. Locked. Besides, they were nine floors up and no ledge outside. She peered into the bathroom. No window. Realizing the burglar must have entered by the door, she rushed over to examine the lock. No pry marks. Anyway, with a guard patrolling the hall, a burglar wouldn't take time to break open a door or pick a lock. Whoever came in must've had a key. The phone was on a leather-covered bedside table. She yanked up the receiver and dialed the number marked *Escritorio*.

"*Sí, aló*," answered a male voice.

"This is room 927. Somebody broke into our room and tore apart a suitcase."

"How unfortunate! Have you made a list of stolen items?"

"No. We just got here."

"When do you believe this happened?"

"While we were having a drink in the lounge. Not sure when the porter brought our luggage up, certainly not more than half an hour ago."

"Do not worry, *Señorita*. The manager will come at once."

"*Gracias*." Jan hung up the receiver and stared at the devastation.

Carrie leaned against the closet door, her face white.

"The manager's coming," said Jan. She perched on the side of one of the beds. "Carrie, without touching anything, can you tell what's missing?"

"Nothing," Carrie replied without looking.

"A good thing you carried your money and airplane tickets in your pack. Maybe the burglar was hunting for those."

Carrie rubbed her cheeks in a nervous gesture. She slipped off her daypack, her hands shaking.

Jan watched her for a minute, noting how Carrie refused to go near her suitcase. "Carrie, did you hide something in your lining?"

"No," Carrie snapped. She went into the bathroom and turned on the sink faucet.

Jan heard her tossing water on her face. "You're acting kind of funny," she called to her.

Carrie came out of the bathroom, wiping her face on a towel. "Just shook up from my fall."

"Of course." Jan regretted her questioning. "A bad way to start a two-week vacation."

"Let's just forget it," Carrie said, tossing her towel on the bed.

"Forget it? Someone broke into our room and tore apart your suitcase. That's criminal."

"I don't want to dwell on any more difficulties. I've had enough." Carrie's voice broke on the last word. She returned to the bathroom and shut the door behind her.

Jan bit the corner of her lip. "Are you sure you're okay?" she called.

"Fine, fine," came the muffled voice.

"Take it easy, relax. I'll handle everything."

No answer.

Jan rose and studied the suitcase. She sniffed, thinking she smelled a faint, musky odor. Was it common in this part of the world? Could it be from him? She sniffed again. The smell was gone, probably never there, only in her imagination. Even if he didn't go to his meeting, why would he break in and search Carrie's suitcase?

Why would anyone?

CHAPTER 4

"Luis is ten minutes late," Jan said the next morning as they sat in the overstuffed chairs near the front desk, waiting.

Carrie shrugged and rubbed her eyes, the skin beneath them puffy.

The only other people in the lobby besides hotel staff were an elderly couple and the man with the goatee Jan remembered seeing last night. They stood conversing near the elevators; she didn't recognize the language—Dutch perhaps. She looked at Carrie, slumped over. "Would you rather go back to the room and rest?" Jan asked her. "We don't have to do anything today."

"No," Carrie replied, sounding annoyed. "I keep telling you I'm fine."

If she's so fine, Jan mused, why did she eat only half a piece of toast for breakfast? And why does she look so weary and dejected? The suitcase ordeal must have affected her more than she'll admit.

The hotel staff had offered little help last night, more interested in checking for furniture scratches. This morning, the day manager was unavailable. She wished Logan was here. With his bulldog determination, he wouldn't stop until he got to the bottom of this.

"Okay," she said, rising, "it's up to me."

Carrie sat up. "What're you going to do?"

"Find out about the burglary."

"Leave it alone. You won't find out anything."

"We'll see." Jan strode to the front desk and plunked the room key on the counter in front of the clerk. She watched him, a different person from last night, pick up the key, swivel and slide it into the correct box out of the hundreds behind him—golden brown cubicles, half full of yellow-tagged black keys like bees in a honeycomb. It amazed her the way the clerk could so quickly deposit the key.

He looked forward again. Straightening his red-striped tie, he issued the flat smile worn by hotel employees. "May I help you?" he inquired, his English soft and smooth.

"Yes. How many keys exist to our room?"

"Two. Both are available for you. Would you like another one?"

"Who else has access to room keys?"

"I beg your pardon."

"The maids, the people who clean the rooms, how do they get into the rooms?"

The clerk stiffened as if an alarm had sounded. "They carry house keys. What is your purpose for inquiring?"

"Last night, while we had a drink in the lounge and your security guard patrolled the halls, someone entered our room, number 927."

Shooting a look at the elderly couple, who stood by the cashier's booth, the clerk said quietly, "Ah, yes, authorities are investigating your difficulty." He spread his hands to signal an end to the conversation. He straightened the brochures in the wire rack on the wall to his right.

Determined not to be cut off, Jan raised her voice. "I wish to discuss our 'difficulty.' I spoke with the security guard on our floor. He claims nobody but the porter got off the elevator last night between 8:30 and 9:00. The head of housekeeping insisted all maids were out of the hotel by 7:00. However, between 8:30 and 9:00, somebody unlocked our door, entered our room and tore apart my friend's suitcase. I went over this with the night manager, who did little except apologize. Since the day manager is unavailable, I'm asking you for information."

While she waited for her words to sink in, she noticed the switchboard blinked, unattended. The cashier must be listening too, for she gazed at a stack of money with the look of a woman who had lost count. The elderly couple also appeared interested, the neck of the white-haired gentleman extending like a pelican ready to pounce on a fish. She was glad to see some people around here were concerned.

Carrie came up beside her and gestured at the glass entry. "Luis is here."

"I'll be right there." Jan leaned toward the desk clerk. "I have questions. Was the porter who carried our bags to the room interrogated? What happens to house keys after the maids leave? How vigilant are security guards? Are your hotel employees trustworthy? Were the police notified? How can you keep an eye on all those room keys behind you?"

Carrie said, "I'll wait outside." She hurried away.

Jan stared hard at the clerk. His eyes had lost their clarity, a defensive film in place. He drew himself up to a larger height and spoke in a clipped manner, focused at a point beyond her. "*Señorita,* in my nine years of duty with this hotel I have learned how to keep a watch on all keys at all times." He adjusted his tie. "I can assure you *El Castaño* is a first-class hotel. Only the most experienced and trustworthy people are hired. No employee of this hotel would ever be involved in a burglary. I can only suppose it was a street person who managed to slip past the guard."

His flat smile returned. When he spoke again, his voice had settled into its former groove. "I trust nothing of value was stolen. We do our best to protect our guests. However, this notice"—he indicated the printed card installed under the glass counter top—"explains the wisdom of placing valuables in our safe. Unfortunately, if an outsider wishes to enter a room badly enough, he will find a way to do so. As to why the police were not called, that is not in my domain."

He fired a few Spanish words at the phone operator, a few more at the cashier. Both resumed work. With a tone of deep concern, he said, "I am terribly sorry, *Señorita.* Something certainly will be done for you."

Still not wanting to let it go, Jan announced, "My good friend, Mr. Acosta, knows the hotel owner well." She adjusted a comb on the side of her hair, pulling in a stray strand. "Should he call while we are gone, please tell him we'd like to discuss last night's burglary and the way hotel management treated our situation."

The clerk nervously adjusted the linen handkerchief in his breast pocket. "*Sí.*"

Carrie was right, Jan realized. No information gained from the clerk. As she walked toward the entrance, Jan considered the options: somebody stole a key, was given a key, or had a key. That person slipped past the guard, unless the guard had the key, which seemed unlikely for a security man. If the porter was the one who tore apart the suitcase, surely he would not have returned to the lobby, where she remembered seeing him when they exited the lounge. Most likely, the burglar came from the street and, given the short time span, he must have known exactly where to go and what he wanted.

At the airport Ignacio had not allowed their luggage to go through customs. At the hotel, he had steered Jan and Carrie into the lounge instead of letting them go to their room with their luggage. Was Ignacio behind the break-in? Most troubling, had Carrie or her father hidden something in the suitcase lining, something valuable? Why didn't Carrie want to pursue the investigation? Did she know who the burglar was?

Through the glass doors, Jan saw Carrie talking to Luis and felt a twinge of regret. Her confrontation with the clerk had driven Carrie out the door. What a lousy way to start a vacation! I should stop acting like a mother hen. It wasn't my bag torn apart. If Carrie wants to drop the matter, I should drop it, too.

The moment she pushed open the glass door, staccato blasts shattered the air. Dust shot in all directions. Her eyes burned. She grasped the door in defense.

Two men inside a roped area along the circular driveway operated a jackhammer aimed into the sidewalk, removing chunks of cracked cement, damage apparently from the roots of a nearby chestnut tree. She hurried toward the Toyota, shielding her face from the debris. Carrie sat in the back seat, her blonde hair visible through the back window. Luis, smoking a cigarette, lounged against the car. Same pose as at the airport. He could be wearing the same white shirt. Did he leave it unbuttoned to the waist because he was hot, or did he like to reveal his muscular, hairless chest?

He grinned as if he enjoyed her confusion. Above the jackhammer noise he shouted, "We leave at once. Your face, my shirt, they get dirty here." He tossed his cigarette into the street and surveyed her through lowered eyes. Everything about him seemed to say, *I know what you're thinking about me.* He opened the rear door and waved her in with a sweep of a hand. She fell into a heap beside Carrie, who looked cool and serene.

With the car door shut, the jackhammer lowered to a snarling growl. Luis ambled around to the driver's side, opened the door, and smoothly slipped inside. Jan wrinkled her nose as a whiff of that shaving lotion, or whatever it was, floated past Jan's nose. Luis switched on the air conditioner and shoved a tape into the deck. As he pulled away from the curb, flute music wailed through the overhead speakers.

Carrie whispered into Jan's left ear, "I asked Luis to take us to the *Museo de Antropologia,* not the *Museo de Oro.*"

"What's the difference?" Jan shouted. She wished the music weren't so loud, wished Luis were another person, anyone else.

Continuing to whisper in her ear, Carrie said, "I told Luis I was more interested in pottery from Pre-Inca civilizations. He suggested we go to the anthropology museum. Is that okay with you?"

"Sure." Jan leaned forward and yelled, "Luis, it's too loud."

The flute continued to cry up the scale until it sounded like a woman's scream. Jan batted him on the shoulder. "Turn that damned music down!"

"The flute," he shouted back, "it is the voice of my country." He burst into laughter. Speeding up, he darted with ease between a bus and a car and around a panel truck that advertised Inca Cola, a hand holding a bottle of golden liquid, ¡*De Sabor Nacional!* Sidewalk faces flashed past—brown, white, black, none smiling.

"Too loud," she cried. "Slow down."

Carrie said nothing. Hands folded, legs arched over her daypack on the floor, eyes closed, she seemed to be listening to a heavenly choir.

Jan gritted her teeth. She pressed her hands over her ears and glared at the back of Luis' head, determined to block out those hellish Peruvian flutes.

CHAPTER 5

The museum collection was housed in a massive stone building built around a central patio, open to the sky, and bare of planting. It was fringed by a colonnaded walkway where numerous dark doors opened. Shafts of light escaped the rooms as people moved in and out. Footsteps echoed against tiled floors like water dripping in a deep cave.

Jan waited with Carrie behind another couple at the ticket booth. From the corner of her eye, she watched Luis conversing with a museum guard. As Luis tilted his head upwards, the overhead light shone on his face and chest, accentuating his smooth brown color and polished skin. His arms arched gracefully when he spoke. The white shirt, cut full, seemed to emphasize his slim hips. To gaze at him was not what she wanted to do, yet she couldn't help it. "Luis," she called, her mouth dry, "do we buy you a ticket?"

He approached her. "No ticket is necessary for me. Often I come here. I give tours to students, so I get in free." He smiled in his knowing way. "I am what you call a fountain of knowledge."

She hadn't considered him an expert in archaeology. Even more surprising was his statement about giving tours to students. What else does this Don Juan do? Break into hotel rooms?

Her plan had been to hurl an accusation when she met him this morning. Force an explanation. But the business with the hotel clerk had held her up, the jackhammer had interfered with her concentration and the flute music had wailed all the way to the museum. She thought of questioning him now, but Carrie appeared to be enjoying herself and Jan didn't want to change her friend's outlook.

Besides, it was hard to imagine Luis a thief. He didn't seem the sort to park his car out of sight, creep up nine flights of stairs, sneak down a hall, open a door with a stolen key, slip inside and rip apart a suitcase. Rather she imagined him announcing his intentions and taking anything he wanted whether you wished him to have it or not.

Carrie said, "Luis, will you give us a tour?" She sounded eager.

His heavy eyebrows shot up. "You think it necessary?"

She nodded. "I love Pre-Columbian pottery. When I taught school, I used their designs in art lessons. I'd especially like to learn more about *Moche* pottery. Some of their ceramics are masterpieces."

"*Sí, magnifico!* I have favorites." He chuckled as if remembering a good joke. "It is best if you ask me the questions."

"Okay. That's what I'll do." Color came to Carrie's cheeks as she smiled at him.

Although glad to see her friend happy again, Jan didn't like Luis being the cause. He might not be a thief, but he certainly knew how to operate around women. Because of another sexy operator, Carrie had lost her teaching job at the Catholic school. Paul got her pregnant, forced her to have an abortion and then abandoned her. Getting involved with another guy like that could only bring on more heartbreak.

In the first room Luis stayed behind, near the door, while Jan and Carrie peered into case after case, moving rapidly over the earliest coastal cultures. In the next room, a larger, colder one, they slowed down at an exhibit of pottery. Carrie bent close to the glass case, concentrating on each piece, her eyes sparkling with excitement. Jan, too, was intrigued. Luis came up between them, and Jan was acutely conscious of his closeness and the musky smell that seemed to radiate from his skin.

The glass case contained smoothly finished jars and bottles in buff and ocher-red colors, most molded into human shapes. Each container had a hollow handle that rose into a long pouring spout. It struck Jan that many of the items in the case were erotic, a few more subtle than others. Those clustered at one end really held her attention. One was a cheerful man with a large penis that curved into the pouring spout. Another was a couple engaged in oral sex. She couldn't believe what she was seeing. Were they supposed to be jokes? *Moche,* said the case label.

She glanced at Luis. His eyes glinted with amusement. Carrie giggled.

Jan quickly moved on to the next case. It held additional pottery pieces labeled *Moche,* each a hollow, cup-shaped figure. She felt more at ease, staring at a group of finely sculpted heads. Much smaller than human size, the individualized faces looked real enough to speak. Also in the case were ceramic sea and land animals. A crab raised a claw as if to fight off an intruder; a pair of monkeys wearing ear ornaments crouched on a tree limb. At one end of the case were effigies of priests, kneeling or seated, and warriors ready for battle. The face of one kneeling warrior reflected the horror of approaching death.

A card in the center of the case gave information in Spanish, simple enough for Jan to translate. She read that the *Moche* culture once inhabited river valleys of the coastal desert more than a thousand years before the Inca Empire. Behind her, on the wall, a map designated an area to the north, around present day Trujillo. So perfectly had the pottery been created, so artistically formed, she found it difficult to believe the pieces were ancient. Shapes, figures, expressions on faces, everything except the clothing, looked modern.

Carrie and Luis moved ahead, stopping in front of another case. Jan caught up, curious about the object of their concentration. It was a globular jar with a stirrup handle that rose into a central spout. The beige-colored surface was covered with intricate, fine-line designs drawn in reddish brown—weird creatures, some part human. In one part of the scene, a spotted animal with fangs hunched over a wild-eyed human. Other humans waited in line. All looked terrified.

"Is that a jaguar?" Carrie asked, pointing to the feline creature.

"A supernatural cat," explained Luis. "The scene here, it depicts a sacrifice. This is called a *Presentation Theme*." His voice took on a studied, professional tone. "These figures, often they stand together on fine-line *Moche* pieces. It is believed they represent a cult ceremony, one that"—he paused, searching for a word—"evolved from the earlier *Chavin* culture. In times of *Chavin*, the people, they had a cat god, a creature with long fangs. The cat on *Moche* pieces, it is more realistic. These figures, see them here, they bring *copas*—what you call them—ah goblets. They bring goblets and other gifts to this god." He pointed to a large figure with rays shooting from all sides. "It is believed to be the sun."

Carrie nodded. "What's in the goblets?"

"Blood. The cat you see there, it draws blood from its naked captive. These figures down here, they are captives. See, hands tied. Blood is drawn from the neck of this one. The others wait to die. This priest is giving the blood to the god. Over here, much feasting, singing and dancing. They celebrate the success of the ceremony."

Jan broke in. "I like the molded figures better." She hurriedly added, "I mean the ones in the last case—the monkeys, the crab, the kneeling warrior—that sort. I don't like the scene on this pot. It's barbaric."

Luis looked at her through lowered eyes. "In the Christian religion, we break bread and drink wine. That stands for the body and blood of Christ. Do you consider that barbaric?"

"Yes, I do."

He gestured at the pot. "Then, this *Presentation Theme*, it is hard for you to understand."

Jan shook her head. "I understand it. I don't like what it symbolizes."

"Symbolizes?" He frowned. "What do you mean?"

"The importance of sacrifice. Killing people for a belief. The priest, the god, the jaguar—they are in control. Other people must must die in their foolish, unjust ceremony."

Luis raised his chin. "You know when a belief is foolish and unjust? You have this wisdom?"

"I don't claim wisdom. I feel for the people caught. Those frightened captives have nothing to say about their lives." She folded her arms around her body. The room was freezing.

"Sometimes sacrifice is necessary," Luis said.

"Human sacrifice? Never!"

Noticing Carrie's disturbed look, Jan stepped away. Let them talk about the pottery without me, she decided.

Luis said, "I am sorry if my explanation upsets you."

"That's not what upsets me," said Jan. "It's the religious scene that bothers me."

"Perhaps I did not describe it well. My words, are they clear?"

She spun around. "Quite clear, Luis. Perhaps you wouldn't mind giving me another explanation. About your meeting last night."

He frowned. "It was not a religious one."

"Did you even go to a meeting?"

"*Sí.*" He moved closer to her and spoke in a tight voice. "*Señorita* Fielding, although it is not your business, I shall tell you about my meeting. It concerned the attempt to obtain water for a community of poor people outside Lima. Not only have they no water, they have no sewage treatment. Mounds of garbage grow higher every day. Children and flies, they play together. It is one of the many ugly places in Peru where people try to live."

"Terrible," murmured Carrie.

"Why did you go to the meeting?" Jan persisted.

"I have a friend who lives there. I care what happens to him, to all of them."

"Luis, please," said Carrie, her voice trembling.

"Last night," Jan continued, unable to restrain herself, "someone broke into our room."

He raised his eyebrows in mock concern. "A burglar?"

"Yes, a burglar!" she exclaimed, her voice resounding.

The two women at the next case glared at Jan as if she were a naughty child.

"Someone," Jan continued, undaunted, "tore open Carrie's suitcase, threw her clothes all over the place and slit the case lining."

"Interesting," said Luis with no change of expression. "You think I might be the burglar?"

"I've considered it."

"If it was me, what then?"

"I would want to know why you did it."

"If it had been me," he snapped, "I would not tell you why."

Carrie cried, "Please, let's enjoy the museum."

The door flew open. A guard entered.

Luis waved to him. "*No problema.*"

Carrie tugged at Luis's arm until he returned to the case, where she spoke to him in Spanish, asking questions about different pieces of pottery. He answered in Spanish. They huddled over the case, soon deep in discussion.

Had Carrie switched from English to Spanish to please Luis? Right now Jan didn't care to look at *Presentation Theme* pots or obscene pots or any kind of pots. She was disgusted with Carrie's peace-at-all-costs reaction. Luis was no better than Paul. Why couldn't Carrie see that?

The room was airless and cold. She grew increasingly claustrophobic, feeling locked underground, dragged under water, afraid she might faint. She charged past the two women spectators, who shot against the wall map as if pulled back by a magnet. "Excuse me," Jan gasped and burst out the door and across the colonnaded walkway.

In the center of the patio she took deep breaths, grateful to be outside. The school pageant flashed into her mind. She was eight. Over her pink tights she wore a red skirt made of layers of crepe paper cut like petals, edges crimped over a pencil. "Don't sit down," her mother ordered, "or you'll ruin your costume."

For an hour she waited in the wings like a mannequin. At last, her cue. Out she walked onto the brilliantly lit stage. "I am the American Beauty Rose", she shouted at the audience. "I represent the United States of America. From a tiny bud, my petals open—" At that point she fainted.

She woke up in the nurse's office, smelling salts under her nose. Mother and little sister, Beth, stood beside the table, looking at her as if she were a specimen.

"You were beautiful," piped Beth. But Mother brushed imaginary dirt from her gloves and said, "A good thing your father wasn't there." Beth spoke up, "Daddy doesn't like us anyway." "Hush," said Mother. "Janet, drop your costume in the garbage can behind the gym."

Slowly Jan walked toward the next gallery and waited for Luis and Carrie. When they came, she apologized for bolting and explained she had suffered a dizzy spell and needed fresh air. During the rest of the time at the museum, she made a supreme effort to wipe all thoughts from her mind. Silently, she followed the two as they moved from room to room, case to case, object to object.

CHAPTER 6

Monday morning, 8:00. Again Jan and Carrie waited in the lobby for Luis to arrive. Jan sat on a bench, duffel bag wedged between her feet. After counting the number of silver-rimmed ceiling lights—fifteen—like full moons on a time exposure, she couldn't think of anything else to do. She didn't feel like talking to anybody. Waiting always bothered her. Carrie stood nearby, holding onto the handle of her luggage cart as if ready to break into a tap dance. She looked rested, back to the Carrie before Paul had clouded her picture.

A flock of German tourists poured out of the breakfast room, the gentleman with the goatee among them. They spread across the lobby like geese taking over a lake.

Luis appeared at the hotel entrance. With cat-like precision, he eased through the crowd and grasped Jan's duffel bag in one hand and Carrie's cart in the other. Indicating with a nod that they should follow, he deftly ribboned back through the hotel lobby to the street.

The sky was gray tipped with brown, as it had been every day since their arrival. Even though the sun refused to come out, it pumped heat into the city. Already, today was hotter than yesterday. From the street beyond the driveway, traffic rattled and growled, squealed and honked. To Jan's relief, the jackhammers were gone but the sidewalk repair, roped off to protect fresh cement, looked disturbingly like a gravesite. Perhaps it held remnants of a tour leader whose group never made it to Machu Picchu, she thought in an attempt at humor. She was glad to be leaving crowded, noisy Lima with its disgruntled tourists, stifling, haze-filled air and frequent reminders of the dead.

Drawn up to the curb was the black Toyota, front and back doors open. Luis piled the luggage and Carrie's cart into the front passenger side. Jan wondered if the reason he hadn't used the trunk was to make certain nobody sat beside him. She climbed into the back seat, Carrie following. With a flourish, Luis slammed the doors and climbed in behind the wheel. The car sputtered to life.

They were to drive south for 303 kilometers, first along the coast, through the towns of Pisco and Paracas, and then inland past fields of cotton, sugarcane and grapes, watered by the Ica River that flowed down from the Andes. Their destination was the resort of *Las Dunas.*

Feeling uncomfortable in the heat, Jan removed the tortoise shell combs that held her hair back, wound her hair on top of her head and shoved in the combs. She caught Luis looking at her in the rearview mirror but pretended not to notice. Immediately, the air conditioner hissed on.

Saturday, after the visit to the museum, she had pinned her hair up in the same manner. That, too, had brought on his stare, an appraisal, as if she were an object up for auction.

Leaning forward, she said, "Luis, I don't mind if you play flute music. The other day I was overtired." He nodded but didn't play the CD.

They drove in silence through heavy Lima traffic. She could see little difference between this and any American city. Cement streets, large, flat-roofed buildings, crowds, modern clothes, cars, lights, exhaust fumes, skyscrapers. What announced South America were the signs in Spanish and the circular plazas that now and then separated the streets. A statue of a national hero commanded each plaza. Often across from it, a church.

An arrow pointed to the Pan-American Highway. Moments later, Lima was gone as if a shade pulled. Luis cracked a window and tested the weather with a hand. He turned off the air conditioner and pushed in a CD—flute music, softer than yesterday, sadder. Rolling the window down further, he called back, "The air, is it good for you?"

"It's great, I love it," Carrie replied, her blonde hair streaming in the wind.

Luis glanced over his shoulder at Jan. "For you?"

"It's okay."

After the museum tour on Saturday, during lunch at the hotel, Luis had asked her what she thought of him as a guide. "I don't think about you," she had shot back. For a moment he stared at her in his intimate way, then cleared his throat and explained how the afternoon could be spent. He could take them to Pizarro's tomb in the *Catedral de Lima*. Or to a fabric shop that sold fine Pima cotton printed with Pre-Columbian designs. Or to the *Museo de Oro*. "The gold objects there are quite beautiful," he said.

Carrie, her face shining, announced she wanted to visit all three. She informed Luis he was not only an excellent guide but a wonderful companion. Miraculously, she didn't look at all tired. Jan tried to join in the spirit of exploration, except when Carrie and Luis knelt to pray at the *Catedral de Lima*. Although she respected their religious beliefs, she couldn't share them. Pretending fascination with a painting, she stood in the aisle, feeling abandoned.

The three concluded the tour with *ceviche*, bread, and tall glasses of Cristal Beer in the patio of the *1900 Restaurant*. During the day, Carrie had shown increasing interest in Luis, taking his arm whenever they crossed the street, riding in the front seat beside him, conversing with him in Spanish, concentrating on his words as if they were precious gems.

When it was time to return to the hotel and she stood with Carrie on the sidewalk, waiting for Luis to bring the car around, Jan felt obliged to say something. "He isn't what you need," she told Carrie gently, "especially now, after Paul."

Carrie frowned. "Stop trying to be my mother."

The reaction astonished Jan, hurt her feelings. "Sure," she answered lightly.

On Sunday, Jan spent the day by the hotel pool. She swam, read a book about the Peruvian Coast, started another on

Peruvian music, ate lunch, drank a Pisco Sour and took a nap. Carrie rested in her room all morning and walked around downtown in the afternoon. It was obvious they wanted time apart. They ate dinner together, but neither mentioned Luis. Instead, they talked in a stilted way about what each had done that day.

Trouble is brewing between us, Jan thought now as they drove along the Pan-American Highway, the road, broad and straight, carved from the rocky desert. Occasionally, rippling sand dunes appeared on the right side with a view of the ocean, a deep blue-green. Most often a hill or a village hid the shore. To the left, tall mountains, wrinkled and brown like an old woman's skin, rose abruptly from the flat, baked land.

Jan unzipped an outer vest pocket and pulled out her bottle of lotion. She rubbed the liquid onto her face, hands, and arms. "Want some?" she asked Carrie, holding the bottle out.

"I have my own lotion," Carrie replied, looking away.

A gasoline truck passed, heading north toward Lima—the first vehicle Jan remembered seeing for ten or fifteen minutes. Since it was a weekday, she supposed few people traveled south, traffic crowding the streets of Lima instead. Probably on weekends cars swarmed the highway. She had read that Paracas, where they were to have lunch, and beaches near Pisco were favorite resorts for Lima's affluent.

An occasional billboard jutted up to advertise *cerveza, cigarillos* or *el hotel mas elegante para turistas*. She could just as easily be headed for Palm Springs. Then she realized the signs were in Spanish.

Ahead she saw a stall surrounded by plastic-webbed beach chairs. Between two poles flapped a line of straw sun hats with gaudy streamers that danced in the wind of an electric fan. A little later another stand came into view, advertising drinks and beach towels.

Jan said she was thirsty and suggested they stop for something cold, but Luis replied, "No. Not safe."

"How come?" she asked.

He waved at the landscape. "*Bandidos*, maybe they wait for us. If we stop, they get us. Always when I drive down the coast I carry a *pistolete*."

Jan swallowed hard. "You have a gun with you now?"

"*Sí.*"

Carrie touched Jan's arm and nodded at the rear window.

Driving directly behind them was a military jeep. As if in recognition of Jan's stare, the jeep speeded up. Luis slowed down. The jeep started to pass. The two vehicles drove side by side, Luis staring straight ahead, his shoulders stiff. The soldier next to the driver carried a machine gun. He eyed them intently. At last he muttered something, and the jeep plowed ahead. Even when it was a speck in the distance, Luis' shoulders looked tense.

Jan decided to question him about the jeep at lunchtime; the atmosphere would be more relaxed then. She caught herself studying the back of his head, his straight black hair, neatly trimmed half way down his brown neck, the starched, white collar beneath it. She resisted an impulse to reach out and touch that band of skin in-between. On the outside mirror, she saw the reflection of his hawk-like nose, sensual mouth and heavy brow. For a moment she saw the face of a priest on a *Moche* jar. She had to close her eyes to stop staring.

What was it about Luis that so affected her? She tried to analyze it. Partly it was his habit of looking at her through lowered lids and smiling in that knowing way. Each time he did, she felt a disturbingly warm dampness. And when she watched the easy movements of his taut body with its polished brown skin, her pulse beat faster. The casual way he wore his loose-fitting white shirt, always a clean one, made her long to bury her face in his chest. She didn't want to be attracted to him. She knew she ought to squash her ridiculous infatuation. But she couldn't. What made it even worse was Carrie's strong interest in him.

Jan's relationship with Logan operated on a different plane. Although she cared deeply for him, during her four years in his law office she found it easy to hide her personal feelings. Jan and Logan worked well together. There were no sexual overtones. She was his efficient secretary; he was her capable boss.

It was different with Luis. What Jan feared most was that something uncontrollable was happening inside of her, a stirring of emotions best left alone.

Nothing along the road now—no signs, no stands, no vehicles, only the monotonous, rocky terrain, framed on one side by bare mountains, on the other by a calm, green ocean that faded into a pale sky as desolate looking as the desert.

Drugged by the repetitive landscape, the motion of the car and the softness of the breeze, Jan was barely conscious of the sounds made by the engine, the flute and the wind. They blended together until they turned into the whimper of a child heard from far away. She felt a need to listen, to cry back. Two faces interceded: her angry mother's; her disapproving father's. She reached out to grasp a hand but couldn't touch anything.

No! Jan straightened up, rigid, fearful she might remember thoughts too awful to acknowledge. Beside her, Carrie swayed to the rhythm of the flute music, eyes closed, blonde hair flying, body relaxed, on her face a blissful expression. What a change! This pale, fragile woman, who only a few weeks ago considered suicide, who two days ago looked completely exhausted, now sat in gun-filled Peru, riding through a bleak, dangerous desert, smiling as if she were off to the fair.

Jan searched for a soothing image.

Logan McCloskey stood in the doorway of his office, hands on the frame, feet apart, an imposing figure, more so when he intended to be, and intimidation was part of his profession. With his suit coat off, shirtsleeves rolled up, red tie askew—his usual appearance by the end of a day—he looked more like a fight promoter than a lawyer.

Life stayed under control at McCloskey, Warner and Jarvis. No matter how desperate she became, how bad her world got, she could sweep it away by going into her cubicle, sitting at the computer, finding the form for each document and turning out precise legal papers.

No correct forms in Peru. No known procedures to follow. Nothing to show her how to deal with dangerous situations, a disagreement with a friend, a strong physical attraction, long buried emotions surfacing. It seemed she had entered a dangerous maze.

During the remaining hour to Paracas, she continually scrutinized the land as if a bandit waited behind every rock.

CHAPTER 7

They arrived at Paracas a little before noon. Luis drove up a hill behind the city to an iron gate; above it on an arch a white-lettered sign read *La Luna Blanca*. He slid out of the car, unlatched the gate and threw it open. It clanged against a metal post and trembled to a stop. Continually surveying the surroundings, he hurried back into the car and sped up the incline toward a round, white building with an oblong wing on its south side. He parked in a level area at the end of the driveway. Producing a large silver key, he unlocked the front door.

Jan followed him into an immense, circular room with a glistening white marble floor and a white stucco ceiling that swept up to a peak like a Bedouin's tent. In the middle of the room grew a garden anchored by three palms that rose some twenty feet to the ceiling. At the base of the trees, among ferns and a ground cover of pea gravel, grew red, stiff-stemmed, heart-shaped, waxy flowers, their yellow stamens protruding like coated tongues.

Carrie pointed to the flowers and said softly, "Anthuriums. My father always keeps an arrangement on his dining room table."

Jan walked over to examine them, her rubber soles whispering against the floor. "They look artificial." Her words echoed between the marble and plaster.

Surrounding the garden were three identical groups of white leather couches, a low, white lacquered table in front of each group. Jan ran her fingers over the arm of the closest couch. The resulting squeak sounded like a maniacal laugh. She shivered.

An archway opposite the entrance opened onto a dark, forbidding-looking porch covered with a green canopy. To the far right of the room stood a counter that reminded her of a mortuary slab. To the left, three dimly lit hallways angled out. The building grew more sinister by the minute. Wrapping her arms around her body, she continued to look about the room, her uneasiness growing. Everything about this place seemed unreal.

It was the stillness she found most upsetting, as if a thief had crept in, stolen the people and wiped away their prints. As if this place required human sacrifice for sustenance.

Across her mind flashed the fear of a bandit attack. The front door was unlocked. Luis had the key. Where was he? "Luis!" she cried. His name echoed in a hiss.

A door down a hallway opened. Luis ran forward.

Jan swallowed hard, forgetting why she had called him. She said lamely, "When do we eat lunch?"

"Soon. Then we leave."

"Leave," she echoed.

"*Sí*. Drive to *Las Dunas*."

"Good." She peered around. "I don't like this place. It feels dangerous."

"You are safe."

"Our room at *El Castaño* was supposed to be safe."

"That was not good." His leather sandals made no sound as he walked over to the curved front windows. He stood there scrutinizing the driveway.

"Is someone meeting us here?" she asked.

Pivoting around, he examined her face. "I hope not."

Unnerved by his stare, she reached over and touched a table, vaguely considering how many coats of paint it took to achieve the sheen.

"Carrie's suitcase problem," Luis continued, "that was an accident. The hotel owner, he was…ah, the English word escapes… embarrassed. *Sí, muy* embarrassed. When you go back to Lima, you must stay at our villa. My father insists." He gestured in finality. "Nothing more to frighten you."

Carrie sank onto one of the leather couches. It made a shushing sound that floated around the room in ghostly sighs.

Jan shuddered and walked over to the marble counter, half expecting to see a body lying on it. In back of the counter, on the curved wall, were ten boxes; each held a silver key.

Behind her a click sounded. She whirled. Luis was inspecting his pistol. After replacing it under his shirt, he walked toward the archway that led to the green verandah, his body seeming to glide—slender hips in tight, black whipcord trousers, white starched shirt, face like a *Moche* priest.

He caught her looking at him and smiled knowingly.

"Keys," she said, pointing at the boxes, her voice husky. "Are we the only ones here?"

"*Sí*. This is a private resort. People come here only by invitation, for parties, weekends usually." He glanced at the front windows and ahead through the archway. Then he walked out onto the covered porch.

She hurried over to see where he had gone. The green canopy reflected its color onto the wicker furniture and marble floor. Everything on the verandah looked under water. Luis had started down the stairs at the far end, his shirt white again. Sweat gathered on her forehead and the back of her neck. What was happening to her? She looked back at Carrie, sitting on the leather couch, looking fresh and relaxed.

A breeze swept in from the porch and brought relief, a smell of the sea. The sea.... Again the breeze. Jan allowed herself to remember, carefully, always carefully. She was seven years old, running on the beach with the wind, her footprints in the damp sand. Trapped behind a piece of driftwood shaped like a hand, was a rainbow-colored abalone shell....

Another shush from the leather couch. Carrie stood up and pulled her daypack onto her back. "I see things differently now," she announced. "I mean from a few days ago."

"What makes you say that?" Jan asked.

Carrie adjusted her daypack straps and swept back her blonde hair. "Before, I might have been impressed by *La Luna Blanca*. Now I see this as a place created to make people feel small."

"It's eerie," Jan muttered and started to walk through the archway onto the verandah. She stopped, balanced on the edge, as if one step further might drop her into the sea.

Carrie walked past her and down the stairs.

Jan pulled her dark glasses over her eyes and forced herself to walk through the arch and onto the verandah. With icy hands she grasped the metal railing. The teal blue sea, about a mile away, looked like a sheet of rippled glass. Above the beach a flock of gulls, their cries faint, swooped and banked, gliding on the wind in changing patterns like signal flags. An iodine odor drifted up. Seaweed, shells, driftwood, white-edged tides. Suddenly Jan felt terribly afraid. It was all her fault. Everything that went wrong that day was because of her. She had failed.

A Spanish conversation filtered into her thoughts. Luis and Carrie stood on the white-tiled terrace below near a crystal-clear pool. Beside them, a round table, three chairs drawn up. So many things come in threes, Jan thought. Three hallways, three palm trees, three sets of couches, three people. The fairy tale ordeal. The odd number. Three strikes and you're out. A fourth is needed to play most games. Why am I thinking in this negative way?

She looked down at the terrace. Empty. Where were they? Whirling around, she saw Carrie in the big room. "Didn't see you pass," she said, realizing her voice was too shrill. "Where's Luis?"

"Checking on our lunch. What's upsetting you?"

Jan hurried back inside. "This place. I don't like it."

Carrie looked around. "It doesn't bother me." She met Jan's eyes. "What *does* bother me is why you don't like Luis."

"I...I don't dislike him."

"Saturday at the museum you were antagonistic. Later you told me to be careful of him. Today you act as if you don't trust him. Something about Luis bothers you. If it's about my suitcase being torn apart, I doubt if he had anything to do with the burglary." Carrie slipped off her daypack and pulled out her brush. Vigorously, she attacked her hair, eliminating the tangles caused by the wind on the drive. "I find Luis intelligent and interesting," she announced. "I enjoy his company."

"Okay, okay. All I meant the other day was I hope you think this relationship through before you allow it to develop."

"Develop?"

"I don't want you hurt again. I never spoke up about Paul, and I wish I had."

Inspecting her brush, Carrie said in a tight voice, "I know you mean well, Jan, but let me decide what to do, even if you think I'm wrong. For most of my life other people have made my decisions. Lately I've realized they haven't always been the best for me."

A male voice spoke up. "*Señoritas,* is your talk finished?"

Luis stood in the archway surveying them. Jan wondered how much of their conversation he had heard.

Carrie replied, "Our talk is finished." She slipped her brush back into her daypack.

"Then, lunch waits for us." They followed him across the dark verandah and down the stairs to the sunny terrace.

CHAPTER 8

Jan finished her salad, the shrimp large, fresh and sweet, the rolls, warm. The lunch had been a pleasure to eat, lightening her mood, diminishing her fears. Picking up a wedge of lime, she was ready to enjoy the rest of her iced tea, when the commotion started.

Brakes squealed. Metal slammed against metal. The sounds came from the front of the building. Excited men's voices, garbled Spanish words. Footsteps clacked across the marble floor.

Alarmed, she held the lime motionless over her iced tea.

Luis rose, quickly wiped his mouth on the linen napkin and stared up at the covered porch. Jan dropped the lime into her glass and exchanged a worried look with Carrie.

A uniformed man in a helmet appeared at the covered-porch railing. Another man. Another. They lined up like ducks in a shooting gallery. They gripped rifles and glared down at the table on the terrace.

With horror Jan realized the gun barrels were aimed at them. She decided against taking a sip of tea. "What do they want?" she whispered to Luis.

He didn't answer, still focused on the porch, his body frozen. The napkin floated from his hand to the tiled terrace.

Two additional military men rushed down the stairway. Both wore holstered pistols belted around their waists and shiny black boots to mid calf. The tall man in the lead had a large black mustache, a swarm of medals on his chest and gold eagles on his shoulders—a colonel. At his approach, Luis raised his hands. The colonel addressed him in a barrage of clipped Spanish accompanied by sharp gestures. Luis cried, "No, no!" The colonel's voice rose. He waved in a threatening manner.

"What's he saying," Jan whispered to Carrie, who sat erect and motionless, clutching the napkin on her lap.

"He's calling Luis a terrorist, part of a guerrilla ambush."

The other soldier, a pimply-faced lieutenant, forced Luis to remove his shoes, then began a slow search, tossing Luis' wallet, pack of cigarettes and box of matches onto the table. With a cry of success, he pulled the pistol from Luis' shoulder holster and held it out.

Taking the weapon, the colonel removed the clip and studied it. With a grunt of disgust, he dropped the clip onto the terrace, where it bounced and nearly fell into the pool. "*Terruco*," the colonel spit out. With the butt of the pistol he struck Luis hard on the cheek.

Luis staggered back, a hand to his bleeding cheek, hatred in his eyes.

Again the colonel raised the pistol as if to strike.

Jan shot out of her chair. "Stop it!" she shouted.

The soldiers on the porch clattered down the stairs and ran forward.

Panic nearly overcame her, but she remained standing, her eyes on the colonel. "Leave him alone." she said, hoping he understood English. "He is not a terrorist."

"*Lo siento, pero lo debemos hacer,*" the colonel said with cold politeness as he inspected the pistol. Ignoring Jan, he stared at Carrie, who remained seated. A sweep of his hand indicated the lieutenant should check the daypack by her chair. There was a quick examination. The lieutenant shook his head and dropped the bag back back by the chair. The colonel looked at Carrie. The only sounds now were the whine of the pool pump and the far-off cry of gulls.

Jan took a deep breath to slow her racing heart. Surely they wouldn't body search Carrie. Her flimsy blouse and cotton skirt couldn't hide a weapon.

The colonel switched his focus to Jan. "Please remove your vest," he said, his English perfect.

She set her vest on the table. The lieutenant patted the pockets. Again he shook his head. "You see," she said, trying to keep her voice steady, "we're not dangerous."

Giving a slight bow, the colonel said, "Excuse me, *señoritas*, but there has been an ugly incident. This morning two military personnel were killed on the road between Pisco and Ayacucho. We believe they were murdered by *Sendero Luminoso*, the Shining Path terrorists."

"What does that have to do with us?"

"A black car was seen in the vicinity. And this man here"—he waved derogatorily at Luis whose eyes still blazed—"is obviously from the Ayacucho area."

"He's from Lima. But even if he were from Ayacucho, I don't see—."

"He carries an automatic pistol," the colonel interrupted. "Although recently it has not been fired, he still is a suspect."

"Why?"

"He has the facial characteristics of men from Ayacucho. Many have been *Senderistas*."

"I can assure you, Colonel—"

"Colonel Huerra." He tapped his feet together with military precision, the automatic pointed downward at his side.

"I can assure you, Colonel Huerra, the gentleman you struck is our guide." She felt her courage building. "He drove us this morning from Lima's *Hotel La Castaña* directly here to Paracas. We are American tourists on our way to *Las Dunas*. You can easily check out our reservations."

She raised her chin, attempting to look assured. "As for the gun in your hand, we asked our guide to bring it along. We've been told this area is dangerous. Apparently it is."

She felt the concentration of the soldiers behind her, their rifles still pointed at her back. Carrie sat like an ivory statue; Luis hadn't moved a muscle. She wondered if her explanation had been good enough. The whine of the pool pump grew louder. Her knees began to shake. She sat down slowly, arms away from her body to indicate her peaceful intent.

The colonel placed the empty automatic on the table and extended his right hand. "Passports," he snapped.

Jan produced hers from an inner vest pocket. Carrie rummaged through her daypack, found the document and handed it to him. The colonel examined the pages, flipping through with his thumb. He tossed both passports onto the table. "They appear in order."

Jan forced a smile as she handed Carrie's passport back and put hers away. The zipper on her vest pocket sounded alarmingly like a saw ripping through wood. Attempting a cheerful voice, she ventured, "You know, Colonel Huerra, you ought to get a job in Hollywood."

"How so, *Señorita* Fielding?"

"Your operation is like a Rambo movie."

The colonel pursed his lips and grunted with amusement, "Hm-m-m, Rambo."

"Ah, so you've heard of the movie."

He nodded. "*Señorita* Fielding, you are a charming young lady." He eyed Luis. "Do you always carry this pistol?"

"No, my father, he lent it to me."

"What is your father's name?"

"Ignacio Acosta."

The colonel's eyes turned to slits. He scratched a corner of his mustache, then smoothed it down. "I know Ignacio Acosta. He has two daughters. I did not know he had a son." He yanked Luis' wallet from the table, opened it and examined the card and picture behind the plastic window. He pulled out several slips of paper and inspected each piece before shoving them all back in and tossing the wallet onto the table. With a slight wave, the colonel indicated Luis should retrieve his wallet, cigarettes and matches, which he did under close scrutiny.

"It is difficult to believe Ignacio Acosta is your father," the colonel remarked.

Jan swallowed hard, determined not to show she was afraid. "Colonel Huerra, let me explain why Luis is our guide. Mr. Ross, the father of my friend"—she nodded at Carrie—"and Mr. Acosta,

Luis' father, are business associates. Because the two fathers were concerned about us traveling alone in Peru, Luis was sent along to show us the ropes."

"The ropes? Ah, the ropes. I see what you mean." Pointing at her empty glass, he said. "Were you drinking iced tea?"

"Yes." She noticed the waiter peering around the edge of the kitchen door under the verandah stairs. His head disappeared.

A laugh exploded from the colonel, a rasping sound that startled his lieutenant as much as Jan. Meticulously he smoothed the center of his mustache. "You ladies should drink more tea."

"That was our plan. The waiter is supposed to bring us another pitcher full."

"Excellent. I am thirsty. It would be a distinct pleasure to join two beautiful *Norteamericanos* for a drink."

Jan swallowed. "Don't you have to rush off to find your criminals?"

"I am apt to be more successful if I am not thirsty."

"What about your men with the rifles?"

"They shall wait outside."

He shouted an order. The lieutenant stiffened and saluted. The colonel saluted back. The pimpled officer barked commands, resulting in a precise maneuver. Then the four soldiers marched single file up the stairs, the lieutenant at the rear. Over the green verandah they moved, through the archway and across the room, their boots clacking in hollow cadence against the marble floor, echoing until they exited the front door.

Jan glanced at Carrie who sipped on melted ice. Luis stood on the opposite side of the table, blood congealed on his cheek in a dark slash the color of wine. Puffy skin encircled the cut. His hands were clenched so hard his knuckles looked ready to burst through the skin. His eyes, dark with anger, concentrated on the colonel. Although the colonel appeared to ignore Luis, Jan felt certain he was alert for the slightest aggressive movement. If Luis tried to grab the gun, the colonel would shoot him. They all might be killed. Tension was building.

"Colonel," she said, her voice not as firm as she wanted, "apparently, we've been forgotten out here. Could our guide remind the waiter about bringing iced tea?"

"Yes. No longer is he a suspect." He looked at Luis. "You may go."

Luis stood there for a moment, his eyes shifting from the colonel to Jan. As though suddenly cognizant of the situation, he picked up his shoes and hurried away toward the kitchen.

His disappearance seemed to ease the atmosphere. Jan adjusted a comb in her hair. Carrie stirred her ice with a spoon. The colonel brushed aside Luis' salad plate and slipped into the chair with the stiffness of a robot. He set his hands on the table as if ready for a banquet. "Seldom," he said to Jan, "do people come mid-week to *La Luna Blanca*."

"I'm beginning to understand why."

He raised his hands in a that's-the-way-things-are gesture. "Did *Señor* Acosta arrange with the owner for you to come?"

"Naturally. Otherwise, no luncheon would have been served."

He half smiled at her answer. "Your friend"—again he smoothed the mustache—"*Señorita* Ross, is that not her name?"

"Yes, that's her name."

"She has a delicate beauty. Such exquisite golden hair. But I wonder why she has not yet spoken?"

"Because you and your men have upset her," Jan replied quickly. "Miss Ross is recuperating from an illness." She leaned forward. "Do I dare be frank with you?"

"Your frankness would be welcome in a world with little."

"My friend and I deplore violence. Your assault on our guide was a shock." She plunged on. "Although we understand the reason for military forces in your country, we hadn't expected to encounter any."

He inclined his head in a patronizing fashion. "A regrettable necessity."

From the kitchen doorway the young waiter bustled toward them, his right palm balancing a silver tray at ear level, a white towel looped over his left arm.

"The iced tea," Jan said with relief.

Surveying the waiter's approach, the colonel said in a brittle voice, "*Señorita* Fielding, are you aware that once again violence has reared up in Peru."

"I realize that must be the case, since there's a curfew and police and guards are stationed about."

With a flourish, the waiter set a frosted glass before the colonel. Beside it, a white linen napkin and a spoon. He poured iced tea from the pitcher, filling the colonel's glass first. Leaving the pitcher on the table, he hurriedly reloaded his tray with empty dishes and flapped his towel at tablecloth crumbs, abandoning those near the pistol. In a final gesture of efficiency, he retrieved Luis' napkin from the terrace floor and hurried away.

The colonel scowled at Jan. His voice took on a biting tone. "Have you heard of *Sendero Luminoso?*"

"Yes, but I thought the group was eliminated a number of years ago."

The colonel shook his head. "*Senderistas* still exist. How many is not known. Even if only fifty, small is big when it comes to terrorism." His fingertips shot together, making a circle. "For a number of years, we have enjoyed peace. Recently, *Sendero* reared up again. Explosions, mostly around Lima. Enough to create havoc, build fear, frighten a population. But, we will find them." He tapped his fingers together. "Many are in prison from earlier uprisings. Among them is their founding leader"—he spit out the name—"Abimael Guzmán."

"Well, if they no longer have a leader...."

"Always they have a leader. After Guzmán came Feliciano, until he contracted a severe tropical disease. Now there are rumors of a new commander." The colonel sighed and took a swig of iced tea.

After a moment, Jan asked cautiously, "What's the purpose of *Sendero Luminoso?*"

"To destroy the Peruvian Government."

"Why?"

"They believe that would solve the *campesinos'* problems."

"Would it?"

"Of course not!" Again he tapped his fingers together. "The *terrucos* claim they will distribute wealth among the peasants—give them land and influence, more of everything. What they will distribute is bloodshed, cruelty and tyranny, nothing of value except to the nucleus. Those who wield the power will be the ones to gain." He took several gulps of tea before setting the glass down.

Carrie spoke for the first time, her voice soft but determined. "It is my impression that Peru is run by politicians and military personnel who don't care about the *campesinos*. When you have nothing, you search for ways to find something."

The colonel looked startled. "We give poor people what we can."

"I doubt it."

Jan could scarcely believe it was Carrie speaking. She stared at her friend in amazement, then concern. The colonel might think Carrie had terrorist sympathies.

The colonel spoke with restrained fury, "*Campesinos* are like grains of sand. Try to build with them and everything gets washed away or dries out and falls apart. Peru has not enough money to handle the poverty here. We are not rich like Americans."

Carrie said, "My impression is—"

"Your impression is idealistic." He finished his iced tea, and then blew out a deep breath, setting the glass on the saucer with a thump. "Did you know *Sendero* hung dogs on Lima's lamp posts—a symbol all capitalist dogs must die?"

Jan winced. "How gruesome!"

"Gruesome indeed. We must eradicate these *terrucos*" He eyed the gun on the table and once more patted his mustache with the napkin. Rising, he dropped the napkin over the weapon. "Return the pistol to your guide. I trust he guards you well. *Adiós, señoritas.* Enjoy your vacation." He tapped his heels together and bowed.

As he strode away, the gold eagles on his shoulders glinted in the sunlight. He disappeared into the shadow of the verandah, followed by the echoing click of his boots across the marble floor. Doors slammed, engines revved, tires squealed. Gradually, the drone of the departing engines became the whine of the pool pump and the distant cry of the gulls.

Jan's shoulders ached. Her muscles felt knotted. With shaky hands she tried to rub them free. Tried to loosen her body so her heart would not beat so fast. The air felt uncomfortably hot and windless. The sun, pulsating in a yellow-tinged sky, had turned the flat sea into a sheet of steel. She pressed the cool glass against her forehead and considered what the colonel would do when he caught the terrorists and what sort of people hung dogs on lamp posts.

Carrie appeared relaxed, slowly drinking tea, not a tremor in her hand. Jan wondered how she could look so calm. Hadn't this encounter alarmed her? Wasn't she upset when the colonel struck Luis? Jan set her glass down and called, "Luis?"

He appeared in the doorway.

"They're gone. Are you all right?"

"*Sí.*" He approached the table, his eyes fixed on Jan.

She reached up and gently touched the wound on his cheek. "I'm sorry he hurt you. We must get your cut treated. Antiseptic or salve. Is there be a doctor at *Las Dunas?*"

He smiled. "It will be fine. Thank you for keeping me from a second cut."

"It was necessary," she replied, a catch in her voice.

Carrie said, "What you did was quite brave, Jan." With a sigh, she picked up her daypack. "I'll meet you two out front. I need to walk around a bit, think things through."

As Jan watched Carrie climb the stairs, cross the porch and disappear, she felt the gap between them widen. Gingerly, she picked up the pistol on the table, warm from the sun. She had never held a gun before. It frightened yet intrigued her. This one had drawn blood on a man thought to be a terrorist, a man whose existence meant more to her than she wanted to admit.

Luis stood by the table, appraising her, but not as before. The moment he had appeared in the kitchen doorway she was aware of a change in their relationship. Nothing she could classify or put into words. Yet she knew that what they thought of each other now was far more acceptable.

"I don't like this place," she said, looking up at the porch, then at the pool and finally at the gun resting in her hand.

"*Sí.*" He picked up the gun clip from the terrace and examined it. "This villa is...*no es muy acogedora.*"

She nodded, not understanding the words but feeling his meaning.

His eyes locked with hers. "Not all is bad, though, *Janecita.*" He touched his wounded cheek. "You came out of hiding."

She nodded and held the gun flat on the palm of her hand.

His fingers lingered on hers. Abruptly, he grasped the pistol and lifted it away. He jammed the clip into the weapon, returned it to his holster and headed for the porch stairs.

CHAPTER 9

Las Dunas was a tranquil, walled oasis of birds, trees, flowers and winding fishponds crossed by little bridges. Immediately after checking in, Jan put on her purple bathing suit and hurried out to the pool. She dove in and came up sputtering and refreshed. Luis joined her. Twice they swam the length and back again, long strokes in unison. Although they never touched nor spoke, she was fully aware of him moving beside her. That awareness, along with the rhythm of their strokes and the pulsation of water across her body, kindled her nerve endings and heightened her imagination. Afraid she might end up embracing him, she broke away on the third lap and scrambled from the pool to dry off and calm down.

Carrie, who had been resting in the room, arrived a little later. For a while she treaded water and talked with Luis. Then, she too swam beside him, her strokes smaller, faster.

Forget Luis, Jan commanded herself. Remember Carrie and Paul. Think about Logan.

Even though it was mid afternoon, the effect of the sun was fierce. Shifting sideways on the chaise lounge, she rubbed more sunscreen on her legs, capped the tube and tossed it into the beach bag. She noticed a tall man, obviously not Peruvian, staring at her from the other side of the pool. His body, bronze and muscular, looked incongruous with the yellow daisy print on his tight Speedo swimwear. Platinum blonde hair haloed his head in a style reminiscent of a Roman statue. Slipping her dark glasses over her eyes, she looked away, not wishing to give the impression of a lonely female.

Except for the Adonis, the lounges around the pool were occupied by Peruvians of various shapes and ages, quietly baking their well-oiled bodies. A few children splashed and laughed in the shallow end of the pool. Carrie, now diving off the board, looked pink from the sun, but Jan knew better than to offer advice. Luis continued to swim in slow, easy strokes, his body gliding with sensuous, masculine grace.

The Adonis flashed a smile. Jan ignored it. Enough of the sun, she decided and snatched up her beach bag. She retreated to a glass-topped table under a palm tree and sat down, listening to the sparrows chirp in the branches above.

The Adonis stood up and made his move, eyes focused on Jan. With a sigh of annoyance, she set her bag on the table. He slipped into the opposite chair and said, "Howdy! I'm Brewster Jacowski." His smile owned the winning lottery ticket.

She was astonished, having expected to hear a deep male voice. Not only did the guy have a Texas drawl, he sounded effeminate.

"Actually"—his hands flew outward—"my name's Marvin. When I was a little boy, I fiddled around Mama's kitchen. 'Honey,' she'd say, 'you all got a knack for brewing up things. A regular brewster, that's what you are.' The name appealed to me, so I've kept it." His laugh shattered the air. He rushed on, "I just knew you all were Americans. That fellow with you must be your guide."

"He's our bodyguard," she answered.

"Oh, really? I thought protection might be more up your alley."

She stiffened. "What makes you say that?"

"Experience, honey. Can I treat you to a drink?"

"No thanks."

"Why not?" Again his hands flew out. He closed his eyes as if in pain. "I won't give you an ounce of trouble. I'm longing to have Americans around for a splash of normal conversation. I've been here a week and nobody speaks English. Have just one little old beer with me."

She shrugged. "I guess that wouldn't hurt."

He waved at a waiter who was serving drinks to four prostrate bodies. The waiter hurried over, his empty tray held aloft. "*A sus ordenes.*"

A giggle escaped Brewster. He replied, "*Dos cervezas. Pilsen Callao.*"

"*Sí.*"

Brewster watched the waiter walk toward the smoothly plastered building. "Ooo, that fellow is so cute. Whenever he says *'a sus ordenes'* it makes the hair on the back of my neck stand straight up."

Jan repressed a laugh, amused at the contrast between Brewster Jacowski and Colonel Huerra.

"Where you all from?" Brewster asked.

"San Francisco."

"On vacation?"

"Yes."

"I gather you two gals are both single."

"How can you be sure? These days, married women don't necessarily wear rings."

"Again, experience."

"Hm-m-m."

"Bet I could even guess your occupation. You're a secretary and your friend's either a librarian or a teacher."

"She's a teacher." Jan raised her chin. "What makes you think I'm a secretary?"

"How you use your hands and the way your eyes say *Everything must be in order.*"

She wrinkled her nose. "You're right. I'm a legal secretary."

"Woopee, I hit the bull's-eye." For a moment he gazed up into the branches as if fascinated by the birds. "I hope you all plan to stay here a while."

"Two nights."

"Where to next?"

"Back to Lima where we catch a plane for Arequipa."

"Oh, I love Arequipa. Beautiful city. Be sure to visit *El Convento.* It'll simply blow your mind." He crossed his legs. "Plan to stay long in Arequipa?"

She paused, wondering why he was so inquisitive. "Overnight is all."

"And after that?"

"Why do you want to know?"

He waved the question away. "Just curious."

She shrugged. "We take the night train to Lake Titicaca."

"Wonderful! I bet you all plan to stay at the hotel on Esteves Island. It's the best place to stay in Puno. You reach it by a causeway."

She didn't reply. Brewster was too inquisitive.

He clapped his hands. "Wonderful hotel. Do be careful in the Andes, though. Policemen and soldiers crawl all over the place, keeping tabs on the *campesinos.*"

"So we've heard."

He gave her the weary look of someone who wants nothing to do with problems. "How're you getting from Puno to Cuzco?"

"I didn't say we were going to Cuzco."

"Oh, but everyone goes there."

"Perhaps we've already been."

"Don't think so." He smiled engagingly. "Now, let me guess your transportation. There's an airfield near Puno, but all planes fly back to Lima first, so, time wise that would be a bad choice. Then there's the road to Cuzco but it's pretty frightful. Nobody in their right mind should drive it. Therefore, I conclude you all plan to take the train."

"You're a clever guy."

"I'm terribly interested in what people do."

She watched Brewster inspect Luis then Carrie. He was beginning to bother her—his manner of questioning, line of reasoning, the way he stared at people. The probability he was gay didn't bother her. Rather, that was a relief, although she wouldn't have known it until he opened his mouth. It did seem odd that a gay man would hang around a family resort where his prospects were few.

"I gather you've been to Peru before," she said.

"When I need recuperation, I head here. I especially find this place relaxing."

"Is your job full of stress?"

"In some ways."

She thought she noted a wary look in his eyes. "Brewster, you don't have to tell me anything about your life. Unless you do, though, stop playing detective games with me."

His eyebrows flew up in mock amazement. "You're a perceptive lady, Miss—" He leaned forward and waited as if for a secret message.

She paused and then said, "Fielding, Janet Fielding."

"And your friend's name?"

"Carrie Ross. I suppose you want to know our guide's name, too—Luis Acosta."

"Any relation to Ignacio Acosta, the prominent Lima businessman?"

"Luis' father. How'd you hear about him?"

"He's well known in Peru." Continuing to stare at Luis, he said, "That's a nasty cut on his cheek. How'd he get it?"

"A piece of metal hit him."

"What kind of metal?"

She was determined to reveal no more. "None of your business."

"Oopsie," he said. "I've hit a teeny snag."

The waiter arrived with tall glasses of beer.

After a few moments of silent drinking, Brewster said, "Honey, I'll reveal myself to you, but don't repeat anything I say to the locals. The reason I ask so many questions is because I'm a writer. Most governments are leery of writers so I wouldn't want that to get back to authorities. On immigration forms where it asks for occupation, I always write *hairdresser*. That's safe."

"Unless you carry a pair of scissors."

His laugh was uproarious. "That's a good one."

She allowed herself to smile. "What do you write?"

With a sigh of resignation, he sipped his beer."Nothing that would hurt a flea."

"I'm sure you're aware that I want to know what sort of writing you do."

He closed his eyes. "Yes, but I'm debating whether or not to tell you."

"Is it academic? Scientific? Political? Mainstream? Some sort of perverse stuff?"

He looked at her intently. "Can I swear you to secrecy? It must be absolute, complete secrecy." His head came within inches of her face. "I haven't got a Bible to swear on but it's that important to keep this secret."

Deciding to go along with the game, she lowered her voice. "Okay, Brewster, I swear on my honor never to reveal what you are about to tell me."

"That's not good enough."

She drew her brows together, then whispered, "Should I ever tell, you may shave my head and brand it with a 'T' for *terruco*."

He giggled. "Honey, you've got a creative mind."

She glanced heavenward.

After assuring their privacy, he gave her a look that predicted the crown jewels would drop from the sky. "I write passionate paperbacks for women who need romance."

"You write that bullshit?"

He drew himself up. "It's good bullshit, lucrative bullshit. I grind out two a year, and they sell damn well. I write under the name of Melissa Morehead. There's a picture of me in a blonde wig on the back of my latest book. Even my agent doesn't know I'm a man."

"I should think the truth would sell more books."

"Women who read me think only a woman can understand their needs. Besides, it's a secret I prefer to keep hidden." He leaned back with the look of royalty.

Jan said, "I'm surprised you told me. After all, I'm a stranger. How do you know I'm trustworthy?"

He smiled engagingly. "Experience, my dear, experience!"

They clinked beer glasses in a toast, laughed, and drank. As she set her glass on the table, she noticed Carrie approaching with Luis, a dark look on his face.

Brewster said, "Oh, oh, here they come. Carrie's got the hots for that fellow. It's written all over her pretty face. Such a shame!"

"Why a shame?"

He rolled his eyes. "Because she hasn't a dribble of a chance with him."

She watched Luis walk toward her, the white towel draped over his shoulder. He moved with little effort, the rich brown skin on his smooth chest catching the sunlight.

Brewster said, "Janet, honey, we better think up a damned good reason for sitting around, snickering over glasses of beer."

Jan smiled at the absurdity of the situation. Her smile disappeared when Luis arrived at the table, his eyes meeting hers with such an intensity that momentarily her breathing stopped. Was it desire, jealousy, possessiveness? She couldn't decipher it.

"I'm going to the room to change," Carrie said serenely. "Luis, when I come back, will you show me that Nazca pottery display you mentioned?"

"*Sí*, it is next to the lobby." Luis wrapped the towel around his lower body and tucked the end into his trunks. "I meet you there."

"Won't take me long," Carrie said and left.

Refusing Jan's offered chair, Luis remained standing. His mouth hardened as he examined Brewster's face. He glanced at Jan's legs, met her eyes and then focused back on Brewster's face.

Jan tried to concentrate on her beer. She cleared her throat. "Luis, meet Brewster Jacowski."

Brewster extended a hand. "Howdy!"

"*Buenas tardes, Señor,*" Luis muttered, ignoring the hand briefly held aloft.

"Join us for a beer?" Brewster suggested.

"*No, gracias, Señor,*" Luis replied. "I have more important things to do." He turned away.

"Mercy, me," said Brewster, watching Luis walk to the lobby. "He does exude sex appeal. Now, don't you worry, Janet, honey. He'll change his mind once he learns what a harmless fellow I am." He reached over and patted Jan's hand. "My dear, I do believe we'll develop a close relationship. It's inevitable."

CHAPTER 10

The dining room, open on all sides like a large gazebo, was 40 feet in diameter with a central dance floor waxed shiny. Crescent rows of tables filled one end, each covered by a yellow cloth and a red-bottled candle that matched the linen napkins. At the other end rose a platform. On it stood five musicians in striped ponchos and leather sandals. They played a soft mix of American and Latin songs that fused into the drone of dinner conversations.

Luis sat between Carrie and Jan at a square table on the fringe of the dance floor. As if on cue, Brewster Jacowski, resplendent in a Kelly green bolero over a voluminous-sleeved shirt ablaze with color swept into the room, sank down in the empty chair opposite Luis and launched into a detailed explanation of how he imagined the chef prepared the chicken they were eating. Luis looked as if he would prefer to cram the bird down Brewster's throat.

"Such a delicate mingling of flavors!" Brewster cried, undaunted. Closing his eyes, he sniffed a morsel on Jan's fork. "Ah, partake of the entwined fragrances."

Jan could only detect garlic.

Brewster spun off in another direction. "How absolutely wonderful"—his hands flew up in a magnanimous gesture—"to be here in this glorious oasis in the middle of the bleak Atacama

Desert, sitting beside two gorgeous American ladies, while across from me lounges a handsome Peruvian gentleman loaded with charm."

Luis leaned back and glared at him.

Jan wondered how Brewster could detect anything when he talked so much. On and on he babbled, seemingly unaware of Luis' apparent dislike of him.

Carrie appeared preoccupied. Dressed in a blue chiffon dress that gave her the look of a saint, she blandly smiled, picked at her food and said nothing. It was as if she had stepped into a glass case and shut the door.

Brewster rushed on, "The service here is excellent, don't you agree, Janet?"

"What? Oh, the service. Yes, great, but you keep changing subjects on me. I'm still lingering over my beauty."

Brewster burst into a loud guffaw and patted her arm. "Honey, you are delightful, and I love your black taffeta skirt and red eyelet blouse. Combined with your dark hair, so marvelously secured atop your head by Spanish combs, and your black eyes that flash fire, I do believe you have turned into a gypsy. Forgive me for rambling on like this, but I am enthralled with the food, the company, the attentive waiters, the quaint dining room, the sensuous music. The whole caboodle blends together and flows about me in a waterfall of delight. I insist on buying you all Pisco sours." He turned to the hovering waiter. "*Cuatro* Pisco sours. And, keep them coming all evening. *Gracias, Señor, gracias.*"

Although Jan found Brewster amusing, his words poured out so fast she could scarcely follow their meaning. She was relieved when the floorshow started, for Brewster ceased talking as if a switch had turned him off.

The music, a combination of singing and dancing numbers, part Spanish, part Indian, sounded good, although, since she had started on her third Pisco sour, she wasn't certain she could detect the quality of anything. The night seemed to be growing colder. Her eyelet blouse was sleeveless, and tiny goose bumps rose on her arms like bubbles in champagne. When she tried to inspect them, her vision blurred. Vaguely, she wondered if fizz had gotten under her skin. Deciding she might freeze and not know it, she excused herself and floated back to the room for her sweater.

She also brought back Carrie's blue shawl, not realizing she had it in her hand until she arrived at the table. "Oh dear, sorry," she murmured, remembering her vow of noninterference.

Carrie, deep in conversation with Brewster, looked up as if she had forgotten who Jan was. With a tinkling-bell laugh, she took the shawl and wrapped it around her shoulders.

Whatever Carrie and Brewster had been talking about must have been fascinating, Jan concluded, for Carrie's glass case appeared to have burst open, and Luis leaned forward as if intrigued with every word the two of them uttered.

"Long live Pisco sours!" Jan cried. The fourth one awaited her.

When the floorshow was over, the band again started to play, the music more Latin, executed with greater energy. One of the musicians shook a pair of maracas so violently they sounded like firecrackers.

"Janet, honey," Brewster cried, leaping to his feet, "let us show these Peruvians how well Americans can dance."

"Sure, why not?"

He swept her onto the dance floor. She forced her mind from its stupor, resolved to uphold the honor of her country and the ancient name of Fielding. Yanking the combs from her hair, she tossed them onto the table and shook her hair loose.

While Brewster led her through a complicated rumba routine, she shed her sweater, peeling it off and swinging it in a circle like a stripper. Next came a hot mambo. She kicked off her shoes and threw herself into it, flouncing her taffeta skirt. This was followed by a cha-cha. At the conclusion, Brewster threw up his hands as if tossing confetti, and Jan bowed so low she nearly fell over. There was a scattering of laughter and applause.

The music slid into a seductive tango. Seizing Jan's waist, Brewster propelled her across the floor, their faces turned tragic, knees bent, torsos straight. His left arm, flat against her right, shot up and down. She whipped her head sideways, then forward, her hair flying about like a dark flag.

Seemingly oblivious of Carrie's rapt attention, Luis closely watched the dance. Jan could feel his eyes. As a result, her style grew wilder, until at the conclusion of the tango, she arched her back over Brewster's arm in an exceptionally deep dip, one leg pointing heavenward.

"*Bravo!*" cried a man at a back table, and the audience clapped approvingly. Jan, laughing, exhausted and sweaty, fell into her chair and wiped her face with the red dinner napkin. She glanced sideways at Luis, wondering what he thought of her performance.

"Now," said Brewster, extending his hand to Carrie, "I request a dance with the lovely lady in blue."

Carrie had the innocent look of a Madonna. "I can't dance that way."

"We shall dance in whatever way you wish."

A smile lit Carrie's face. "Ask them to play a waltz."

Brewster shouted to the band, "*Señores, por favor,* a waltz.*"*

To the music of "The Blue Danube," Brewster and Carrie circled the floor, around and around, faces serene, whirling like dancing dolls, the kind Jan remembered from her childhood. Aunt Theresa's clock had a pair that danced every hour. Once she had watched them dance twice, would have watched a third time, but her mother had appeared, angry that Jan lost track of time. Always, the anger.

Jan sipped her drink and watched Carrie and Brewster dance. The room moved, lights turning, tables rising, music descending from the sky. She grew more and more aware of Luis in the chair beside her, the cuff of his white shirt rolled back, a wrist exposed, his slender fingers clenching a glass a few inches from hers. She met his eyes often, but not for long, her vision too confused for safety, the world too soft-edged for support. She didn't dare speak and he said nothing. Instead, they exchanged intimate smiles, occasionally brushed shoulders and touched hands in passing. Each time, her heartbeat quickened, and she had to look away from him and attempt to concentrate on the dancing dolls, Carrie's chiffon dress flowing around her, Brewster's neon sleeves billowing.

Luis shifted in his chair and muttered something in Spanish. He stood up. Jan held her breath, afraid he would ask her to dance, certain she would pass out if he took her in his arms. He didn't ask. Instead, he launched into a suggestive dance around his chair, concluding with a series of flamenco stamps. She giggled. So did he. When he started to sit down again, he nearly missed his chair.

We're both drunk, she thought hazily. Got to be careful. In a moment of clarity she instructed herself to cut the connection to him. Cut it now. Not yet, a voice whispered from deep inside.

Later in the evening, Carrie got the hiccups and spilled her drink. When Brewster threatened to haul "the handsome Peruvian gentleman loaded with sex appeal" out to dance, Luis leaned back in his chair and made the sign of the cross. He stood up, smiling and swaying, arms extended like a priest, shirt whiter than snow. "There are three main evils," he announced. "*Primero:* lying to your friends, unless a lie is necessary for survival."

"*Sí, sí,*" agreed Jan and Carrie.

"*Segundo:* stealing what belongs to another man. Unless it, or she"—he smirked at Jan—"is left unguarded."

"*Sí, sí, sí,*" cried Brewster.

"*Tercero:*"—Luis nearly fell over backwards, but with dignity regained his balance—"killing those you love. Unless they become your enemies."

Carrie's eyes widened. "No, no," she whispered.

Jan blinked, not sure what his words meant.

Brewster sniveled, "Great Priest, I have many sins to confess."

Luis held onto the back of his chair. "Time for you to go, *Señor*," he said, waving Brewster away. "Neither of us is what the others think."

Shortly thereafter, the band dissolved and all of the guests wandered back to their rooms. Waiters blew out candles and gathered the remaining dishes and napkins. Systematically, they moved along the crescent rows, retrieving bottled-candles and finally, the tablecloths.

CHAPTER 11

Jan left Carrie, lily-like in her chiffon dress, sitting on the floor of their room. "I need air," Jan told her and sauntered out into the garden.

The night smelled like bubble gum, the kind her sister used to chew on the way home from school. Most likely the aroma came from flowers. So slight was the breeze carrying the scent that not a leaf moved. Would she know if one did?

Stopping in the middle of one of the bridges, she peered into the pond below and vainly searched for something alive—a goldfish, a frog, anything. Pathway lights sent a metallic sheen across the water, except for a black, fortress-like shape caused by the bridge railing and posts. She raised her arms and swept them from side to side, amused at how her shadow looked on the pond. "Here stands Janet Fielding, guardian of the fort," she announced to the night and then rested against the railing, resigned to the delightful haze of Pisco sours. With her eyes closed, she attempted to concentrate on whether the air was warm or cool.

"*Buenas noches.*"

A male voice. She spun, lost her balance, and fell back against the railing.

"Luis?" She could barely make out his face. "You scared me. I nearly fell into the fishpond."

"*Lo siento.*" His voice contained a smile. "I was not sure that was you."

"It's me."

"*Sí.* I am glad you did not fall in."

They laughed as if the situation was extremely funny.

"What're you doing out here?" she asked.

"I cannot sleep. I came outside to think." He lit a cigarette and tossed the match into the water.

"You should quit smoking. It's bad for your health."

He snorted and waved his cigarette through the air. "Americans always say what is good, what is bad, what we should do, what we should not do."

"I apologize. Let's go back to square one."

"Where is that? What do you mean?"

"It means we should forget what I just said and start over."

"I see. We go back to square one then."

They leaned on the railing and looked down into the water. He said, "You dance well, *Señorita Janecita.*"

She liked the soft sound of the name. "I got carried away."

"I enjoyed watching. You move with good rhythm, with... I have trouble finding the right word." He raised his cigarette hand in a curve. "Energy, that is it, much energy, a loose body." He took a drag on the cigarette and then tossed it into the pond, blowing smoke after it. "You like this Brewster man?"

"He's amusing, certainly not a boyfriend for a woman."

"You think he is, what you call it, gay?"

"Of course."

"I think he is not. Something too much about him."

"I had the same feeling at first." Wishing it wasn't so dark and she wasn't feeling so giddy, she peered into Luis' face. With the index finger of her right hand she attempted to trace the cut on his cheek. "Did he ask you about that?" she inquired.

He grasped her hand and held it. "*Sí,* he asked about it."

"What did you say?"

"Nothing. Carrie, she told him everything."

"Everything?" She was conscious of his hand holding hers, tightly. The night felt cold against her bare arms.

"*Sí*. That time you went back to your room for your sweater, that is when this Brewster man asked Carrie questions. Many questions. He asked about her home, her father, when her mother died, her teaching, why she came to Peru. She told him everything, even about her bad love affair."

"My God! What else did she tell him?"

"About her ripped-open suitcase, about Colonel Huerra, about this cut to my face, about you and the man you work for, this Logan McCloskey in San Francisco."

Jan tried to pull her thoughts together, to focus on what Luis had said. Although she understood why Brewster had questioned Carrie, she couldn't figure out why Carrie had told him so much. Did it matter? Probably not. And yet....

"I know why Brewster's so nosy," she said with a triumphant grin. "He swore me to secrecy."

"And you believe him?"

"Shouldn't I?"

He shrugged. "Nothing is right about this man."

The pressure of Luis' fingers were firm as they explored her hand. She closed her eyes, enjoying the sensation.

He said, "Your skin, it is very soft."

"Please, I—"

"Sh-h-h. Why did you help me at *La Luna Blanca*."

"I didn't want to see you hurt."

His other hand reached over and caressed her left shoulder. The fingers slipped down her bare arm and stopped on the wrist, massaging it. "Your help was a great surprise to me."

Her breathing turned ragged. "A surprise?" she faltered.

"*Sí*, I did not think you liked me. In Lima, I know I upset you. I thought, this lady does not care to know me."

She wet her lips. The musky smell from him was faint and appealing. Heat radiated from the dark V of his bare chest.

He drew her right hand up against his lips and gently kissed it. With a catch of breath, she pulled her hand away.

He said, "You do not like your hand kissed?"

She swallowed. "I like it."

"Why did you take your hand away?"

"Because there's something I...I must say." She barely spoke the words. Her body ached for him. She wanted to feel his arms around her. Taking a deep breath, she desperately tried to think. It was the alcohol, she concluded, definitely the alcohol that made her want him. She must push aside the haze.

"Carrie's my friend," she said defiantly. "My best friend. She's gone through a tough time." She rushed on, afraid she might burst into tears. "Luis, you know how she feels about you. I won't, I can't be the cause of her unhappiness."

"I do not love Carrie."

"Then, tell her before it's too late."

"Why?" He took hold of her hand again, his other hand still massaging her wrist.

"If you don't want to be her lover she needs to know."

He frowned. "You make too much of this."

"How can you say that? Aren't you concerned about her feelings? I don't understand you."

"I see no reason to be upset."

"If that's how you feel, then just leave me alone."

He let go of her, stepped back and reached for another cigarette. "Is there someone else? Someone back home? Is it this Logan man?"

"Even if there weren't anybody else, I couldn't, I mean, even if I wanted you, and maybe I do...." She realized it was impossible to explain.

"If a man and woman wish to make love, there is no reason why they should not." He lit his cigarette. "You make life too complicated."

She shivered and peered down at the water. "It seems," she said stiffly, "that I live by a different code."

He sighed.

She clung to the railing.

"Are we back to square one?" he inquired.

"Yes, that's where we are."

She no longer thought of the shadow on the water as a fort. It was nothing but a black blob. She couldn't look at Luis, didn't want to believe he stood there, fearful she might regret her decision.

"So, there will be no square two," he said, hurt creeping into his voice, belying his arrogant words. "I will not try again. *Buenos noches, Señorita.*"

As Luis' footsteps faded, Jan remained at the rail, gripping it tightly, willing the night air to clear her head.

When she finally returned to the room, Carrie wasn't there. A note on her pillow said, *I've gone to spend the night with Luis.*

Jan crumpled the paper into a hard ball and hurled it at the wastebasket. Had Luis, unable to get her, rushed to their room and picked up Carrie? Or, had Carrie charged off to find him, to offer herself?

She yanked off her clothes, not bothering to hang up anything. Her coral silk nightgown lay in the dresser drawer, the damned silk nightgown Harley claimed made her look seductive. Harley, that pathetic affair of four years ago. Wadding up the gown, she threw it at her reflection in the mirror. Naked and trembling, she climbed under the bed covers and switched off the lamp.

Across her mind flashed a picture of Logan picking up his briefcase as if it were a scruffy dog in the wrong place. Logan, always ready to tackle the next problem.

Sitting up, she fumbled until she found the phone. She dialed the front desk. "I'd like to place a call to the United States, to a Mr. Logan McCloskey in San Francisco, area code 415."

"Sorry," said a female voice on the other end. "The switchboard is closed for the night. Please place your call in the morning after 7:00."

Jan clutched the phone as if it were a life preserver. "Isn't there any way to…I mean, what do you do if there's an emergency?"

"Do you have an emergency?"

"No."

"If you give me the number," the voice continued without expression, "I will have your call placed when the operator comes on duty in the morning."

"That won't be necessary. It isn't important."

She replaced the receiver, deciding she was glad the call hadn't gone through. What would she have said to him? *Even if you don't give a hoot about me, please come, I need your help?* No, she wouldn't have been able to say those words. She couldn't ask for help. Why risk being turned down or thought weak. Instead, she would have made flippant remarks: *Has Linda kept up with your barrage of dictation? Have you murdered any defense attorneys lately?*

Logan probably had no idea she was in *Las Dunas*. With so many clients to please, why would he bother to check the itinerary posted above her office desk? He would have said, *Hey, where are you? What time is it down there? You sound drunk. What the hell's happening? Give me details.* She would have burbled about drinking too many Pisco sours and dancing a wild tango. Once again, doing and saying the wrong thing. Thank God, she hadn't been able to call.

She sat up. I'm drunk and nothing matters, she told herself. Carrie and Luis can do what they want. I'm going to forget how I danced. Forget Luis. His words meant nothing. He's one more guy on the make, and like a fool, I fell for his line. Forget it all.

In spite of her determination not to cry, tears came. She slipped back under the covers, forced herself to stop crying and at last fell asleep.

CHAPTER 12

Jan woke up the following morning to an excruciating headache. The waiter had assured her Pisco sours didn't give hangovers. Either he was wrong or she suffered from too much tango.

Carrie's bed was empty, the spread neatly folded over the pillow. The room was a mess, Jan's taffeta skirt crumpled on the floor, her eyelet blouse hanging from the lamp shade, her coral nightgown lumped before the mirror and her bra, panties and shoes scattered about as if a wind had gotten hold of them. Never had she left a room in such disarray. She closed her eyes, not wanting to remember how it all happened.

For a while she stayed under the covers motionless, hoping the pain would disappear, but it only grew worse like a knife-edged band cutting into her brain. Soon the sun reflecting through the glass doors would strike the mirror and the beam might blind her. I must crawl out of bed now, she decided.

The thought of breakfast made her stomach churn. She staggered into the bathroom to fix a glass of Alka-Seltzer. While the tablet dissolved, she tottered back into the bedroom and hung up her blouse. She hurled her coral nightgown into a drawer, banging it closed, wincing at the noise. Perched on the edge of her bed, she took a deep breath, blew it out in a slow stream and drank the Alma Seltzer all at once.

Gradually the band around her head loosened. Her stomach stopped jumping. Determined to get the room back in order, she methodically gathered up the rest of her clothes and put them away. The last item she faced was the balled-up note from Carrie; it sat on the floor in a pool of sunlight, a vivid reminder. She thought it best to treat the paper as something unimportant. Scooping it up as if it were a dust ball, she dropped it into the wastebasket.

After a long, lukewarm shower, the idea of toast and coffee seemed possible. She put on her burnt orange slacks and matching striped shirt, an outfit bought especially for the trip, thinking bright clothes would give her courage. She glanced at her watch, 10:00.

My God, the flight's at 11:00, she remembered. When had she ever slept this late? At least most people would be done with breakfast. She didn't feel like seeing anybody.

Unfortunately, the dining room was still half full. Even worse, Carrie, Luis, and Brewster sat at the same table and in the same seats as last night—a replay in brilliant sunlight.

Jan returned Brewster's "Howdy" with a tight smile. Although her dark glasses needed cleaning, she wasn't about to bother with them. Fine if she couldn't see a damned thing.

Brewster rose, draped his napkin over his papaya, pushed his chair back and assisted Jan into the vacant seat. "We've been waiting for you." He adjusted his lavender silk cravat and sat down again. "We wanted your approval before we solidified our plans."

Jan squinted at the three. Brewster looked thoroughly gay. Carrie sat in angelic silence, still in her rumpled chiffon dress, her skin no longer swimming-pool pink, her face as pale as the day after the abortion. Luis, the shadows under his eyes like dark crescent moons, lightly tapped a spoon against the table as if accompanying music in his head. He appeared edgy as if expecting an attack. Both he and Carrie looked exhausted. Jan wished the smudges on her glasses had blurred her vision more. With an effort, she raised her cup and caught the eye of a waiter who circled the room with a large carafe. While he poured her coffee, she said to Brewster, "What plans?"

"Carrie tells me you all are flying over the designs at 11:00."

"If you mean the ancient Nazca Lines, yes. Carrie wants to photograph them." Jan gulped her coffee, wishing it were hotter. "Our travel agent insisted we fly in the morning because desert afternoon winds are treacherous."

Brewster shook his head like a wet poodle. "Winds are not a problem for experienced pilots. Now, I have a suggestion. Since I too want to fly over the Lines, and I happen to know that at Ica Airport only three-passenger Cessnas are available, we must take two flights. You and Luis in the first flight; Carrie and I in the second, which I'll pay for."

Jan unfolded her napkin. Not feeling together enough to try her Spanish on the waiter who hovered near their table and hoping he understood English, she said to him, "Please, another cup of coffee. This one's not hot enough."

The waiter nodded, whisked away her cup and a moment later returned with a fresh cup balanced on a napkined tray.

She sipped, relieved the new brew was hot and strong. *"Gracias,"* she managed to say. Maybe now she could handle this situation, whatever it was. She glared at Brewster. "Since you come to this resort often, how come you've never flown over the Nazca Lines?"

He threw up his hands. "Oh, I have flown over them. Many times. I've located and identified all anthropomorphic, spiral, and geometric designs, even those hidden in the mountains. I've studied theories as to how they got there, when, and why, and I've even concocted a theory that—"

Jan interrupted, "Mind if we discuss your theories later? I'm not up to hearing about them now."

"Of course not, honey. We're all suffering from last night's fling. I predict our misery will soon dissipate." He leaned forward. "You agree, then, two flights, the second one in the afternoon. Same plane, same pilot. I know him well. He's an expert at handling chaotic winds."

She surveyed him over the top of her cup. "If you've flown over the Nazca Lines so many times, why go again?"

"It's rare to have someone along who speaks English."

"Why not go with me? Why with Carrie?"

"Oh, I don't mind," Carrie said quickly. "I want to take the flight with Brewster." She crumpled her napkin onto her plate and flashed a smile, deepening the darkness under her eyes.

"My reason is simple," said Brewster. "Carrie waltzes with such divine, impersonal grace that I feel safe with her, while you, honey, are such a sexy gypsy that if we flew together in a plane, I might forget my preference and insist we fly on forever."

"Nonsense!" Jan sighed and waved at the waiter, pointing to her empty coffee cup. The refill came at once.

Luis said in a business-like voice, "This Brewster man's arrangement, I agree with it. He wants to fly with Carrie. Carrie wants to fly with him." He appraised his spoon. "And the sexy gypsy does not frighten me."

Jan couldn't tell if that was sarcasm or a joke but Brewster' shattering laugh hit every nerve in her head. Raising her dark glasses and rubbing her eyes, she said, "Apparently these decisions were made before I arrived this morning."

Brewster spread his arms in a gesture of innocence. "Not fully, although I'll admit I spoke with my pilot friend." He patted Jan's arm, a look of mischief in his eyes. "I took the liberty of canceling your pilot and arranging for you and Luis to fly with my friend."

Jan frowned. "You're a pushy guy, Brewster." Suddenly his image of her as a sexy gypsy seemed funny. Resting her elbows on the table, she looked sideways at Luis. "Shall I bring along castanets?"

Luis stopped tapping his spoon. "If you do, I might forget where the lines are drawn."

Again Brewster's laugh exploded, causing sharp pains to shoot though Jan's head.

Carrie said softly, "Excuse me. I'm going back to the room to change."

Perplexed, Jan watched Carrie's progress down the path and across the bridge. Why did she want to fly with Brewster after spending the night with Luis? And what was the real reason why Brewster wanted to fly with her? Assuming he was gay, it wouldn't be sexual, although, maybe Luis was right. Maybe Brewster was straight. If so, why pretend to be gay? Odd how Carrie and Luis never once looked at each other. Not the usual way lovers acted. The whole setup was peculiar.

Here I am, Jan thought, about to be hurled into the air with a guy who doesn't care which woman he took to bed. She stole a look at him. Wearing a clean white shirt like a coat of paint, musky odor faint, hands toying with a spoon, he stared at an oblong pattern of sunlight on the floor. What's on his mind? What's Brewster's motive for planning this trip? What's Carrie thinking about? She tried to quell her fears, not used to facing situations over which she had no control.

CHAPTER 13

They arrived at the Ica Airport in Luis' Toyota, Brewster in front next to Luis, Jan in the back seat. The runway baked in the late morning heat and the windsock hung limply from the pole like a dead bird. On one side of the airport stood a small, square, stucco terminal, the same dun color as the desert. Except for two Cessnas, one dark blue, one silver, the small airport looked deserted.

Inside the terminal, at one end was a Formica-topped counter. The only other object in the room was a dusty wooden bench under an equally dusty window. Jan sat down, thought better of it, and stood. Luis stayed near the doorway. Brewster ran behind the counter and rummaged on the shelf beneath. "Don't you all worry." he said, pulling out a clipboard. "Felipe's usually late. I'll sign us in."

A few minutes later, an engine sputtered to a stop outside. A car door slammed. A short man in a black leather jacket with ragged cuffs and a pair of goggles too big for his face, tapped on the window. He poked his head through the doorway and yelled, "*Ayudeme.*"

"Ah, Felipe," cried Brewster. He shook the man's hand and accompanied him down the runway to the blue Cessna, where they unfastened the tie-downs.

Luis walked outside and stared at the two men. Jan waited in the doorway, thinking the silver plane looked far newer. The more she looked at the blue Cessna, the older it appeared.

Felipe gave them a cheerful wave and shouted, "*Espere un momento, Señorita y Señor.*"

Luis' expression was serious. Jan said to him, "Have you ever flown over the Lines?"

"*Sí.* Once, with a friend, a pilot for Aero Condor. This, I think it will be different."

"Think it's safe?"

He shrugged. "This Brewster man says so."

Jan swallowed hard and watched the pilot run around the plane, tapping here and there, inspecting underneath, leaning inside the cockpit. "At least he's checking it out," she muttered.

The pilot beckoned for them to come.

Luis climbed in first, after suggesting Jan sit with the pilot for a good view. Jan crawled into the front passenger seat and slammed shut the tinny-sounding door.

The cockpit felt cramped. The glass in the plane was as dirty as the window in the terminal. It struck her that if the plane took off into the sun, which seemed the plan, the filthy glass would cause such a glare the pilot wouldn't be able to see and neither would they.

"*Un momento.*" Felipe reached under his seat and brought out a newspaper. "*El sol. Hace dano.*"

To her horror, he taped the newspaper over the windshield, completely covering it. She glanced back at Luis and noticed perspiration on his upper lip.

Felipe hunched toward the windshield. Carefully he tore out a two-inch-square strip of newspaper in front of him. With a smile of triumph, he wadded the scrap and tossed it over his left shoulder. Obviously he used the newspaper to diminish the sun's glare and believed a small aperture was enough for the take off.

Forget this plane ride, she decided. She would leap out right now. Where was the door handle? There wasn't one. The engine roared to life. "Wait!" she squealed, but realized nobody could hear her. Something above her head vibrated like the twang of a bedspring. The engine grew louder. The twang picked up tempo. She jammed the end of her seat belt into the slot. No catch. Again and again she tried. Felipe's seat belt must be broken too. Either that or he didn't bother with it.

Behind her, Luis sat straight and stiff, his belt fastened. With a nervous laugh, she leaned back in her seat. The frame collapsed onto Luis' lap. "Sorry," she yelled. In a frantic scramble, she regained her upright position and clutched the sides of her seat.

The plane bumped down the runway, then wobbled into the air, banked into a turn and headed south. Reaching up, Felipe loosened the newspaper, tore it off the glass and pushed it onto Jan's lap with a gesture for her to fold it up. She stared at the pile of paper and pretended she didn't understand. He tapped her shoulder and gestured again. With a feeling of certain disaster, she let go of the seat, hastily folded the paper, and again grasped the seat. He shoved the paper under his legs, probably saving it for future use, she thought.

As they flew over a range of hills between the Ica Valley and the pampas of Nazca, she felt a sense of imbalance and a fear of falling into nothing. She couldn't lean back. She wore no seat belt. The engine roared like a sick lion. Rattles in the plane multiplied until they sounded like a ton of BBs hitting a tin roof. Surely, the plane booked by the travel agent would have been better than this one. Was Brewster playing a macabre joke on them?

Gradually she realized the stupidity of clutching the seat. That didn't keep this rattletrap in the air.

"It will be all right," Luis yelled over the noise but he didn't sound full of assurance. He pushed the back of her seat forward and leaned against it. Extending his arm over her right shoulder, he pointed toward the side window and yelled, "See below? The town of Nazca."

She nodded.

About fifteen minutes later a group of straight lines appeared on the ground. Many intersected at a central point or created complex abstract patterns. Especially interesting was a long, yellowish trapezoid that narrowed at one end. Its precise, clean-cut form contrasted sharply to the gray-brown desert. The shape reminded her of a landing field. "What is it?" she shouted, peering through the murky window.

Luis stretched forward to see. "Nobody knows for sure," he shouted. "Some think an aid for astronomy. Others say a ceremonial site. Fertility, maybe a..." His voice was lost in the roar, the twang and the rat-tat-tatting of falling BBs. He yelled anew, "Some call it a pathway to..." Again his voice was overwhelmed.

"To what?" she cried.

"To the Gods," he bellowed.

She grasped the ledge in front of her, praying the Gods would be kind and nothing would break off in her hands.

For forty minutes they circled above multitudes of intersecting lines, some like spokes on a wheel. Occasionally, she saw spiral and geometric forms and anthropomorphic figures. All appeared etched into the desert floor, designs so large they could be seen only from above. She found it hard to believe these designs had been created by an ancient people who had no way of seeing them. No planes, no airships of any sort. What intrigued her most were the outlines of creatures. There was a monkey with a great spiral tail, a hummingbird with a long bill and intricate wings, a spider, a condor, a lizard, a bizarre creature with huge hands.

Over the noise, Luis explained how the designs were formed by removing rocks from the desert surface and exposing the light-colored earth beneath. He told her that measurements taken on the straight lines showed incredible accuracy. The precision of the prehistoric creations, formed without computers, without modern tools, astonished her so much that for a while she forgot she was flying in a plane. She appreciated how hard Luis was trying to be informative, even if she couldn't hear all of what he said and couldn't bear the thought of his sex life.

As they flew back over the hills, she considered the grandeur of the Nazca Lines and felt privileged to have seen them. If this weren't one of the driest, most isolated places on earth, she felt certain the ancient Lines would not have survived.

The landing was a rattling success. Felipe had to be a good pilot, she concluded, to have flown this bucket of bolts.

Brewster sauntered out to the plane and opened the cockpit door. "Did you all have a pleasurable time?" he smirked. They nodded like robots. "Good, good. Now drive back. After Felipe refuels the plane, I'll use his car to pick up Carrie. We'll meet you by the pool at 4:00."

For the return to the resort Luis suggested Jan ride in front beside him. Apparently encouraged by her interest, he spoke about the early coastal cultures and explained more theories about why the Nazca Lines had been created.

"One theory relates them to weaving," he said. "Another claims they are pottery designs. Still another, that priests made the lines. Maybe prayers for rain." His free hand flowed about to help illustrate his words. "They had to be drawn first—models made. Designs were...ah, what is the word—scaled, that is it. *Sí*, scaled and laid out with ropes or poles. Perhaps both. Very straight lines. Some go many kilometers." He slowed the car down and looked at her through lowered eyes. "Did you like seeing them?"

"Yes," she replied, "the lines are amazing." The way he used his eyes bothered her. In a husky voice she said, "I appreciate your information, Luis."

They were silent until they said formal good-byes in the parking lot.

In the gift shop she purchased a book about the Nazca Lines. As she passed through the dining room she ordered a ham sandwich to go. From a soft drink machine she bought a bottle of Inca Cola. Carrie wasn't in the room. Across her bed lay the blue chiffon dress. Operating on automatic, Jan hung the dress up. Realizing what she had done, she considered tossing it back on the bed but decided she wanted no visual reminders of last night.

A little after 2:00, while Jan sat in the small patio eating the sandwich and sipping the golden drink, the blue Cessna appeared in the sky. The plane made a slow circle then headed north, a direction that seemed strange to her. She had thought all Lines were to the south?

Resting her bare feet on the low table, she read until she fell asleep. At 3:45 she woke up, surprised she had slept an hour. Carrie hadn't returned. Time for a quick shower.

Luis met her at a table by the pool. Both ordered soda water and laughed about it. "No alcohol for me tonight," Jan said, and he agreed.

At 4:30, she expressed concern that Carrie and Brewster hadn't shown up.

Luis shrugged.

However, at 5:00 he announced it was time to worry, for soon it would be dark. Twice after that Jan hurried back to the room to see if Carrie had returned. Luis asked a hotel clerk to check on Brewster's room. Both places remained empty.

"Where are they?" Jan said, not wanting to say what was on her mind—a plane crash.

Luis pushed aside his empty glass and stood up, surveying the sky, already black and star-filled. "Maybe no lights on the runway. I go to the airport and see."

A bellboy appeared, carrying a tray, the kind used to present a bill. "*Señor Acosta*," he called out, "*Señorita Fielding.*"

"*Sí,*" both said in unison.

Jan chewed on her bottom lip as the bellboy approached. "*Un mensaje telefonico.*"

Luis took the message from the tray and deposited a tip in its place. Unfolding the paper, he read it silently. With no change of expression, he sat down and handed the paper to Jan.

She read the message: *Forced to land in Nazca because of engine trouble. Must stay here tonight for repairs. See you at breakfast. Brewster.* She looked at Luis. "Think that rattletrap will make it back safely?" She tried to hide the concern in her voice.

He raised his hands in a futile gesture.

Along the hotel pathways, lights glowed, but the bridges across the ponds were lost in darkness. An idea nagged her, a disturbing one that made no sense: Carrie and Brewster planned this before they left.

"Might as well eat dinner and watch the floor show," she said to Luis.

"Is that what you wish to do?"

"No, but I can't sit in the room worrying."

People began to fill up the tables. Several men briefly met her eyes and smiled as if they hoped she might do another memorable dance. A woman stared at her in a disapproving manner.

"Luis," she said quietly, "let's move to a back table."

He raised his eyebrows in a questioning manner.

"In light of my dazzling performance last night, I'd just as soon blend into the scenery this evening."

He observed her through lowered eyes. "Unfortunately, *Janecita*, you are not an easy lady to forget."

CHAPTER 14

"Let's talk," Jan said from the patio doorway.

It was the next morning. Carrie had just arrived and was tossing clothes into her open suitcase.

"About what?" Carrie said, not looking up.

"About where you've been, what you've been doing."

"No time. It's almost 7:30. I bet Luis is waiting out front." She gave Jan a sideways look. "Did you eat breakfast?"

"As much as I could stomach. Look, there's enough time to let me know a few things. Last night I was so worried I couldn't sleep. I feel as if I'm traveling with a time bomb."

Carrie's laugh sounded artificial. "Don't worry, Jan. Everything's fine." She held up her cotton print skirt. "This needs washing but I'll have to wait till Arequipa." She stuffed the skirt into the suitcase and hurried to the closet, bringing out her chiffon dress. "Are you all packed?"

"Sure, I had to do *something* while you were lost in the middle of the desert." Jan sat down on her bed, arms and legs crossed. "Where'd you sleep last night?"

"In a house—one of Brewster's friends. Please, Jan, don't interrogate me." Carrie snapped the suitcase shut. She grabbed the brush from the dresser and assaulted her hair, leaning to one side, then to the other.

Jan studied Carrie's reflection in the mirror. Although the shadows under her eyes weren't as deep as yesterday morning, she seemed twice as nervous, her hand trembling between downward strokes. Maybe she should probe Carrie later, perhaps during the drive back to Lima. No, Luis would hear and some questions were about him. Maybe at the Lima Airport. No, Luis' father was supposed to meet them. On their flight to Arequipa? Impossible. They'd be welded to Luis. Her next time alone with Carrie wouldn't be until this afternoon when they reached their new hotel room. Hours of built-up worry if no explanations now.

Carrie pulled strands of hair from the brush. Briefly she met Jan's eyes in the mirror "Don't stare at me," she said.

"Anything else I shouldn't do? *Don't give advice. Don't interrogate. Don't stare.* Should I disappear?"

"Of course not. I'll explain everything when we have more time." Carrie released the hair strands over the wastebasket and watched them float down. "Anyway, there's nothing much to discuss."

"Nothing much? Night before last you slept with Luis. Yesterday you flew off with Brewster and didn't come back until this morning. Isn't it natural I'd want to know where you went and why you did these things?"

"All right! All right!" Carrie turned around with an exasperated look. "I spent the night with Luis because he's sexy and I was drunk and lonely. Do you want details?"

"No." Jan inspected her sandals.

"As for Brewster, I flew with him because I think he's funny and I like to laugh."

"That doesn't make sense, knowing you."

"Maybe you don't know me as well as you think you do."

"I thought I understood you pretty well. I thought we were good friends. At this point, I don't know what to think. For God's sake, Carrie, I'm not trying to hurt you."

"You keep pumping me."

"I'm worried about you."

"I can take care of myself." Carrie held her brush against the light and plucked out a few stray hairs, her hands shaking. "Brewster knows a lot about the Nazca Lines," she added as if an afterthought.

"Did you take pictures?"

There was a pause. "No. I studied the Lines and listened to Brewster's information."

"You said you wanted to photograph the designs."

Carrie leaned back against the dresser, her free hand fingering the drawer pull beside her. "There wasn't time. The engine trouble developed quickly. Felipe made a forced landing at Nazca."

"Your plane didn't head that way. I watched it from the patio."

Carrie took a quick breath. "Yes, well, first we flew north and Brewster showed me a design on a mountainside. After that we circled around and flew south. Then we had trouble with the plane. While Brewster stayed behind to help fix the engine, his friend drove me to his house where I had a restful night. This morning Felipe flew Brewster and me back to the Ica Airport. After we landed, he drove us here. There, I've accounted for all of my movements. Are you satisfied?"

"Not really. The whole trip sounds fishy to me."

Carrie shrugged. Turning away, she examined her face in the mirror. "We may meet Brewster again," she said softly. She shot a look over her shoulder. "But don't mention that to Luis."

"Why not?"

"Luis doesn't like him."

"I don't either. The guy gives me bad vibes—the way he maneuvered the plane rides, the forced landing, other things. He's off base in a way I can't identify."

"That's because he's gay and you're used to straight guys."

"That's not the problem." Jan leaned forward. "Do you really trust Brewster? Do you enjoy being with him more than with Luis?"

Carrie jammed her brush into the daypack and fastened the cover strap. "I'm not a child who must explain how I feel." She pulled the pack onto her shoulders and wheeled around to face Jan. "How about if I grill you for a change? Tell me about your experience last night with Luis?"

"We didn't sleep together if that's what you want to know," Jan replied in an acid tone.

"So, what did you do?"

"Nothing. What's gotten into you?"

Carrie folded her arms and snapped, "I want details about what happened and I want them now."

Jan unfolded her arms and tried to keep anger out of her voice. "You don't have to mimic me. I get your point. Luis and I ate a quiet dinner. We both had broiled tuna. Then we watched the floor show. Afterwards, when the band broke into a rumba, we left for our separate quarters. No clay-pot chicken, no Pisco sours, no dancing and no jokes. We were concerned about you and Brewster."

"A shame you wasted your evening worrying about us."

"Sarcasm isn't natural for you, Carrie. You sound phony. Obviously something's bothering you." Jan rose stiffly. "However, from here on, I won't question you. Sorry if I've shown concern. In the future I'll try not to care."

"I didn't mean to make you mad," Carrie said gently. "Yesterday's engine trouble still has me upset." Even more gently, "Could you help me set up my baggage cart? You know I don't have an ounce of mechanical ability."

"And I'm great at getting you organized."

"You're a good friend. You've helped me a lot, and I appreciate your concern."

"Sure!" Jan yanked Carrie's cart out of the closet and thrust it open. She slammed the suitcase on top and stretched the bungee cords around it, fastening them onto the bars with a twang.

"Go ahead," Carrie said, "bang everything to pieces if that makes you feel better."

"Your conveyor is ready, *Señorita*."

Carrie sighed and grasped the handle of her cart. Opening the front door, she held it back with a foot as she pulled the cart outside. Jan yanked up her duffel bag and stalked after her.

"I forgot to check the itinerary," Carrie called over her shoulder. "What time's our flight to Arequipa?"

"Eleven twenty-five," Jan yelled so loud that a woman walking on a pathway turned around to look at her.

Carrie broke into a run, the cart careening noisily after her. She dashed across the pond bridge as if it might blow up at any minute.

Jan continued her stolid march, never breaking step until she reached the Toyota parked in front of the hotel. "To hell with everybody," she muttered.

At Jan's overly polite suggestion, Carrie climbed in front next to Luis. Jan crumpled into a back seat corner, announcing she needed sleep.

On the way to the coast, they passed fields of sugar cane and rows of grapevines. Polite Spanish chatter between Carrie and Luis wafted past Jan's ears, simple sentences even she could understand, not the sort of language expected between lovers. She caught Luis looking at her in the rearview mirror and chastised herself for noticing. She felt like the naughty kid relegated to the corner during recess, only nobody had sent her there.

After Paracas, it was bleak desert again, the ocean to their left. Luis turned off the air conditioner and opened his window to let in a breeze. From the speakers floated Peruvian music played by stringed instruments. Jan was thankful not to be assaulted by wailing flutes. The soothing melodies and balmy air lulled her to sleep.

The next thing she knew, Ignacio tapped her arm. "*Señorita Fielding*, you are curled up like *la gatita*."

She rubbed her eyes. The large body of Luis' father filled the car doorway. They had arrived at the Lima Airport.

"You are a little cat," he continued. "From now on I shall call you *Gatita Fielding*." His fat cheeks puffed out in his usual smile. He gestured for her to get out. "Come, come. I have confirmed three seats on the plane to Arequipa and the luggage is unloaded from the car." He indicated the Peruvian boy who waited near the entrance, Carrie's cart in one hand, Luis' satchel in the other, her duffel bag slung over his shoulder. "All we need is *La Gatita*."

Ignacio led them past a series of guards. "Board the plane from that room," he announced, indicating the way to go. "Have a splendid time." He flashed his usual smile and waddled away as if more important business was elsewhere.

On the plane, Jan insisted on sitting behind Luis and Carrie, in the seat originally assigned to Luis. As she collapsed into it, Luis gave her a worried look. "Are you ill?"

"No, just tired."

It was more than that. She felt like excess baggage, a prying fool, nobody's friend, least of all her own. She lamented her ten more days in Peru. If only she weren't so obsessed with finishing every damned thing she started, then she could fly back to San Francisco to the safety of the law office, to Logan, to a place where she belonged.

The plane seemed scarcely to move, so smooth was the flight. The engines droned softly. Quite a difference from the last plane ride, she thought. The old lady in the aisle seat next to her began to snore, lips wrinkling as if she tasted sour grapes. Jan watched the side of her black mantilla move in and out with her breathing.

The flight was less than two hours. As the plane started its descent, outside the window loomed a mountain, capped with snow and laced with clouds. She pulled the travel brochure from her inside vest pocket and read the caption under the photo: *The volcano, El Misti, casts an early morning shadow over the white colonial city of Arequipa, cradled in the foothills of the Andes—a city where it is always spring.* Looking down at the city, she was surprised at its whiteness.

She heard Luis explaining to Carrie. "It is because of the sillar. It makes the domes, steeples, walls, everything shine in the sun."

"What is sillar?" Carrie asked.

"White *petrificar.* How do you say *petrificar* in English?"

"Petrified lava," Carrie replied. "It certainly lightens up the city."

Jan concentrated on the view out the window. *As the inner world darkens, the outer world must lighten.* Where had she heard those words? Then it came to her. The priest in Carmel—five years ago, his words beside the casket.

A vivid picture of Beth flashed across her mind. They played in the surf, splashing water on each other. Quickly she erased the sight, afraid she might remember more, and she couldn't bear to relive the details of her sister's death.

CHAPTER 15

At first glimpse, *La Posada del Puente,* their hillside hotel in Arequipa, appeared to be a modern sculpture. However, from the entry stairway, it looked more like a puzzle waiting to be pieced together—a mix of geometric shapes terraced down the west bank of the *Rio Chili.* The river had overflowed onto lower sidewalks and churned against the pylons of the bridge on the nearby street.

"*Pasaportes, por favor,*" thundered the rotund clerk, who sat on a tall stool behind the wooden counter. He slipped his book onto a shelf below his knees. "*M-m-m, norteamericanos.*" He raised one eyebrow at Luis.

The clerk inspected each passport page in the manner of a scientist searching for hidden contaminants. "To reach the bar and dining room," he intoned without looking up, "proceed through the glass doors"—he gestured toward the doors at the far end of the foyer. "To reach your rooms, walk down the passageway"—his hand sailed backwards to indicate the windowed hallway near the desk. As for our lobby, you'll find it through the archway directly behind you"—his hand extended forward, eyes still studying the pages.

Jan, Carrie and Luis turned to view the lobby. A dark-complexioned, black-mustached man in a tan shirt sat on the couch, reading a newspaper.

The desk clerk continued in his rumbly voice. "The fireplace in the lobby is only lit on cold evenings. The conference room, not visible from this point, is located to the left of the fireplace. Should you wish to use it, reserve the time here. As for the garden paths, presently it is too dangerous to walk on the ones by the river. They are flooded due to heavy rainfall in the Andes. And now, *señoritas y señor*...."

The three faced him again. He raised his bushy, gray eyebrows, straightened his back, and pushed out his chest, his stomach extending with it.

Jan felt certain the gentleman had perfected his spiel with much practice, his gestures and eyebrow movements timed perfectly. Not only did she find the desk clerk's looks and actions amusing but the man on the couch also looked funny —his mustache reminded her of the letter "M," a miniature symbol of McDonald's. Everything about the hotel seemed comical.

The desk clerk plopped the passports on the counter. With precise movements, he produced two registration cards, one for Jan and Carrie and one for Luis, followed by two identical pens.

After the three had signed the cards, the desk clerk filed them away. With a dramatic sweep of his hands, he shouted, *"Botones"* and stared at the ceiling as if the porter might descend from there. His brows drew together in an ominous line until a young man in a white uniform appeared by way of the glass doors. "*Aquí,*" the desk clerk growled at the boy and handed him three keys. "*Numero catorce para las señoritas. Numero quince para el señor.*" With a nod, the boy gathered up the baggage.

The desk clerk reached under the counter and brought out his book entitled *Mas Vale Tarde Que Nunca,* opened it to a marked page and returned to his former and apparently more desired occupation. It was as if the people who stood before him no longer existed.

Carrie whispered in Spanish to the bellboy, who then handed Carrie her room key. She announced, "I'm going to look around for a bit," and walked across the foyer and into the lobby.

Jan followed the porter down the passageway, Luis behind her. Although she couldn't imagine why Carrie wanted to look around before going to the room, she had no intention of inquiring. The inquisition was over.

After the porter deposited the luggage and left the room, Jan threw open the window to let in fresh air. She was startled to see a tethered llama outside, munching on the lawn. The creature paused as if she were an unwelcome intruder. With an imperious look, it urinated. Jan giggled.

Even though she had a slight headache, probably due to the altitude, over 7,000 feet, life looked better now than it had this morning. The car nap had helped as well as the relaxing plane ride and she had enjoyed the encounter with the pompous desk clerk. The llama was comical too; it reminded her of Mrs. Beauchamp, one of Logan's haughty clients. Imagining what might happen if Mrs. Beauchamp urinated on the oriental rug by Logan's desk, Jan laughed so hard she had to pull out a tissue to wipe away the tears. It felt good to laugh again.

Wondering what to do next, she decided to wash her face and take two aspirins. Then, she sat in front of the window, observing the clouds on *El Misti*, watching the llama eat grass, and noting the flooded paths by the river. She contemplated the biggest problem she faced now was how to recover her friendship with Carrie. Best to be polite and cheerful and ask no questions. The same with Luis. She wouldn't let either of them disturb her newly found equilibrium.

No sense waiting for Carrie any longer like an impatient mother. She would locate the bar and have a beer.

When she reached the foyer, the desk clerk was still reading his book. She walked softly past him and peered into the lobby. Empty. She looked toward the conference room. To her surprise, Carrie sat at a table, huddled in conversation with a man in a tan shirt. He looked up. It was the same man who had been on the couch reading the newspaper.

Abruptly, Carrie rose and with a murmured, "See you later, Jan," shut the door.

"Well, I'll be damned," Jan sputtered. One night Carrie sleeps with Luis, the next night she spends with Brewster, and now she picks up with a stranger and shuts the door on her best friend.

Jan stomped across the foyer, ignoring the clerk who looked up with arched eyebrows. She flung open the glass doors, and charged across the deserted patio. At the bar, she ordered a beer. "Any kind," she announced and brought a brimming mug back to a patio table where she fell into a chair and took large gulps.

Through the glass doors, she saw Luis furtively enter the foyer from the passageway and slip out of the hotel. Where's he going? Unable to quell her curiosity, she left her beer on the table and re-entered the foyer, tip-toeing past the still engrossed desk clerk. She stole out the hotel entrance door and hurried to the edge of the stairway. Luis stood on the sidewalk below. After a quick look about the sidewalk, he eased into a taxi. The cab shot off toward the bridge. Across the street, a gray car pulled away from the curb. It also crossed the bridge. The driver wore a tan shirt. From her vantage point she watched the taxi move along the street and turn toward the center of town. Not far behind, rolled the gray car.

If Logan were here, Jan knew he would soon find out what all this meant. He always knew how to learn the truth—who to trust, who to watch, who might be a friend, who an enemy. She doubted if she could do as well, but she had to try.

She returned to the hotel foyer and glanced into the lobby. Empty. The door to the conference room was open, the table deserted. Peering down the passageway, she saw Carrie standing by one of the windows, surveying the garden. How long had Carrie been there? Had the man in the tan shirt slipped out of the hotel while she ordered her beer?

Remembering her beer, Jan hurried back into the patio. As she sipped, she reviewed the strange events of the past few days: Carrie's suitcase torn apart, Luis attacked by a colonel, a gay guy nosing into their lives, Carrie running off to sleep with Luis, Brewster dictating their flights over the Nazca lines in a battered plane piloted by his friend Felipe, Brewster and Carrie disappearing into the Nazca Lines, Carrie meeting a tan-shirted guy with an M-shaped mustache, possibly the same guy following Luis, although that might be taking the intrigue too far. Then there was the way Carrie had acted since *Las Dunas*, as if Jan no longer was her friend.

It seemed that Carrie and Luis were involved in situations they didn't want each other to know about. And definitely neither of them wanted Jan to know about anything. Somewhere in the middle sat Brewster. On the edge lurked the pilot Felipe and the man in the tan shirt.

She believed she would get nowhere by asking questions. Best to keep a sharp eye, listen to conversations and pretend no concern. It seemed of utmost importance to piece together this puzzle and by God she would succeed even if the completed picture might be one she didn't care to see.

CHAPTER 16

All evening Jan pretended to be cheerful. She smiled and chattered with Carrie and Luis about the beauties of Arequipa and which points of interest they might visit the next day. Carrie didn't mention the man in the tan shirt, Luis didn't explain where he had gone in the cab and Jan asked no questions.

Breakfast was dinner conversation warmed over, harder for Jan to swallow. By the time Luis ushered her into the taxi for the trip to the convent of Santa Catalina, her facial muscles ached from smiling and her teeth felt wrapped in ice.

She scooted across the back seat, Carrie climbing in after her. In a surprising move, Luis ran around and eased into the other side. He waved Jan to the middle.

Acutely conscious of his musky scent, Jan quipped, "Hey, since I'm the chaperon on this field trip, I'd prefer to sit on the side." She started to clamber over Carrie.

Luis muttered, "It is better if you stay in the middle."

"No, I—"

"Hush," said Carrie, her smile benign. She eased Jan back to the center. "Sit still and no more arguments." Her laugh sounded forced.

Jan didn't find it funny. She figured Carrie didn't either. It seemed as if they were trying to hold onto a relationship that no longer existed in order to hide what did.

Yesterday, after finishing her beer, Jan found Carrie in the room taking a nap. Leaving her alone, Jan had walked out into the garden to survey the flooded river below. An hour later, while she stood in the foyer, perusing the tour pamphlets in the rack near the front door, Luis returned, rushing into the hotel, shirtsleeves rolled up. He attempted to conceal a large manila envelope, holding it behind him as if it were a stolen gem, and mumbling a greeting to Jan, who replied, "Hi." It was all she could think of to say. The desk clerk, still involved in a book, frowned at the interruption. Luis rushed into the passageway.

Evasion fluttered in the wind. Jan continued to hide her concerns beneath a veneer of gaiety and waited for evidence to slip out. With this in mind, she sat sandwiched in the taxi, babbling about the scenery. She laughed at the slightest joke, tried to pretend Luis was her brother, and treated Carrie like a close friend, feeling she no longer was.

The tour of the Santa Catalina Convent took more than an hour. A solemn woman, her hair drawn into a severe bun, showed them around. She explained how this small inner city of winding streets, beautiful gardens, patios, arcades and cell-like rooms had been a nunnery for 400 years.

"Today," the woman proclaimed in a dry voice, "Santa Catalina stands nearly empty—a tourist attraction. Once, however, inside these high walls lived 330 nuns. Many came from the Spanish aristocracy, girls entering the convent at the age of fourteen, often accompanied by their maids. A nun never left the convent. Eight hours a day she prayed, her life cloistered, even her death, for she was buried in a cemetery within the convent walls."

The thought of a young girl forced to kneel and pray for eight hours a day boggled Jan's mind. What would a girl say to God if not allowed to experience life? Would she repeat meaningless phrases, over and over in a mind-numbing chant? "Keep me innocent, oh Lord. Tell me, heavenly Father, what I should say, what I should do, what I should think?"

Suddenly, she saw her sister's face, only thirteen when she drowned, she too plucked from the brink of life.

Jan hadn't thought about Beth for years, but since arriving in Peru, she often appeared, dreamlike—her face, her mannerisms, their times together. Frightening pictures sometimes filled her mind and she had to force them away.

"Please note," continued the guide, "the inner face of the outside wall, which surrounds the monastery, is painted red. This symbolized leaving carnal desire behind, indeed all worldly sins. Inside these walls a state of serene virginity prevailed."

Jan studied a scene painted on the sillar wall of an arcaded walkway. The fresco showed a handsome man approaching a beautiful woman. She said to the guide, "Is this the lover some nun dreamed about?"

The guide stiffened. In a tight voice she said, "The nuns painted a number of frescos. This one depicts Divine Love as a dashing Spanish cavalier. If you read the white words coming from the mouths of these figures, you will understand that the scene illustrates the life of the soul."

"Oh, excuse me." Jan looked heavenward. "My Spanish is poor."

Luis' mouth twitched in a half smile. Carrie walked ahead to study another fresco. From outside the monastery walls, brakes squealed, a horn blared and voices of men and women chattered and laughed.

The smile still occupied Jan's face at lunchtime. They sat in the trellised patio of the cafe, *Sol de Mayo.* Jan ordered *anticuchos*, skewered pieces of spicy meat, and Carrie ordered *rocoto relleno*, hot peppers stuffed with meat, rice and vegetables. When Luis' *cuy chactado* arrived, Jan's appetite disappeared and her smile was difficult to maintain. Splayed across his plate was a broiled guinea pig, limbs extended, head attached, front teeth protruding, eyes bulging like large peppercorns. She had read about this Peruvian dish but wasn't prepared for the sight of it, like a half-burned rat. When Luis tore apart the tiny body and began to eat it with relish, she fought back an urge to throw up.

To Jan's amazement, Carrie asked for a taste. Luis ripped off a leg and handed it to her. She bit into the meat, chewed thoughtfully, and pronounced it better than rabbit. Pushing aside her stuffed peppers, Carrie ordered *cuy*. At this point, Jan's carefully preserved smile dissolved.

"*Sí, inmediatamente,*" cried the waiter. "*Al instante voy por la bella señorita.*"

Jan tried not to watch Luis and Carrie wrench apart and devour rat-like creatures with frightful heads. She understood why Luis enjoyed this gruesome food. It was part of his culture. But she couldn't figure Carrie's fascination. This fragile, soft, vulnerable girl Jan knew in San Francisco was turning into a tough woman who could handle things Jan couldn't.

After lunch Carrie informed the taxi driver she wished to be dropped off at *La Compania*, located at the southeast corner of *Plaza de Armas*. "I've read about this Jesuit church," she explained to Luis and Jan as the taxi drove them away from the convent. "I want to go there for half an hour." She cleared her throat and added, "And I want to go alone."

Luis frowned. "Why alone?"

"I'm still bothered by things that happened to me in San Francisco. What I did may have been wrong. I'm upset about it. I need time by myself to pray."

With a shrug, Luis said, "All right, we wait outside for you."

"No, no. You two go on ahead. Tour the old mill. After that, come back to pick me up."

"I find it odd," Jan said quietly, "that at this moment you want to rush off and pray."

"It's important to me," Carrie said impatiently. "Do I have to discuss my religious needs?"

"I'm not asking you to do that."

"You know I'm Catholic, Jan. I taught at a Catholic school. Many mornings I went to Mass."

"Okay, sure, but...."

Jan started to say she didn't think it wise for Carrie to traipse off into a Peruvian church alone, but she knew her advice wouldn't be appreciated and was a breach of the promise made to herself.

"But what?" Carrie asked, her eyes flashing.

"Nothing," Jan answered, looking down at her folded hands.

Luis leaned forward and scrutinized Carrie. In a curt tone he said, "The old mill, you said you wished to see it."

Carrie wet her lips and cleared her throat. "I do, yes. Why don't you two visit *Artisanas* for 30 minutes. Then, come back for me. We'll tour the mill together."

The taxi pulled up before a church with a carved facade in Spanish Baroque style. Carrie jumped out and pulled on her daypack. Luis called out to her. "Watch out for thieves. They slash that bag on your back. What you carry, it can be gone, poof."

"Thanks for your concern." Carrie slammed the cab door and ran toward the church entrance, her yellow pack a bright spot against the white sillar walls.

"*Artisanas*," Luis directed the driver. Leaning back, he tapped his knees in a gesture of annoyance. "Carrie surprises me. Why does she not pray in the big *Catedral*." He waved toward the large building on the other side of the square."

Jan tucked a loose strand of hair behind her ears. "Apparently, she prefers this church."

"*Sí*. Apparently."

Their eyes met briefly. She moved over on the seat, glad not to be as close to him. She felt his stare touch every part of her body. Unable to swallow, panic rising, she fumbled in her skirt pocket for a cough drop and then remembered she hadn't brought any.

He said, "It is not good for Carrie to wander about alone."

"Then, why didn't you stop her?"

"I have no authority."

"Being on intimate terms would seem reason enough."

"Intimate terms? What does this mean?"

"You know."

He frowned. "I do not know."

"She spent a night with you," Jan burst out. "You slept with her."

"That is not true."

Jan glared at him. "You're lying. At *Las Dunas*, after you left me on the bridge, you slept with her."

"I tell you, I did not sleep with Carrie"

"But she left me a note...."

His eyes grew fierce. "*Janecita*. I spent that night alone. I sat by the pool."

She took a deep breath and looked away, attempting to calm down. Where did Carrie spend the night if not with Luis? With Brewster? If Brewster wasn't gay, why did he pretend to be? Had the man in the tan shirt been at *Las Dunas*? Had she slept with him? Barely conscious of her voice, she murmured, "Maybe he's the man she's meeting."

Luis grasped her arm. "This man she meets, who is he?"

Startled, she tried to pull away. "I...I'm not sure."

"You have an idea," he insisted, increasing the pressure on her arm.

"Why is it important to you?"

"Tell me."

She tried to free her arm but he held on. "The man in the hotel lobby," she sputtered. "The guy reading the newspaper."

"What makes you think she meets this man?"

Feeling claustrophobic she blurted out, "They met in the conference room. Carrie shut the door. Later he left the hotel. Now let go of me."

"When did he leave?" Luis moved closer, his breath warm on her face.

"Before you did."

"You saw me go?" He tightened his hold on her arm.

"Yes."

"Did this man follow me?" He blew the words into her face.

"I don't know," she gasped. "Someone drove after you."

"What color car?" he demanded.

"Gray." She struggled. "Luis, you're hurting me."

"¡*Madre de Dios!*" he swore and released her. With a scowl he turned away.

She rubbed her arm, the marks of his fingers still there, the skin red around them. Trying to keep her voice steady, she said, "I don't know what you're up to, Luis, or how Carrie's involved but something is terribly wrong."

"*Dios, Dios,*" he muttered.

"What's happening? Tell me."

In a flash of anger he cried, "You have no right to know. You came here to see pretty sights. I show them to you. So, see them and do not question me."

She drew back into the corner. All she could think about was getting away from Luis, from Carrie, from the whole confusing, miserable mess. Her chin shot up defiantly. With a shaky hand she tapped the cab driver's shoulder. "*Por favor, Señor, La Posada del Puente.*" She repeated louder. "*La Posada del Puente. Pronto!*"

During the trip back to the hotel, Jan buried herself behind a shield of silence.

CHAPTER 17

It was dusk when they checked out. By the time their taxi reached the Arequipa train station, night had descended.

Near the depot entrance, Luis announced, "Watch your luggage. Thieves around."

"I can't watch everything," Carrie cried. She dragged her baggage cart after her, the case askew from her hurried set-up after leaving the taxi. "Why must you walk so fast?" she called after him.

"Only ten minutes left," he shouted. "No regular train to Puno. If we miss this chartered one, we have to take bus." He disappeared into the station.

Carrie lurched after him, her cart balanced precariously.

Jan followed into the crowded terminal that smelled of rancid bodies and wet wool. Shifting the duffel strap on her shoulder, she peered from side to side for potential thieves. Dull eyes stared back. Nearly everyone was brown-faced and barefoot. Tattered children eeled in and out of hollows. Clothes rustled, feet padded against the tile floor, and voices echoed in undecipherable sounds.

She emerged onto the train platform, thankful to reach fresh air and see a smaller crowd. The overhead string of lights bobbed in the wind, creating shadows that flit across the station like bats. It was cold, and she hadn't dressed warm enough.

The train engine grumbled and white clouds hissed under the passenger cars that lined the platform. Luis led them past two cars. A clump of boys, ragged and dirty, their hands buried up their sleeves, squatted near a post. Men, bending under heavy loads, knit caps pulled skull-tight over their ears, trudged by in striped ponchos. Women, their vacant faces framed between double braids that hung down like ropes, felt hats low over brows, shuffled stoically along in bell-shaped, multi-layered skirts. Bundles were tied to their backs with shawls; often bobbing from the top was a child's head with eyes like shiny beads.

A squeal escaped from under a railroad car. Jan clutched her bag. Another squeal. Another. Only brake testing, she realized. Her sigh of relief sent a white stream into the air.

She hurried past five old men who stood in a circle like statues, a bulge distorting the cheek of each man—coca leaves, she surmised. Looking back, she noticed the same kind of bulge on other cheeks, a way to numb the senses from the cold, she imagined and shivered, her denim vest giving little protection. Unfortunately her sweater lay at the bottom of her duffel bag, impossible to retrieve now, what with thieves about and the train ready to leave at any minute. Luis wore a waist-length jacket of black wool, his white shirt hidden; Carrie wore her blue shawl. It surprised Jan that they were more prepared than she. *Am I losing control over my life?*

"Here," Luis shouted, pointing to a doorway at the end of a car. He ran up the steps, then turned on the landing to make certain they followed.

At the foot of the steps, Carrie couldn't locate the bungee cord hooks to remove her suitcase from the cart.

"*Apurate, apurate,*" Luis cried down to her, his voice full of exasperation. He beckoned for her to get onto the train.

Carrie pulled the cart up the steps, its wheels squeaking like a bewildered mouse. Jan followed close behind. On the landing, Luis pulled open the heavy metal door to the forward car. The three hurried down the narrow corridor, passing the bathrooms, and into the warm seating area. Occupants stared at the intruders but looked away when Luis located their seats in the middle of the car: two together, one across the aisle.

Carrie slipped off her daypack and succeeded in unfastening the bungee cords around her suitcase. "How do these seats translate?" she asked Luis.

He grabbed her suitcase and shoved it up onto the baggage rack. "Translate? What do you mean?" He jammed her folded cart on top of the suitcase.

"I mean, how do these seats turn into beds?"

"We sleep on the seats. This is not a tourist hotel."

"I realize that. You don't have to growl at me. I just wondered about it, that's all."

He glared at her."The seats are adjust—I don't know the English word."

"Adjustable," Jan suggested coolly as she located her sweater in her duffel. She attempted to lift her bag up onto the rack.

"*Sí,* adjustable." Luis yanked the bag off Jan's shoulder and crammed it up onto the shelf. "Heat and blankets, they are provided in this car. Not so for the rest of the train." With an exclamation of disgust, he collapsed into the single seat and heeled his satchel beneath it.

Jan sat down next to the window, pulled on her sweater and inspected her fingernails.

Ever since this afternoon's disturbing taxi ride, anger between the three had broken out at intervals. When the cab, dispatched to retrieve Carrie from the church, arrived back at the hotel, Luis had confronted Carrie in the foyer. Jan pretended to read a magazine in the lobby while a barrage of Spanish, too fast for Jan to understand, shot between the two. The desk clerk looked shocked. Afterwards, Carrie fled into the passageway.

Dinner was early so they could make the night train to Puno. Luis didn't appear at the table. Carrie spooned her *sopa de pollo* with a grim look. Jan, abandoning her plan of non-intervention, interrogated Carrie, demanding truth. Where had Carrie gone that night at *Las Dunas*? Why had she lied, saying she had slept with Luis? Who was the man in the tan shirt with the M-shaped mustache? Did she meet him in church?

"I'm not going to tell you anything," Carrie announced. A moment later, she slammed her spoon on the plate and left the table.

Now she stood in the train aisle and surveyed the passengers as if she were their tour guide. At last she sat down beside Jan and crossed her arms, a new pose used more frequently since leaving *Las Dunas*. Jan folded her hands primly in her lap and stared at the back of passengers' heads, at people's profiles, at peasants out the window, at anyone and anything except at Carrie and Luis.

She noticed the people in the car looked different from those who milled around the station—lighter skins, Spanish features, modern clothes, animated eyes. Obviously, they were well-to-do. They didn't have to carry heavy loads or go barefoot or chew coca leaves to survive.

The train jerked away from the city on time and slipped into darkness, leaving a group of stone-faced Peruvians on the platform. Jan wondered if they were waiting for another train? Or were they so poor they gathered at the station for want of a better place to go? The scene—blank faces, strange sounds, unusual clothes, coca wads, bare feet—tumbled through her mind and made her stomach feel queasy. Best to wipe the misery away, she told herself. Nothing she could do about it.

The engine gained speed, and the car settled into a clicking rhythm. The conductor punched tickets, dispensed blankets and switched off the lights, except for those near the aisle floor which gave a twilight look to the interior. Wrapped tightly in the wool coverlet, Jan slept for several hours.

When she awoke, her shoulders felt stiff. Outside, complete darkness. Rain tapped tiny fingers against the window. Silver raindrops slid down the glass and fell away. The reflections of passengers in various attitudes of repose appeared ghostly.

Needing to go to the bathroom, she rose and dropped the blanket on the seat. Carefully, she stepped over Carrie, who was asleep. Luis was awake. For a moment he stared at her in what seemed a questioning manner. Then, he closed his eyes and turned on his side. The train swayed and jerked.

She grabbed the metal handles on the backs of seats and lurched up the aisle toward the car entrance. As she watched her progress in the black glass windows, she felt no relationship to her reflection. It was as if someone else walked in the night. Near the front of the car, the fragrance of women's perfume, scents like gardenias and lilacs, intermingled and grew heavy. The silence, the smells, the warm interior wrapped her in a mind-dulling cocoon.

Reaching the narrow corridor, she held onto the smooth, brass railing along the wall and looked back into the car. Everyone had successfully shut out the world, blankets pulled around shoulders, bodies curled up or stretched out, eyes closed, mouths open, cheeks sagging, a few frowns as if dreams were bad. The face of a man in the last row came into her focus. Something familiar about him. She squinted. His mustache—M-shaped.

Her mind snapped out of its haze. With the blanket under his chin, she couldn't tell if he wore a tan shirt. The light was too low to see his face clearly. He turned over and pulled the blanket higher. A man in the next row had a similar mustache. Perhaps her first impression was wrong. Even if it was the same man from the hotel, no reason why he couldn't be on the train, except that when Carrie stood in the aisle surveying everybody, she must have seen him, yet hadn't spoken with him. Jan decided she would have a closer look at his face when she returned to her seat.

After she had finished in the lavatory and stood back in the corridor, she started thinking about how many cars made up the train. Was the one behind theirs second class? What was it like to travel that way? Perhaps if she looked through the entry door she could see into the other car. She pressed her nose against the glass. All she could see was a lighted window in the door beyond. Nothing much of the inside revealed. Then her eyes, adjusting to the outer darkness, caught something else.

An Indian woman stood on the landing, hat down to her eyes, shawl tightly drawn, a cheek bulging with a wad of coca, body buffeted by icy wind and soaked with rain. Low accordion gates on either side were all that kept the woman from falling off the train.

Shocked, Jan drew back, steadying herself on the corridor railing. The woman was freezing out there. She must let her in. But if she did, most likely the Peruvians in the car would insist she didn't belong. They would force the woman back out, be furious with Jan for interfering. Even worse, assuming the woman was hitching a free ride, she might be thrown off the train. Yet, how could Jan stand here, protected and warm, while a woman suffered in brutal weather? Was there anything she could do? Her sweater. She could give away her sweater. Hand it out to her. Not much, but it might help. She slipped it off.

The metal door was locked from the inside. She shoved back the bolt and struggled to pull the door open. A blast of frigid wind struck her. "*Aquí, aquí,*" she cried, holding the sweater out.

The Indian woman stared ahead as if Jan weren't there.

Jan made emphatic gestures for her to take the sweater.

The woman turned and faced the other way.

Jan didn't know how to make herself understood. She touched the woman's back, the shawl wet, slippery, cold. "Let me help you," she cried. The woman pressed herself against the door to the next car.

Hands grasped Jan's shoulders from behind and propelled her back inside. It was Luis. He shut the door, bolted it, and faced her in the narrow passageway.

Jan tried to push past him to get outside again.

He pulled her back. "You cannot do that," he said quietly.

"But she's freezing. She"—Jan's voice broke—"she might die."

"*Sí.*"

"I've got to help her."

He shook his head. "It is not your battle. Besides, she will not let you help." Pulling a handkerchief from his pocket, he wiped Jan's cheeks. "Why do you cry, *Janecita?*"

"It's only the rain." She lowered her head so he couldn't see her face. His musky odor drifted and mingled with the damp smell of her hair. "I'm tired, and there are so many poor people. I want to help. I don't know how." In frustration she hurled her sweater at the door and rubbed an arm across her wet eyes.

"Her suffering, you want to stop it. Is that why you cry?"

"Yes," she replied in a small voice, turning away. "But I...I can't reach her." She leaned her forehead against the wall and clutched the railing. She was unable to check the tears, unable to erase the picture of the peasant woman. Afraid of the image because the woman's face became her sister's. "Beth," Jan whispered helplessly.

Luis turned her around and pulled her into his arms. "This is not your fault," he said.

She buried her face in his chest. Ever since her sister' death she had fought against feelings that the drowning was her fault. The undertow was too strong. No way she could have reached her. It took all her remaining strength to fight back to shore. But the facts remained: Beth died, Jan lived, and Mother never forgave her.

They stayed in the narrow aisle, the train rocking them from side to side. He patted her back and murmured, "*Janecita, Janecita,* I know how you feel. It is sad." He held her close. She was thankful for his assuring words and the warmth of his arms.

At last, her crying stopped. Although the light was dim, she could see the expression on his face, compassionate and tender. She reached out and traced the cut made by the butt of the colonel's gun, a thin line on his cheek. He kissed her fingers. His lips moved toward hers. She closed her eyes and kissed him as if he were the answer to all her questions and it no longer mattered what her problems were.

CHAPTER 18

"Padrino, how many hours did it rain?" Luis asked the little man who stood by the tracks at the Puno depot, his knit hat clutched in both hands like an offering. Wrinkles carved terraces down his face, and his nose was shaped like a beak. He was about five feet tall, wide-chested and copper-skinned. Beneath his red wool poncho, black, baggy pants ended at the knees. His sandals appeared to have been cut from an old rubber tire. While he talked he fingered the llama designs on his hat as though counting the number of stitches in a pattern.

In heavily accented English, Padrino replied, "It rained ten hours, I think."

Jan found that difficult to believe, for the early morning sun shone fiercely in a royal blue sky, Yet, puddles of water sat around the station, and a procession of clouds marched above the bare mountaintops. She dug in her duffel bag for her dark glasses to cover her eyes, puffy and sore from crying.

Padrino continued, "Last night, heavy rain."

Luis chewed on his lower lip. "Floods?"

Padrino nodded. "Much water in Urubamba River, in Vilcanota—all over. Many villages, no way in, no way out. Roads, bridges, whoosh. Big trouble driving here. Fields full of water."

He raised his arms, his poncho appearing like wings. "Many people soon hungry," he cried.

Jan had a notion he might sail off into the sky.

Luis frowned. "The train to Cuzco, is it running?"

"Today, no," Padrino replied. "Some tracks under water. Maybe tomorrow if no rain."

He answered other questions about the condition of roads and villages until his arms collapsed to his side. With a sigh, he wrung his hat as if it too was full of water.

The train sat behind them, its windows dark, engine mud-spattered and silent. The platform was empty except for the conductor, standing near the sleeper car. A few minutes after arrival the crew and passengers disappeared into the town. Jan wondered if the peasant woman on the icy landing had survived.

Two young soldiers with hard faces and ready rifles stood on either side of a door to the small depot. Luis continued to talk to Padrino, glancing about as if not wishing to be overheard. The station reminded Jan of a deserted outpost, a place where no one would care to stay for long.

She had expected Puno to be cold. since it was over 12,000 feet. Instead, even though it was early morning, rays baked through the back of her vest. Taking it off, she neatly folded it into her duffel bag and then rolled up her blouse sleeves.

Luis and Padrino walked around the side of the station. Carrie followed, dragging her loaded cart, its creaky wheels squeaking like a pig led to slaughter. By the end of the trip, Jan thought she might need earplugs. She slung her duffel over her shoulder and started after Carrie.

The red-roofed city of Puno, pressed between desolate mountains and Lake Titicaca, had the look of a worn out creature. The smell of sewage hung in the air. Jan tried to imagine herself living here where breath came hard and even the houses seemed tired. Across the street stood three citizens with solemn faces and faded clothes: a woman in a doorway; two men hunched against a wall. If forced to live under the same conditions, Jan wasn't sure she could survive.

A large, black bird soared in a circle high in the sky, its tail spread in a fan, fringed wing tips streaming like narrow banners.

A condor, Jan surmised. Ominous the way it slowly circled, its short, white-banded neck pitched downward, rotating from side to side as it searched the ground below.

From the town side of the station, Luis called her name. She ran forward, stumbled over a rock and nearly fell. Parked in the street was a battered green truck with a missing fender. Fracture lines radiated from a small hole in the rear window as if a bullet had pierced it. On the truck bed bulged a partial load covered with canvas.

"What about the mine?" Luis asked Padrino.

"Water not reach. Everything high and safe." He pointed to the truck bed. "I brought detonators and dynamite."

"Dynamite?" said Carrie. "What's that for?"

"My father's mining business," Luis replied easily, but he frowned at Padrino, who twisted his hat tighter. "Load the *señoritas'* baggage," Luis commanded him, "and drive them to *Isla Esteves*. After that, come back for me."

Padrino pulled his knit hat halfway onto his head so it rose to a point like an elf. He shoved Carrie's loaded cart against the boxes on the truck bed. Turning around, he extended his hands for Jan's duffel bag.

The idea of bouncing down the street in an old truck loaded with dynamite didn't appeal to Jan. She looked questioningly at Luis.

He raised his eyebrows humorously. "I promise you nothing will explode while you ride in Padrino's truck. He is careful and dependable. For many years he has been the foreman of my father's silver mine. Although he speaks no Spanish, he is good with English.

"How did he learn it?" asked Carrie.

"From a nun who runs a school near here. She taught his wife too. Their son Rafael is my friend. We went to school together." He removed the duffel bag from Jan's shoulder and handed it to Padrino, who set it next to Carrie's suitcase. "I must stay a while at the station. I have work to do here."

"Unloading a shipment?" Carrie inquired.

He examined her with narrowed eyes. "What makes you say that?"

"You said you had work to do here. Since this is a train station, I assume you'll either unload something or load something. Which is it?"

"Why do you ask questions?"

Carrie's face was full of innocence. "I'm just curious."

"There may be harm in too much curiosity." With a firm grasp, he assisted her into the cab. "What I do here does not concern you." His voice was sharp. "Particularly you, who do not always speak the truth." He moved away from the vehicle and stood beside Jan.

The truck sputtered into action and backfired. Jan flinched.

"Only the effect of altitude," Luis said, drawing her to the side of the truck where they could not be seen from the cab. He pressed his body against hers, brushed his lips across her hair and kissed the side of her neck. "Meet me in an hour," he whispered.

"Where?" she asked breathlessly, wanting him even closer.

"By the hotel dock."

"How do I find it?"

"The far side of the parking lot. Follow the path down hill." He helped her into the cab. After closing the door, he gave her his all-knowing look through lowered eyes, then stepped back and lit a cigarette.

The truck vibrated as the engine gathered strength. They rattled down the street and past a large stadium, then turned onto a road that led toward Lake Titicaca, glinting gold and silver in the sunlight. Carrie asked Jan to roll up her window, saying the stench of sewage was too strong. Jan obliged although bad odors didn't bother her. Neither did the vigorous bouncing of the truck, nor its battered condition. She even forgot they carried dynamite. Everything else faded as she recalled Luis' lips and the feel of his body pressed against hers.

Carrie kept glancing back through the rear window. Once, when the truck hit a sharp pothole, she grabbed Jan's arm, fear in her eyes.

They drove onto a smoother surface, a causeway several miles long. The elevated road led across a corner of the lake to an island, a flat-topped hill rising from the water. The elegant-looking, government-owned hotel crowned the hill. Three cars and a small bus were in the parking area. Jan noted an indentation on the far edge of the lot—the start of the path.

Padrino pulled up before the hotel entrance and set the brake. He ran around to help them out of the cab, then dashed to the back of the truck and lifted off their luggage. As he started toward the hotel, Carrie said, "No, no, please, set my cart down. I'll take it inside. *Gracias, Padrino. Adiós.*" Grabbing the handle, she hurriedly squeaked her way into the hotel.

Still thinking about Luis, Jan relieved Padrino of her bag. The little man flapped his arms as if embarrassed at his inability to further assist. He took off his hat and fingered it a moment before climbing back into his truck and driving away.

Inside, Carrie stood by the counter. "I've filled out the registration cards," she said as Jan arrived. "Here. Check that I got your passport number right and sign your name.

Only vaguely aware of what Carrie said, Jan signed her name and stared through the large picture windows at Lake Titicaca. The water had lost its hard glitter; it was a soft blue of a robin's egg. An eternal hour to wait, she thought.

"May I suggest," said the neatly-groomed Peruvian lady behind the counter, "that the *señoritas* relax this afternoon. The high altitude can give you a bad headache and problems with breathing. In your room is *mate de coca*. If you drink several cups of this hot tea, it will help against the *soroche*, the altitude sickness."

The lady fished a key from a box. "Room 107. Your friend awaits you."

Jan blinked at Carrie. She wasn't certain she had heard correctly. "Is someone in our room?" she asked.

"Yes," Carrie replied.

"Who?"

"Brewster."

"What's he doing here?"

"Sh-h-h!"

The lady said, "One moment, please. A porter will carry your luggage." She held the key in the air and, with her other hand, tapped a counter bell.

"We don't need help," Carrie said, snatching the key from the woman's hand. She sprinted down the hall, her noisy cart bouncing after her.

The lady's hand remained up as if the key still in it.

Jan reshouldered her bag and rushed after Carrie, her mind now fully operating. Carrie must have planned this meeting with Brewster, concocted some sort of a deal not to be shared with Jan, the outsider.

A momentary guilt hit Jan. As far as she and Luis were concerned, wasn't Carrie the outsider?

It doesn't matter, she rationalized. Carrie's not in love with him. She's got a screwy relationship with Brewster—flying over the Nasca Lines with him, meeting him here. What's going on between them? And what about the guy in the tan shirt? How does he fit into Carrie's interests? I should have investigated these angles on the train. Should have pumped Carrie about them. Should've gone back and examined the face of the man with the mustache. If I hadn't been so wrapped up in my own emotions, I might have discovered what was happening.

From another time her mother's face ghosted, and her shrill voice cried, *Janet, once again you have failed.*

CHAPTER 19

The first thing Jan saw when she entered the room was the picture window. Beyond it, a panorama of water and sky in muted blues and greens fading into each other. The second thing was the back of Brewster's blonde head rising from one of the two overstuffed chairs that faced the lake. His denim-shirted arm reached out to the table between the chairs and poured a cup of steaming liquid from a teapot. *Mate de coca,* Jan realized, the medicinal odor drifting up.

She dropped her duffel bag on the nearest twin bed and sat down stiffly beside it. "Why are you in our room, Brewster?" she snapped, indignantly.

Brewster peered around the edge of the chair and waved his cup at her as though saluting her presence. "About time you two arrived," he said. What took you so long?"

Carrie answered in a mechanical voice, "An Aymara Indian called Padrino drove us here in his old truck." She wheeled her creaking cart into the closet.

"Did you learn his connection?" Brewster asked.

"He's the foreman at Ignacio's silver mine. He delivered a truckload of dynamite and detonators to Luis." Carrie disappeared into the other chair. "Luis is still at the train station. 'I have work to do here', he said." Her hands appeared as she poured herself a cup from the teapot. "Luis is upset about the floods. The train to Cuzco might not leave tomorrow."

"Yeah, it rained like hell up here yesterday afternoon and most of the night."

Jan burst out, "Brewster, what happened to your southern drawl? Where's the gay Texan who wrote pulp romances and danced the wild tango?"

"Got rid of him. Didn't need him any more." Again he peered around at her, his smile cold, his eyes piercing. "My latest information indicates you are deeply involved with Luis."

Jan shot a look at Carrie, who still faced the lake. "I don't know what you're talking about." She set her dark glasses on the nightstand. Her eyes burned and her head ached. Unzipping her duffel, she pulled out her coral nightgown. The flimsy material struck her as absurd. She shoved it under her pillow. She fingered the spiral designs on the bedspread, tracing the lines as if that would bring order to her mind. What did Brewster mean "deeply involved with Luis"? Her finger turned white from the pressure.

"Brewster," she finally blurted out, "damnit, what's going on here. If you don't square with me, I'll call a security guard to get you out of here."

With a chuckle, Brewster said, "Janet, I've always admired your direct approach."

There was a soft, insistent knock on the door—four fast raps. Brewster didn't seem surprised. Setting his cup on the table, he rose quickly. In three strides he reached the door.

It was the dark-complexioned man in the tan shirt, the man with the M-shaped mustache. He slipped into the room, glanced at the occupants and then stood by the dresser.

"Meet Carlos," Brewster said to Jan.

"I've seen the guy around."

"You sound tense. Relax. Would you like this comfortable chair?"

"I prefer to stay where I am."

"Suit yourself." Brewster returned to his chair. He swiveled it around to face the interior of the room. Leaning forward, elbows on knees, hands clasped under chin, he once more concentrated on Jan. "We couldn't tell you anything before," he said. "We had to wait for developments."

Jan wondered why Carrie didn't also turn around to be part of this conversation.

"Before I explain," Brewster continued, "I must issue a warning about your precarious situation. You and Carrie are no longer ladies who've come to Peru just for a vacation, although you better pretend you are. Around here certain people enjoy snuffing out lives of people who know too much."

"I gather you're trying to scare me."

"Yeah. Scare you into being careful and cool-headed."

"You've succeeded. What's next?"

"No matter what emotional attachments you've developed for a particular person, you must get rid of them." He paused. "I'm speaking of Luis."

Jan took a quick breath. Carrie remained hidden in the chair. "You have no right to dictate how I should feel about anyone."

"Perhaps I don't," he said harshly, "but, as Carrie can tell you, in my world leverage outstrips rights."

Carrie didn't turn around, but in a small voice she said, "Do whatever he asks, Jan. It's dangerous not to."

Jan drew a quick breath. She focused on Carlos, "How do you fit into this scenario?

"DEA."

"What's that?"

"Drug Enforcement Agency."

"Peruvian?"

"No, American, but I blend into the local population."

Brewster poured a cup of *mate de coca* and brought it over to Jan. She stared into the brown liquid then looked over at Carlos. "Isn't this stuff illegal?"

"Not in this part of the world. Drink it. Helps with headaches and I'm sure you've got one from the high altitude."

The tea felt good as it slipped down her dry throat. Her head throbbed but she figured it came as much from tension, lack of sleep and the crying jag on the train as from the altitude.

"Is Luis in trouble?" she asked Carlos, trying to sound casual.

"We think so."

She took more sips, closing her eyes each time she swallowed. "What's he done wrong?"

"Nothing yet, but he's on the brink."

"Why drag me into this?"

Brewster spoke up. "Because Luis has fallen for you."

Jan took a larger swallow. She realized she held the cup so tightly the handle might break off. Loosening her grip, she said, "What makes you think that?"

"For starters," Brewster said, "your meeting with him on the bridge at *Las Dunas*."

Jan banged her cup down on the nightstand, spilling the liquid. "You hid in the bushes and eavesdropped."

"No. Carrie did."

Jan stared at Carrie's chair, not wanting to believe what she had just heard.

Brewster's tone was matter-of-fact with a hint of sarcasm. "When Carrie ran off to find Luis, I just happened to be sitting on a garden bench with a pair of binoculars. I watched you wave your arms on the bridge and Luis come in for a final approach. Then I saw another person. I couldn't see who it was, shadows too deep, but I had a hunch. The figure stopped near the foot of the bridge. A moment later, it slipped around the post and huddled on the bank. After Luis left and you staggered away, I confirmed it was Carrie."

Jan rubbed her hand hard across the rough-textured bedspread as if to eradicate its design. She cringed at the thought of how Carrie must have felt as she heard Luis, the man she had hoped to spend the night with, proposition her best friend.

"Carrie, did you"—Jan concentrated on her words, but couldn't find any that might help—"did you hear everything Luis and I said?"

Carrie remained silent, still staring through the window.

A faucet gurgled on next door followed by the faint sounds of splashing water. In the hall, a door slammed, a key turned. Two women with English accents chattered about the price of alpaca sweaters. As their footsteps moved down the hall, their voices faded out.

Jan swallowed hard. "It was never my intention to do anything to hurt you."

"I know." Carrie sounded weary. "I'm not blaming you. Luis is charming and persuasive. You found that out on the train."

"You listened there, too?"

"No. That was Carlos."

Carlos pulled at his mustache. "En route back to my seat I related everything to Carrie."

Jan sank back against the headboard, her face flushed.

Brewster asked, "When do you see Luis again?

Not comprehending his words, not wanting to listen to anybody, Jan rubbed her forehead and wished she were someplace else, anyplace.

He spoke louder. "Janet, when do you next see Luis?"

"At 10:30," she said in a voice that didn't seem hers.

"You've got fifteen minutes to get there."

She shook her head. "I'm not going."

"Of course you are."

Tears formed but she blinked them back. With sudden energy, she grabbed her coral nightgown from under the pillow and stuffed it into her duffel. When she tried to zip it shut, part of the gown caught in the zipper. After two frantic attempts, she finally got it closed. She snatched up her dark glasses and jammed them on her face.

"I'm taking the next plane home," she announced. "I shouldn't be here. I don't want to be here. I don't want to see anybody connected with this goddamned place ever again."

"Be sensible," Brewster said.

"Go to hell!"

"I've been there."

"Go back," she yelled. "That's where you belong."

"Calm down."

Slinging the duffel over her shoulder, she charged for the door. Brewster leaped forward to intercept her. He pulled the bag off her shoulder and threw it on the bed. Grabbing her shoulders, he said, "I'm here to give you instructions."

Her cheeks burned. Her knees shook uncontrollably. "I won't take orders from you."

His grip tightened. "Yes, you will."

She looked about wildly. Carlos guarded the door. There was no way to escape. Her shoulders slumped. He released her.

Retreating to the bed, she collapsed, chest down, face hidden in the pillow, sides drawn up around her head so she could scarcely breathe. She didn't want to breathe. She only wanted to get rid of the pain.

"Please, Jan"—it was Carrie's soft voice, her hands gently trying to detach Jan from the pillow—"let me explain."

Jan pulled away. She turned her left cheek onto the pillow, cool against her hot skin, a respite, something to cling to as she gulped for air.

"I'm sorry I hid by the bridge," Carrie said. "I was carried away by Luis' charm. I wanted to know his feelings. And, well, we were all pretty drunk that night." She hurried on, "After you both left the bridge, Brewster came over to me. He seemed genuinely sorry about my situation. He led me to his room, wrapped me in a blanket to stop my shivering and gave me several cups of coffee. When his accent disappeared and he told me the situation, I realized he wasn't being kind."

Jan raised her head slightly. Brewster stood before the window, gazing at the lake, his hands clasped behind him. Carlos wasn't in sight, probably still by the door. "So you spent the night with Brewster." Jan spit out his name as if it were bitter.

"Yes, but not in the way you might think. We talked, and when we finished, there was no more night. He explained how Ignacio and Luis were involved in a drug-smuggling ring. He said it was necessary for me to help."

Jan turned over and looked at Carrie, who sat on the edge of the bed, arms clasped around her body as if to hold in warmth. "Was this why your suitcase was ripped apart?"

Carrie nodded. "One of Ignacio's men tore out the lining. My father hid money in there—payment for cocaine shipments."

Abruptly, Jan sat up. "Your father's a cocaine dealer?"

"More than that," said Carlos. "We've photographed him collecting money from dealers in California, Oregon and Washington. We've traced a number of his laundering practices for Ignacio."

"Why hasn't he been arrested?"

"We need to find out more about his operations."

Carrie said, "For a long time I've suspected my father. He was always secretive about where his money came from and vague about the companies he dealt with. I wanted to know the truth. The main reason I came to Peru was to meet Ignacio. I thought he might be the key. When I saw my suitcase lining torn open, I realized my father must've hidden something in there." She looked down at the floor. "Buying a new case for me should have tipped me off, since his usual gift was money."

Jan's headache felt worse, a throbbing pain that clouded her mind. She massaged her temples and attempted to think clearly. Never had Carrie hinted of her suspicions about Ignacio, not a word about her father, the wealthy businessman who hovered over columns of figures, annual reports and fax machines. No wonder he could buy a Pacific Heights mansion and own so many businesses.

"Why didn't you tell me, Carrie?"

"At first I wasn't sure about my father's business. Then, after I learned the truth, Brewster insisted I say nothing to you."

"You shouldn't have listened to him."

"I had to"—Carrie wet her lips—"for your safety. Otherwise, you would've been…hurt." She looked at Brewster's back. "He made the threat sound real enough."

Jan frowned. "So you flew with Brewster to Nazca where the two of you made-up a plan to use me, assuming I'd get in deeper with Luis?"

"They didn't fly to Nazca," said Carlos. "They flew to Huanaca. I met them there for a briefing."

"Is Brewster also with the DEA?" Jan inquired.

"No," Carlos answered emphatically. "We don't operate in his manner."

Brewster turned around and exchanged a hard look with Carlos.

Jan narrowed her eyes. "Brewster, there must be a compelling reason for you to be here in Peru, acting out your peculiar roles. What is it? Why are you here?"

His eyes turned to slivers of steel. "I see you've recovered from your emotional outburst. It's time for you to meet Luis."

"If I won't go, what then?"

Slowly he iced out his words. "If you won't follow orders, your friend Carrie could have a short life."

Jan scooted back against the headboard. "The implication is that you'll eradicate *me* if Carrie doesn't do as you say, and you'll eliminate *her*, if I won't follow your orders. How dare you use death threats! What happened to the gentleman who danced a waltz with the lady in the blue chiffon dress?"

"He was a phony," Brewster said quietly. "Carlos, give Janet a glimpse of why threats are necessary."

Carlos straightened his back. As he talked, he stared at the ceiling. "What's left of a formerly large and active guerrilla group called *Sendero Luminoso* has taken over the jungles of the Haullaga Valley. They protect coca farmers and their fields, for a price. That's partly how they're financing their planned revolution against the Peruvian Government. *Sendero* has spread into other coca farming areas for the same reason."

He looked from Jan to Brewster and back again. "These guys are so fanatical about their cause, they kill whoever stands in their way. Torture is common. The last time I drove to Tingo Maria to meet an informer, I found him face down in the middle of the road, hands tied behind his back. He'd been beaten then slowly strangled with a rope twisted by a stick of wood. For five days they let him lie there, bloated, stinking, on top of *Sendero* graffiti, a warning to anyone who might follow his example."

Jan drew a quick breath, trying not to visualize the picture.

"That's not an isolated incident, "Carlos continued. "Executions occur daily. Anyone who interferes, who fails to support their doctrine...." He drew the edge of his hand across his throat.

In an effort to keep herself together, Jan rubbed her cheeks. She had no doubt Brewster would carry out his threats. He instilled as much fear into her as Carlos did with his talk of terrorists and traffickers. If only she were back in Logan's office. She longed to see him standing in his doorway, to be safe at her computer, pushing the right keys, producing required papers, doing what she understood.

Carlos said, "Luis has a truckload of explosives and detonators. I checked them out at the station. Don't know why he has them; do know he bought chemicals from an Arequipa warehouse and shipped them to Puno on the train. Most likely they are for processing cocaine at a new lab, location unknown. We've heard rumors that Ignacio intends to build enough labs to break the connection with Colombia, where most cocaine is now processed." He leaned back against the dresser.

After a moment, Jan said wearily, "Okay, Brewster, what do you want me to do?"

Brewster returned to the swivel chair. "At the present time, you're closer to Luis than anybody else. Easily, without causing suspicion, try to learn what plans he has for his supplies, especially the explosives—their destination, who takes delivery and what they're for. Luis is not to know Carlos and I were here. I'll contact you again in Cuzco." He paused. "One other thing."

She felt his eyes as she opened her duffel to pull out her sweater. "What is it?" The steadiness of her voice surprised her.

"There's a strong probability Ignacio is not Luis' real father. Should that be true, I must know who his real father is and his present location."

A shiver ran up her back and through her arms. Across her mind flashed the image of the woman who stood outside in the cold on the train, her face a mask hiding private feelings to endure her hardship.

"Is that all?" she asked, looking at him.

"For now." With a half smile playing around his mouth, he added, "Enjoy your lover's rendezvous."

CHAPTER 20

From the top, the path looked steep and rocky, twisting down through stunted trees and brush to a shadowy inlet below. Jan couldn't see a dock and figured one must be located beneath the overhang that jutted out near the bottom.

Behind her, nobody in sight. On the parking lot, the same few vehicles as when she and Carrie arrived but now they loomed ominously. And the hotel that had seemed so elegant before, protruded from the flattop hill like an ugly wart.

She wondered if she could be clever enough to handle Brewster's orders. Could she pretend feelings for Luis yet not feel them? Or would she feel them and not be able to pretend? How could she ask Luis the necessary questions and not make him suspicious? Her watch read 10:32. She was late.

Starting down the path, her sandals slipped on the loose gravel. In trying to regain her balance, she dropped her sweater. For a terrifying moment she imagined herself hurtling over the side, smashing onto the rocks far below. Standing perfectly still, she realized she should have worn sneakers. After Brewster issued his orders, her mind hadn't functioned properly. She remembered going to the bathroom like a zombie, throwing water on her face, blinking, adjusting the combs in her hair, trying to pull herself together. That sandals might be a problem hadn't entered her mind.

Carefully she picked up her sweater and brushed off the dirt. She tied the sleeves around her waist and adjusted her dark glasses, gone askew on her nose. Not enough sleep last night. Should have eaten breakfast. Acid churned in her stomach. One moment she loved Luis, the next she hated him. He scared her, yet she was scared for him. He was arrogant but sensitive to her feelings. Although she feared him, she found him overwhelmingly attractive. Was he really part of a drug ring? Was he a terrorist? As she continued on down the path, her temples throbbed like muffled pile drivers.

A spell of dizziness hit. Grasping a branch for support, she envisioned herself in the crepe paper costume on the brightly-lit stage shouting, *I am an American Beauty Rose*. Inwardly, she heard her mother shout, *You're a failure*. But then Logan's voice overrode her mother's, *Jan, you're a hell of a good office partner*. Yes, she thought defiantly, I'm not a failure. Damn the past.

Determined to keep control of herself, she breathed deeply and exercised her shoulders in small, circular motions. For the rest of the hike down, she kept her eyes on the path, making certain the ground beneath each step was stable.

Luis sat on a boulder by the dock, his black jacket gone, his shirt grayed by the shadow from the overhang. He smoked a cigarette and surveyed the lake. Tied to the dock was a green and white motor launch about twenty-five feet long with a small cabin in need of paint. The boat bobbed on the water like a toy in a bathtub, creaking against the dock as if anxious to get loose.

When he saw her, Luis tossed his cigarette into the water and smiled. "Ah, you are here. I was afraid you might not come."

She tucked her dark glasses into her pocket and laughed lightly. "I had to," she said, thinking how ironic those words were.

"Where is Carrie?"

"In bed, altitude sickness."

"Does she know where you are?" he inquired.

"Yes, but not that I'm with you." The lies were coming easily. "I told her I planned to hire a boat."

He chuckled. "That is true. I am the captain." He gestured at the boat. "If Carrie sees this from her window, we are tiny figures, too small to recognize."

"How much does your tour cost?" she asked, affecting a flirtatious tone, intrigued at how his chest muscles caught the light through the opening of his shirt.

"You are the payment," he said, hugging her.

She pressed the side of her face against his bare chest. His musky aroma was strong. With surprise she realized it came from cigarettes, the pack in his shirt pocket. She listened to his heartbeat deep and regular.

He tipped up her chin and studied her face. "You look tired, *Janacita*."

"I've got a problem with the altitude."

He nodded. "I, too, am light in the head, and I come here often."

"To Lake Titicaca?"

"And other places in the Andes."

"Working for your father?"

"*Sí*."

"In his silver mine?"

She was trying to sound natural, but the words rang false in her ears.

"Questions, questions," he said. "Forget them."

She smiled. "It's an old habit. All my life I've looked for answers."

"Even when you find them, they may not stay the same." He cupped her face with his hands, leaned down, and kissed her softly. Her eyes remained closed while she savored the velvet touch of his lips. When he drew back, she opened her eyes and murmured, "I've forgotten my questions."

"*Bueno, bueno.*" He slid off the rock and led her toward the boat. "This ride on the water, it is pleasant. We eat roast potatoes from Padrino, a broiled chicken from the hotel and Cristal Beer from me. All is aboard the boat. We have a *comido de campo*—what do you call it?"

"A picnic?"

"*Sí*, a picnic. Also, a ride on the water, a time to know each other. We talk about life. We motor over part of the lake. Then, we drift through channels over there." He pointed to reeds in the distance.

It sounded good to her. What if she forgot Brewster's orders? What would she say when she saw him again? *I felt so sick I forgot what I was supposed to do.* No, no, better to say, *I tried but he refused to tell me anything.*

"We will visit a floating Uros Indian village," Luis announced.

"A village that floats on the lake?"

"*Sí.* A number of villages do that. They are built on layers of reeds."

"How do the people cook? Build their houses? Walk around? Do anything?"

"Very quickly. They must, or they sink in the water." He grasped her hands. "You are such a pretty lady, *Janecita*. To be with you makes me happy."

"I'm glad," she replied, a slight catch in her voice. "I don't want to make you unhappy."

Again they embraced. When he released her, she had to lean against him for support. More than anything she wanted to be lost with Luis on Lake Titicaca, floating among the reeds, held in his arms, adrift in a place of no worries. Anxiety shot through her. Had she fallen in too deep?

As she stepped aboard the boat, the smells of fish, algae and damp wood revived her. Slipping past the wooden wheel, she entered the cabin. The vessel rocked from side to side. Most of the white paint was gone from the ribbed frame that rose up from the narrow-planked floor. Noting the open windows all around, she concluded it was a sightseeing boat. Beneath the windows was a worn, leather-padded bench shaped like a horseshoe. On the bench was a brown and white wool pouch, stuffed with bottles of beer and the picnic lunch. Beside it, his black jacket. She touched a sleeve.

Shifting to a port-side window, she watched Luis free the boat from the dock, first the bow, then the stern. He tossed the lines aboard, then leapt on after them, his movements perfectly timed, footfall easy, a feline grace to his body. Watching him made her body feel hot. Damn this attraction, she thought. Untying her sweater, she dropped it on top of his jacket, hiding it as if that would make her feelings disappear.

The water beside the boat looked dark and still. A strange face stared back at her. She leaned over and looked closer, thinking the darkness of the water must be what made her look so pale and unrecognizable. I will set aside a patch of time for Luis and me. For a little while, that's all. For the rest of the afternoon I'll turn cold and logical. A ripple shattered her reflection.

Luis started the engine and edged the boat out of the cove. She put her dark glasses back on, emerged from the cabin and stood beside him at the wheel. The lake, eerily quiet and empty of boats, appeared as large as a sea, spreading to a barely discernible horizon of mountains. To the north, a forest of brownish-green reeds jutted up from the water. Clouds overlapped the sky in shades of white and gray.

He put an arm around her waist and she leaned against him.

Not until they were in the middle of the lake did they speak again. Luis slowed the engine and maneuvered over a series of waves caused by a speeding motorboat. "What about Peru?" he asked, gesturing over the water. "Do you find it beautiful?"

"The scenery, yes. Other things, well, no."

"What is not beautiful?"

She sat down on the bench. "The poor people. They seem resigned to awful conditions—dull eyes and often a wad of coca in their mouths."

He rubbed his hands hard over the wheel, slivers of varnish flaking into the air. "Coca finds a home with poverty." He cut the engine and silently they drifted.

"Tell me more," he said. "I want to know your thoughts on Peru."

She tried to relate how sad she felt about the shanties on the hill outside Lima and the destitute people who milled at the Arequipa train station and how helpless she felt about the woman on the train who stood all night in the icy rain. But she couldn't make her feelings clear, so she gave up, thinking maybe the cultural difference was too big. "Their eyes are empty," she finally whispered. "It's as if they don't want to see where they are."

With an abrupt turn of the wheel he shot the boat into a channel between the reeds. "When life is difficult," he growled, "feelings must be dulled for the body to go on." He slowed the boat to a crawl and glanced at her sideways. "Do you have poor people in your country?"

"Yes, but not as visible as here."

Perhaps he didn't know what she meant by *visible,* but he didn't question her further. A relief, because her head still ached badly from the high altitude and lack of sleep. Formulating precise answers was too difficult.

If she didn't feel better soon, she didn't see how she could follow Brewster's orders. She knew that prying out information must come as a natural outgrowth of conversation, but she didn't feel like conversation. Maybe she would try after lunch but the thought of food turned her stomach. It bothered her that she could sit in this boat, caring about a man yet ready to betray him. She didn't want to find out anything about his life. It didn't matter to her what he had done or what he was going to do. What mattered was who he was now right now, here with her. If only she could forget about Brewster and Carlos.

The sky hid under gunmetal clouds. She folded her dark glasses and tucked them into her shirt pocket; she adjusted the combs in her hair; she brought her sweater out from the cabin and slipped it on in case the weather turned cold. The methodical processes gave her a sense of control. She felt it was important to be ready.

From where she sat in the cockpit, she could see Luis' face over her shoulder, his prominent nose and high cheekbones similar to those of the Indian people on the streets of Puno. Yet because of his penetrating eyes and the sensuous way he moved, he was more handsome. His voice, occasionally hard and sharp, was frequently soft with innuendoes. The way he always wore his shirt, revealing his hairless chest and warm skin the color of koa wood, was sensually appealing. When he glanced down at her, she forced a smile and thought it safer to examine the scenery.

They chugged slowly along a narrow channel, cattail reeds rising on both sides like a bamboo forest—straight, woody stems less than an inch thick, dense growths as tall as the boat. Side channels appeared every hundred feet or so. On one, she saw a reed-bundle boat with a prow shaped like a canoe. A man sat in it. He wore a red-striped poncho and a pointed knit hat and he held part of a fish net. His eyes met hers in a blank stare.

A heavy mist moved in and draped the reeds, hanging a low ceiling over the channel, turning it into a tunnel. The air smelled like seaweed on a beach at low tide. She wrapped her arms around her sweatered body, not that she was cold, for the cockpit was warm, heated by the engine under the deck, its soft throb reverberating against the wood beneath her bare feet. What bothered her was the darkness and the narrow path of water and the feeling of being carried out, swept away from everything she understood.

"In our country," she said, her voice strange to her ears, "we don't suffer the weather extremes of Peru. Sure, we have places with lousy weather but I don't think anybody lives at 13,000 feet."

"Many of our poor no longer live in the Andes," he said. "They go down to the cities, hoping for better lives. Only their lives get worse." After a pause he continued, "In your country, how often do you see poor people?"

"Not much. Homeless people sleep on benches, under bridges, in out of the way places. Sometimes they wander the streets or sit on sidewalks but I stay away from them. I'm afraid of getting robbed. A woman alone has to be extra careful."

He snorted, "In Peru the rich do not see the poor at all."

"You sound angry."

"Not with you. I am angry at the situation. And with myself. I think of my friend, Rafael."

She stiffened, on alert. "Padrino's son?"

"*Sí.* he struggled to get through school. Two jobs, little sleep, hard work. Not for me. Always I have money, a rich father, a big house. Rafael, his family, they have nothing. While at the university, where did he live? In a tin shack."

He yanked out his pack of cigarettes and looked at it as if it were another of his benefits. With an exasperated grunt, he squeezed the pack into a ball and hurled it into the water. "When I was a student, not once did I go to see him there."

"I don't visit my school friends either," she said, wanting to ease his torment.

For a few moments he stared at her without speaking and she stared back unable to find more words. Then he asked, "You work in San Francisco for this man Logan?"

"Yes."

"He is a, what you call it, *abogado?*"

"A lawyer, yes."

"Then, he, too, is rich."

"Not really."

He wrinkled his nose as if he didn't believe her.

The reeds grew taller, dimming his face. She squinted up at him and chose her words carefully. "You think about this a lot, don't you, about differences between the rich and the poor?"

He nodded. "Our country, it is divided not only by color but by class. The two are linked. Today we have new degrees of poor." He waved his hand in a sweeping gesture. "And the rich whites get richer. Do they invest their money in Peru? No! They send it to Swiss banks or invest in foreign companies. They desert Peru when they no longer profit. Who will be left? Poor people. Caught between a corrupt government, propped up by the military, and terrorists who must attack the government."

"Should the government be destroyed?" she asked quietly.

"*Sí*, crushed," he hissed, his eyes more fierce, his breathing heavier.

She caught her breath, fearful the boat would plow into the reeds.

With a brittle laugh, he steered back on course. "What does the government care about the *campesinos* and *cholos* in shantytowns, the *pueblos jovenes* they call them. They know nothing of coca chewers who live and die. Nothing about *mestizos* who labor in the jungles. They do not wish to know."

He jerked a package of matches from his pants pocket and felt the empty shirt pocket where his cigarettes had been. With a groan of annoyance he tossed the matches overboard.

She touched his arm. "I'm sorry about all these problems."

He glanced at her hand, then focused on her lips, her chest and further down, his mouth softening into the smile that indicated he knew her reaction to him.

Her nipples stiffened. Her breasts ached. In a panic, she looked away.

The channel widened and the mist dissipated. The sun shone brilliantly for a few moments before again hiding behind a layer of clouds.

Suddenly Luis cut the engine and pointed ahead. "There—the floating village." He retreated into the professorial tone used at the museum. "The Uros Indians have lived on Lake Titicaca for hundreds of years. They know nothing of rich or poor people, governments or rebels. They live apart."

The village glowed, its dried yellow reeds a bright contrast to the water, black as ink, and the sky, the color of lead. Huts, built of reed poles and mats, lined three sides of a plaza, open to the channel. Two boats were drawn up at the open edge. Reed bundles lay in piles between the houses or angled upward like haystacks. Six women, wearing colorful long skirts, shawls and black bowler-style hats, sat in the plaza. Two children in ragged, modern dresses waited for their boat to dock.

"These women," said Luis, gesturing at the seated ladies, "they make crafts to sell to tourists. The children are guides. They help us walk on the reeds."

He sprang to the bow as it drifted onto the reed matting. "You can tell the Uros on the mainland by how they walk—lightly, like a wave, so as not to sink through the reeds. You must do the same here." He threw the bowline to a girl, then stepped easily from the boat.

When Jan stepped ashore, a girl of about ten, with dirt-smudged face and arms, tangled dark hair and large, serious eyes, led her to the seated ladies. "*Rapido*," the girl kept repeating, pointing to Jan's bare feet that sank whenever she stopped.

The village smelled of rotten vegetation and sewage. She had a vision of sinking into the lake. Should she have worn her sandals? No, everyone was barefoot except Luis. His shoes looked out of place, probably would smell for weeks. At least she could wash her feet when she returned to the boat.

The women sat in a row, staring at her. She felt their eyes but didn't stare back. What must they think of her in matching wine-colored slacks and sweater, her face white and clean? It was humiliating to be the center of their attention, to be so out of tune, so wrong.

She tried to inspect the items for sale: models of reed boats and embroidered wool weavings of village scenes. She paced back and forth in front of the women, her knees bent, afraid to stop, feet recoiling from the slime that oozed up between the reeds when she didn't move fast enough.

She would buy a souvenir to take home, a conversation piece. When friends came by, she could say, *I bought this when I visited a primitive tribe in the Andes at 13,000 feet. Would you believe it, they live on Lake Titicaca, in reed huts on a reed raft. Quaint people, those Uros Indians!* But she knew she wouldn't say that. She'd only say, *It was made in Peru.*

"All the weavings are nice," she said, a tremor in her voice. "I'd like to buy one, but I don't know which to choose or how to buy it." She turned to Luis, her eyes pleading for help.

He picked up a weaving about three feet long and two feet wide, the scene heavily embroidered with two fishermen in reed boats drawing up a net filled with fish, a giant condor with outstretched wings above them. After bartering a few moments in Spanish, Luis gave the woman money and handed the weaving to Jan. "My gift to you," he said.

The smell was overwhelming; the reeds hurt her feet; her toes were black-rimmed. "*Gracias,* she managed to say to him. "I want to go now."

"*Rapido,*" the little girl called out as she led her back toward the boat. "*Rapido.*"

CHAPTER 21

For twenty minutes after they re-boarded the boat they drifted through fog-shrouded reeds. It was cold, and Luis now wore a jacket, his white shirt hidden. He leaned against the boat wheel, one foot on the cockpit bench. "You should eat something," he said and continued to chew on the second drumstick.

"I'm not hungry," she replied and moved away from his shoe.

"A beer?"

She shook her head.

"You do not look happy."

"I can still smell the village on your shoes."

"It is not what you are used to?" he said with his smile." He brought his foot down and threw the bone into the reeds. Leaning over the side, he washed his hands in the lake. "Our picnic, it is not turning out well."

"It's the altitude. My head aches and my stomach hurts. Let's go back to the hotel."

She stood up and balanced her way into the cabin where she sat down and stared at the black lines between her toes. Although she had tried to wash her feet over the side of the boat, much of the oily grime still clung to her skin.

He peered at her through the doorway, his look sultry, seductive. "Shall we make love on the boat?" he inquired.

She bit her lower lip. "No."

"Do you suffer because of the altitude and the village smell on my shoes? Or is the bench too narrow and the floor too hard?"

"You're being sarcastic."

"Have you thought about what it is like to make love in a floating reed village?"

She turned away from him.

"Of course not. To you, love must come in a gentle scene, on a soft mattress with perfume and sweet music."

"I can't help where I come from or what I am."

"You could try."

She didn't know how to answer that. Their lives seemed too far apart. Facing him, she said in a stiff voice, "Let's get back to the hotel before it rains."

He sighed. "All right, we do what you wish." His laugh was hollow. "But the sky tells me rain will not start today. It will come tonight. Big rains then. Floods maybe."

"Floods?" Instantly alert, she asked, "Could it be enough to stop the train? Is there a possibility the train won't go to Cuzco?"

"*Sí*. That is possible. If so, I use Padrino's truck and drive to Cuzco by myself."

She lurched to her feet. "You'd go alone? Leave us here in Puno?"

"There is an airport at Juliaca. Or, close by, a military airfield. If necessary, I call a pilot friend to fly you and Carrie."

"I don't understand why you wouldn't fly with us?"

"Impossible. I must make a delivery."

She tried to sound casual. "That's right, I forgot. You have a truckload of dynamite and detonators to drop off."

He narrowed his eyes. "*Sí*."

"But surely, if there's a flood, we can all wait until the weather gets better."

"No, I must be in Cuzco by tomorrow night."

"Why?" she asked.

"I do not care to tell you," he replied.

"So, you don't trust me."

"I trust nobody except my closest friend."

"Rafael?"

"*Sí*, Rafael."

She sat down again and tried another tack. "Does he looks like you?"

"What do you mean?"

She shrugged. "Rafael is an Indian and your features look Indian."

"We do not look alike. Rafael is Aymara. I am part Quechua—a *mestizo*. Many people in Lima have Indian blood."

"Then your mother must be Indian," she said, "because your father looks Spanish and you don't look—"

"Ignacio is not my father."

"Who is?"

Luis pursed his lips. With his thumbnail, he chipped a loose piece of paint from the doorframe and flicked it into the water. "I should not have told you about Ignacio. Do not repeat my words to Carrie. Forget them." He stepped into the cabin and raised Jan's chin to closely meet her eyes. "Say nothing to Carrie. Is that clear?"

"Sure. All right." She swallowed hard. "Where is your father?"

He let go of her chin. "I do not wish to tell you. All I will say is this. He saved Ignacio's life once. So Ignacio took me when my mother died in childbirth." He frowned as if regretting his words. "You must never repeat any of this."

"I'd like to meet your father. I'd like to meet Rafael, too."

"I pray you never meet either of them."

"Why not?"

He threw up his arms. "Questions, questions. I thought you would give them up."

In a soft voice she said, "That's where the dynamite is going, isn't it, to Rafael and your father?"

"*Janecita*." He backed away. "Why is it necessary for you to figure things out? You are too clever. That part of you bothers me even more than your need for a comfortable place to make love."

"You don't want me to be clever?"

"I would prefer you not question me. There are things I must do that are dangerous. I do not want bigger difficulties. Already, I am worried."

"I can see that." Carefully she chose her next words. "Luis, I only want to know why you're so upset. Surely you can tell me what's worrying you."

He sat on the bench opposite her. "One worry is about your friend Carrie. She does things I do not like. She tells you she slept with me when she slept in another place." His words speeded up. "She flies to Nazca with Brewster and does not return until morning. She talks to a man in Arequipa who follows me. She tells me how much she wants to see the city sights; instead, she runs into the Jesuit chapel. Who does she meet there? I think it is the man who followed me in the gray car. Carrie, she gives me much to worry about."

"It's only because she has a crush on you."

"A crush? What is that?"

"She's in love with you. Women do strange things when they're in love."

"It is more than that. She is mixed up in other matters. It is important for her to forget them."

"Them?"

"The people, their dealings. They are deadly."

Jan tried to laugh but couldn't bring it off. "I don't get it."

"Tell Carrie to stop working with people who are against me."

"She isn't working with anybody."

"I believe she is."

"No, no. Besides, what's there to be against? I don't see why you're so—"

He shot over beside her. "Look at me when you talk about this. You are frightened for your friend. That I can understand. But my two fathers, I tell you they would not like what she is doing. He spoke between clenched teeth, "If she continues, if anyone interferes in our business here in Peru, business important to us, they will be taken care of."

"Taken care of?" she echoed.

"You know what I mean. You know."

She nodded. "I know more than you think. Although I don't know what the dynamite's for, I know you're part of a drug ring."

She hadn't meant to say it. It had come out so easily, leaving her with a sense of relief combined with alarm.

He grasped her shoulders. The boat tipped precariously. "What makes you believe I am part of a drug ring?"

"You tell me you're involved in a deadly business. You say Carrie will be taken care of if she doesn't stop doing whatever she's doing. If it's something else, tell me."

"Do not talk about these things." He gripped her tighter. "Do not think about them."

"I don't want to. I wish I knew nothing. You're in trouble, Luis, deep trouble."

With a look of fury, he shoved her back until her neck arched over the windowsill. His body pressed against her, a weight crushing her chest. Sharp pains jabbed at her temples and whipped down her spine. Her mind froze in one track: *he's going to kill me....*

"You know too much," he cried.

Terrified, she beat her fists against his back. She needed air. With a burst of energy, she beat harder. Losing strength, she flailed at nothing.

With a groan, he released her and lurched away. She gulped air and fell sideways onto the bench.

"*¡Madre de Dios!*" he whispered hoarsely. "If they were here, they would kill you in an instant. Do you know that?" He turned back to meet her eyes. "I gave an oath to my people; I cannot let my heart interfere."

She managed to sit up, feeling her throat, her eyes locked with his.

"*Janecita*," he moaned as if only then aware of what he had done. Kneeling, he cradled her body. "I hurt you. I did not mean to hurt you."

She felt the anguish and frustration under his words. Her arms encircled him. "I know, Luis. I understand."

Gently he rubbed the back of her neck, holding her close, his breath quickening. "Forgive me. That I did such a thing to you fills me with misery. Please, please, forgive me."

In a trembling voice she said, "It was my fault, Luis. I asked too many questions. I played a silly game with you, but it's over."

He buried his face on her lap. "I love you too much," he said, crying now, his shoulders shaking with his muffled sobs.

She stroked his hair and murmured reassurances as if to a child. Then, raising his head, she gently kissed his wet cheeks.

"I taste your pain," she said, tears spilling down her own cheeks. "Now it is mine."

"*Mí Janecita.*"

"*Sí.* I am your *Janecita.* And it doesn't matter where or how."

He spread his jacket on the floor of the boat. She lay down on it and brought him to her. They made such intense love that she forgot where she was or where she had been. She forgot about Brewster and Carlos and Carrie, about the Uros village and the Indian woman on the train, about Logan and her computerized life. Her body rose to meet Luis, rose and fell in a smooth rhythm, faster and faster until nothing else mattered. There was only her passion with Luis.

CHAPTER 22

"You've been gone five hours," Carrie said as she let Jan into the room. "I was worried."

"Is Brewster still here?"

"No, he and Carlos left after you did."

"Good. Double lock the door."

The dead bolt clicked.

"Is someone after you?" whispered Carrie.

"No, just scared."

Jan's heart thumped so fast it seemed to run outside her body. She hurled the Uros Indian weaving onto her bed and staggered into the bathroom. Kicking off her sandals, she grabbed a towel and fell to her knees on it, hanging her head over the toilet, her stomach contracting, her whole body caught in dry heaves. The altitude, she thought miserably. The altitude, Luis, Brewster—the whole shitty business.

Carrie held her shoulders. "What are you afraid of?"

"I can't talk about it now."

Gradually the nausea subsided. Her heartbeat slowed. She leaned sideways against the white-tiled wall, smooth and cool on her face. It was a relief to kneel on the towel, to press her cheek against the cold wall. Water was running. It took her a few moments to realize the sound came from the bathtub.

Carrie, the blue shawl draped around her shoulders, hovered over the tub, adjusting faucets. A faint odor of lilacs rose on the steam.

Pain stabbed Jan's neck. She flinched and grasped the toilet seat. A frightful apparition appeared, disembodied, swinging grotesquely in the air—Brewster's cruel face. With a whimper, she pressed her forehead against the wall.

Carrie said soothingly, "I added foam crystals. You'll feel better after a bath."

"I won't feel better until we get out of Peru." Abruptly she turned around and seized Carrie's arm. "Brewster can't force us to meet him in Cuzco. Let's fly home in the morning."

Carrie gently pried Jan's fingers from her arm. "Try to relax."

"How can I? Don't you see the danger we're in? Don't you realize what might happen to us?"

Carrie studied her for a moment. "All flights at Juliaca are canceled. The airport runway is flooded."

"Then we'll take the train. We'll go back to Arequipa."

"The tracks may be under water by morning. If they aren't, then, yes, you take the train down to Arequipa and arrange your flight back to San Francisco."

"You too, Carrie."

"No!"

"No?" Jan tried to stand but couldn't get her legs to work. Holding onto the toilet seat, she cried, "So what if Paul was a bastard and your father launders dope money and those nuns at your Catholic school fired you. Go home. Start a new life. Everything'll work out. You'll find a job. Something with children. You're a great teacher. I'll help you get a job. I can help. I know I can."

She rattled on, scarcely conscious of what she was saying. "It's ridiculous to stay here. I've caused trouble for Luis. Hurt you. Made a mess of this trip. Damnit! I've got to get back to the office. To Logan. My cubicle where everything's easy to understand. Pour out perfect pages on my computer. Forget what's happened. No more threats. Oh, God, I'm so frightened. We have to get out of here. We need to feel safe."

Carrie said softly, "Safety isn't my concern."

Jan let go of the toilet seat. "What in hell do you mean?"

"You're upset. This isn't the time to—"

"Whatever we decide," Jan shrilled, "we do it together. Together!" She fell against the wall.

She became aware of the cool tiles against her face, Carrie massaging her shoulders, the sound of running water. "It's the altitude," she moaned. "I'm overtired. I haven't eaten. I raced up the hill."

Carrie took hold of Jan's arms. "Come on, get up and undress. Climb into the tub."

Leaning heavily, Jan rose. "You're stronger than I thought," she muttered.

"I'm learning." Carrie elbowed the toilet seat down and steadied Jan to sit on it. "Can you undress by yourself?"

"Sure."

While Carrie tested the water and adjusted the faucets, Jan managed with trembling hands to untie the sweater from her waist. She took off her blouse and her slacks and then peeled off her underwear. As if performing a ritual, she dropped each piece in a pile on the floor.

"Where did you leave Luis?" Carrie asked.

"At the dock. I was an idiot to run up the hill."

"Why did you?"

"Don't know."

"You must've had a reason." Carrie shut off the water. "What happened to your feet?"

Jan inspected her toes curiously as if they belonged to somebody else. "They're dirty," she announced.

Carrie edged the sandals away and picked up Jan's clothes. "I got us a bottle of soda water. I'll pour you a glass." She left the room.

What a switch, Jan thought. At home, it was efficient Jan who always rushed to the rescue, nursing Carrie after the abortion, listening to emotional outbursts from her, dispensing reassurance. Now it was calm, capable Carrie who lent Jan her strength even through she, too, must be suffering.

Slipping off her wristwatch, Jan tried to read the time, but couldn't focus on the hands. She stood up, shaky. Holding onto the sink with one hand, she set the watch on the shelf under the mirror. What did time matter anyhow? What did Luis matter? Too much, it seemed. Too much.

Their lovemaking had been the most satisfying she had ever experienced. Intense but tender. Passionate and fulfilling, exchanging the essence of each other. Afterwards, during the ride back to the dock, it seemed as if she moved through a dream, her head on his shoulder, his arm around her waist, a slow passage through a cradling reed forest, across an enchanted lake.

But the moment the boat touched the dock, her fears returned in a jumble. Fleeing from her own confusion, she leaped out of the boat and charged up the hill without even saying goodbye.

Now here she was, naked and trembling, looking at herself in the mirror. She raised her chin and attempted to straighten her shoulders. Could this woman apologize to Luis for running away? Could she tell Luis about Brewster and Carlos, and then beg him for help?

Not likely, she concluded. The worry about a repercussion was too strong, the risk to Carrie too great. Brewster knew that. He knew this woman better than she did. He knew she would dance the tango for a lark but choose the safest route home.

Dizzy again, she clutched the edge of the sink, determined to stay upright. The dizziness passed. She pulled out the side combs, piled her hair atop her head and shoved the combs back in. Carefully she stepped into the tub and sank into warm, satin-smooth water. Bubbles rose in peaks like miniature volcanoes, hissing across the top of her body. Closing her eyes, she slipped farther down so that water surrounded her neck to soothe its ache.

Holding up a handful of foam, she considered the unfairness of life. The Uros Indians would never know how it felt to lie in a tub of hot water. Neither would the woman who stood out in the cold on the train. She wished it weren't so, but it was and she couldn't change it. Because they couldn't enjoy a hot bath, should she forgo it? Should she not love a man because he was wrong for her? Should she have died because her sister drowned?

She reached for the washcloth and sat up to scrub herself, first her face, then her neck and arms and on down.

Carrie returned, her shawl gone, the color of the blouse matching her cheeks, pink from the heat of the bathroom steam. She handed Jan the glass of soda water.

Jan nodded thanks and took a few sips, then leaned back and balanced the glass on her chest. "I appreciate your help, Carrie."

"That's what friends are for. You're the one who taught me how to be a friend."

"It was easier for me. I didn't have to go through your ordeals. Besides"—she thought of Luis—"I had no interest in Paul." She noticed that most of the bubbles in the tub had burst. In the glass of soda, bubbles began to disappear. Soon all the bubbles would be gone. She said, "I'm sorry about Luis. About your father, too."

"I know." Carrie picked up Jan's sandals. Turning on the sink faucet, she used her fingertips like a stiff brush to scrub off the dirt. When finished, she switched off the water, shook the sandals, and wrapped them in a white hand towel.

A strain of iron runs through her porcelain body, Jan thought, while I've turned fragile like a rice paper lamp.

"Have you eaten anything today?" Carrie asked.

Jan shook her head and sipped more soda.

"It's past 3:00. I'll order soup."

Jan jerked up, spilling liquid from the glass. "No, don't let anybody into the room. It could be dangerous."

"Why?"

"I don't know. I'm paranoid about these drug guys. Give me time to pull myself together and I'll explain. Anyway, I'm not hungry. Is there any coca tea left?"

"Yes but it's lukewarm."

"No matter." Jan finished off the soda.

Carrie took the glass. "At least eat a couple of crackers so you won't get sick again. I brought back two packets from lunch."

"Okay." Weariness flooded through her.

"And you better get out of the hot tub or you might pass out." Carrie yanked up the lever to let the water down the drain. "Need any help?"

Jan watched the water level lower. "I don't think so."

Carrie nodded and left the bathroom.

Holding onto the side of the tub, Jan carefully rose to her knees, then her feet. Gingerly, she stepped out of the bath, still holding on with one hand, the other hand reaching for a heavy, white towel. Although her muscles were weak, her stomach felt better, dizziness gradually retreating. She wrapped the towel around her body and walked into the bedroom. Carrie sat in one of the swivel chairs. Jan rummaged in her duffel bag until she found her cotton robe. She laid the Uros weaving in the bottom of her bag, underneath everything. No sense keeping reminders in sight.

The crackers were on Jan's bedside stand along with a cup and the teapot. After adjusting the pillow against the headboard, she leaned against it, her legs stretched out on the bed, and poured herself a cup of tea.

Carrie said, "Heavy rain is forecast for tonight. If that happens, the desk clerk thinks no trains'll come in or go out. No telling how long Juliaca's airport'll be flooded." She folded her hands in her lap. "We may be stuck here for a while."

"That's okay. We'll hole up. If we can't get out, Brewster and Carlos can't get in. It's only Luis we have to worry about, unless drug traffickers or *Senderistas* lurk in the corridors."

"Are you ready to tell me what happened with Luis?"

Jan cleared her throat and swallowed hard. She stared at the spread, at the spiral design that reminded her of a flattened bedspring. It seemed important to concentrate on something abstract while she talked. "He thinks you're working against him, Carrie. That you're conspiring with other people. He said that if you continue to do this, they, whoever they are, will take care of you." She looked up. "What he meant was they'd kill you."

There was no change in Carrie's expression. Jan hurried on, her eyes back on the spread. "We took a trip on the lake in a motor launch. Visited a Uros Indian village built on a reed raft. That's where I got my feet dirty, walking around there. Afterwards, we talked and I said too much. Made the mistake of confronting him about the drug ring. At first I thought he was going to kill me. Now I'm more afraid someone else might."

The lake scene rushed across her mind. Luis, the dark water, her body pressed against the boat until she couldn't breathe, his face, wild and furious, suddenly changing from anger to sadness to love. How had she allowed this to happen? Her feelings for Luis were not the same as those for Logan. Was it love she felt for

Logan? If she weren't so tired, she might be able to sort this out, work the right keys, come up with definitive answers.

A pain cramped her neck. She squeezed her eyes closed and rubbed the muscle hard. The pain subsided. When she opened her eyes again, she noticed Carrie's mouth had softened in the old way and her eyes had their former look of innocence.

"Luis will protect us," Carrie said.

"Don't be so sure. He doesn't trust anybody except"—she decided not to mention Rafael's name—"his best friend, and I don't trust anybody except you. For a while, I didn't know about you. We shouldn't rely on anybody here. I'm leery about traveling on the train to Cuzco with Luis."

Her hand shook as she lifted the teapot and poured the rest of the tea. Holding the cup with both hands, she drank it all.

There was a soft rap on the door. She exchanged a startled look with Carrie.

"Who's there?" Jan called.

No reply.

As Carrie started forward, Jan whispered, "Wait." She set her cup on the stand and crawled to the foot of the bed where she could see the door. "Luis?" she called.

Silence.

A white, oblong envelope appeared under the door.

Carrie hurried over and scooped it up. Inserting a fingernail under the flap, she ripped it open and took out a piece of folded paper.

"Who's it from?" Jan asked.

"No signature, but I bet it's from Brewster." Carrie handed her the paper.

Jan read it silently: *Say nothing about our business to my new weapon or you risk his life. For his sake, you must go to Cuzco.* "What does he mean by *my new weapon?* Luis? If we don't go to Cuzco, do we risk his life?"

Carrie reached for the paper and reread the words. "Luis isn't a new weapon."

Jan crawled back to the headboard and leaned against the pillow. "The note must've been delivered by Brewster's spy. Someone at the hotel. We're being watched, Carrie." She shivered and slipped her legs under the covers.

The phone rang, startling them both.

On the third ring Carrie answered and then held the receiver out to Jan. "It's a person-to-person call to you from Cuzco."

"Brewster?" inquired Jan.

"The operator didn't say."

Jan took the phone. "This is Janet Fielding," she said in her office voice.

"You may proceed, *Señor.*"

"Hello, Jan?"

"Yes."

"Are you okay?"

Her hand tightened on the receiver. "Logan?"

"Yeah, who'd you think it was?"

"I had no idea. I couldn't imagine." She felt weak again.

"Are you okay?" he repeated, more insistent.

"I'm fine. What're you doing in Cuzco?"

"Worrying. Yesterday I had a phone call from a guy. He told me you were in trouble. Said if I didn't meet you in Cuzco, you might not survive. I was worried sick. Grabbed the night flight to Lima and the first flight this morning to Cuzco. All day I've been trying to get through to Puno. Not a damn line open until now. What's more, ever since I landed, some little guy's been tailing me. Don't know who the hell he is or what's going on. Are you really okay?"

Jan clamped her hand over the mouthpiece and whispered, "A man phoned Logan to say I was in trouble, that he better get to Cuzco. Since Logan landed, he's been tailed."

Carrie pressed her lips together, "Logan must be Brewster's new weapon."

Jan caught her breath. "And if I don't go to Cuzco—"

"Jan," Logan yelled on the other end of the line, "answer me!"

"It's a hoax," she blurted into the receiver. "Somebody's playing a joke on you."

"I don't buy that."

"What else could it be? Look, I'm sorry about this, about your flying all the way to Peru. How'd you know where I was?"

"Every day I've checked that itinerary you posted above your desk."

Her eyes burned. "I didn't think you'd be interested."

"Well, I am. When I thought something had happened to you I was frantic. We should talk about this, Jan. About us."

"Well, yeah, sure, I'd like to do that."

"When are you arriving in Cuzco?"

Jan chewed her lower lip.

Logan said, "Why the silence? Are you sorry I came?"

"No, no, I'm glad. It's great you're here. It's just—" Frantically she searched for the right words. "It's, well, I'm thinking about your law practice. Won't it suffer?"

"Jarvis is handling my cases. Jan, something's wrong with you. I can tell."

"I'm...I'm worried about the floods."

"No problem here in Cuzco. I've been told no problem in Puno."

"Not now. But tonight it's supposed to rain hard. Tomorrow the train might not be able to leave."

"Juliaca has an airport."

"The runway there is flooded." She cleared her throat. "It's bad all over Peru. You really shouldn't have come."

There was a pause on the other end of the line. When he spoke, his voice was low and serious. "I had to make sure you were okay."

His concern brought tears to her eyes. "I'm okay, really."

"What about your friend, Carrie?"

Jan wiped her eyes with her sleeve. "She's fine. We're both fine. Well, not exactly. I'm suffering a bit from altitude sickness—headache, stomach, the works. That's why I sound so strange. Right now I'm drinking coca tea and it isn't hot enough."

"Yeah, I've had two pots of the stuff and I'm walking on air."

She laughed nervously. "Where are you staying?"

"Hotel Libertador."

"That's where our reservations are."

"I know."

Once more she cleared her throat

"Have you got a cold?" he inquired.

"No. Look, Logan, do me a favor. Rest in your room. Have your dinner brought up. Don't go sightseeing until I get there. The altitude can hit you hard. Besides I'd like to be with you when you explore." She rubbed her neck. "And be careful about that little man following you. He may be a thief or a murderer or who knows what. Don't let him catch you alone in the hall or anyplace. Promise me you'll stay inside the hotel until I come. I don't want anything to happen to you."

"It's been a long time since anyone was interested in my welfare."

"I've been interested for a long time." She added softly, "More than that." Taking a deep breath, she returned to a business voice. "Look, I'll get to Cuzco as soon as I can. Hopefully tomorrow. Meanwhile, be careful."

"Right." He paused. "Jan, I've missed you."

"Missed you, too," she replied, a lump in her throat.

"See you soon."

"Sure. Goodbye."

Carrie took the receiver and replaced it in the cradle. In an even voice, she asked, "What'll you do about Luis? He won't want Logan around, and I doubt if Logan will put up with Luis."

Jan threw back the covers and sat on the edge of the bed. "I've got to get to Cuzco and act as if nothing's wrong." She fidgeted with the teapot lid, lifting it and setting it down, trying to think the problem through. "The minute we get to Cuzco," she continued, abandoning the lid and sitting cross-legged on the bed, "the three of us must find a way to fly out before Brewster locates us. I'll beg Luis for help. When he realizes we won't interfere with his business, he'll be eager to help us get out of Peru."

She had no idea what Luis would think or do. The words had simply flowed out.

Again the phone rang. Jan grabbed the receiver before it could ring twice. "Hello."

"This is the desk clerk."

"Yes."

"Is *Señorita Fielding* there?"

"This is *Señorita Fielding*."

"I have a message for you from *Señor Luis Acosta*. He said to tell you he is sorry to leave but feels it necessary. He checked out of the hotel a few minutes ago."

Jan caught her breath. "Where did Luis go? What are we supposed to do?"

"He arranged for his pilot friend to fly you tomorrow morning to Cuzco."

"From where?"

"The nearby military field."

Attempting to keep her voice steady, Jan said, "What time is our flight?"

"At 10:00."

"Did he say where he'd meet us in Cuzco?"

"He said to tell you he cannot meet you there. He wished me to express his unhappiness about the weather and all the other bad events. He hopes the rest of your trip in Peru will be more pleasant."

Jan's fingers turned numb. She loosened her grip on the phone. "Thank you." She replaced the receiver. In a monotone she said, "Luis is driving Padrino's truck to Cuzco."

Carrie's eyes widened. "The road between here and Cuzco is terrible."

Jan nodded and studied the other designs on the bedspread: birds, fish, a strange kind of cat. Where had she seen shapes like these? The Nazca Lines, and on the pottery and burial weavings at the museum in Lima.

"With the rain," said Carrie, "and the washouts and that beat-up truck, I don't see how...." After a moment she asked, "Did he say when he planned to reach Cuzco?"

"No." Jan started to repeat what the desk clerk had told her but found the words too difficult. "He...he won't be seeing us again."

Carrie pulled her shawl around her shoulders. She sat down facing the window. In a small voice she said, "It's started raining."

Jan sighed and wished for another cup of tea, a hot cup to take away the cold she felt inside. Carrie got over Paul, she told herself. She'll get over Luis, and so will I. I'll forget I ever met him. I have to. And when I get to Cuzco, I'll find a way to protect Logan.

The sky and lake grew dark, deepening layers of gray down to navy blue. She could scarcely see the outlines of the two chairs, Carrie completely hidden. Tearing open a package of crackers, Jan began to eat, the snap and crackle a relief from the silence.

"We'll go to the dining room for dinner," she announced. "I'll wear my orange slacks and striped blouse. We might as well make ourselves highly visible for Brewster's spy." She took a deep breath and exhaled forcefully. "What do you think?"

"It could rain all night," Carrie answered as if she hadn't heard the question.

CHAPTER 23

All night it rained, often heavy, water striking the window like pellets, waking Jan up. By dawn, though, the storm was over. As the sun rose, the sky turned a royal blue, processions of clouds marching across in loose formation. From their room high above the lake, Jan peered down at a reed boat, its sail curved by the wind, a tiny figure bent in the prow. The vessel skimmed across the slate-colored water textured by shifting white dots.

She wondered if Luis was still in the truck, creeping along the backbone of the *altiplano*. Or had he been waylaid by a flooded road? Stopped by a washed-out bridge? Bogged in a muddy ditch? A terrible vision broke across her mind: the truck, unable to round a sharp curve, hurtled off a cliff and exploded in a ball of flame that tumbled over and over, smaller and smaller until it reached the bottom where it glowed momentarily then disappeared.

Dressed only in bra and jeans, she stood in front of the window. Bumps rose on her arms like whitecaps raised by the wind. She rubbed them vigorously but refused to move away from the cold glass until the boat disappeared among the reeds.

Shivering, she turned away to pull on a warm flannel shirt, adding her denim vest for insurance. Today she would see Logan. Soon everything would be under control. Into the duffel bag went the wine colored sweater and slacks, the last things to pack, the last clothes worn with Luis, items difficult to see and touch again. "Let's head out for breakfast," she called to Carrie in an attempted cheerful voice.

The dining salon was closed. A staff member directed them to a narrow, windowless room that looked more like a chapel. At the far end was a long buffet table lit by recessed ceiling lights. On either side of the aisle stretched rows of wooden tables with benches. Six women and four men occupied one table. Jan remembered them from the dining room last night—an English tour group, the only other guests at the hotel. They hunched over their cereal and solemnly crunched. Occasionally a spoon clinked against a bowl.

The buffet table was crowded with cereals, muffins, fruits, juices and a thermos of coffee, along with neatly stacked china and napkin-wrapped silverware. Carrie shook corn flakes into a bowl. Jan took a blueberry muffin and poured herself a cup of coffee.

The swinging door behind the buffet flew open. A young waiter with amber skin emerged in a crisp uniform that matched his black hair and eyes. The overhead light transformed his high cheekbones and the bridge of his nose into gold. In a measured voice, he proclaimed, "We have eggs scrambled, fried or boiled. We have bacon, sausage or ham. What do you wish?"

"Nothing," they replied in unison.

The young man bowed and sprinted back through the swinging door that flapped behind him like a broken wing.

"Could be Brewster's spy," Jan murmured, amused at the encounter. She and Carrie sat down at a table on the opposite side from the British tourists.

Jan thought it strange so few guests were at this hotel. *Las Dunas* had been crowded with vacationers from Lima. Was there more to fear from terrorists up here in the Andes? The thought sent a chill through her.

The tour group's director rose, his white mustache twitching. Holding his body stiffly erect, he tapped his spoon against a glass. "Most of you are aware that the plan this morning was for the minibus to transport us up the mountainside to visit the ancient stone burial towers called *chullpas*. I regret to say we cannot visit the *chullpas* because the causeway that links us to the mainland has disappeared."

"Disappeared?" cried an elderly woman, her eyes wide.

"Indeed. Presently it is under quite a load of water."

There were anxious murmurs. Jan exchanged a concerned look with Carrie.

"Barring further downpours," the director continued, "I am told the causeway may reappear tomorrow."

Carrie whispered, "How do we get off the island?"

Jan jammed the last piece of muffin into her mouth and finished her coffee. "I'll check on the situation with the front desk. Meet you in the room."

No doubt Brewster knew about the flooding, she thought. His spy would have told him, and Brewster would have figured a way to get them to Cuzco. Or Luis would have a card up his sleeve. Surely floods had occurred here before. What if she was assuming too much and nobody had made arrangements? What would happen to Logan if she didn't show up in Cuzco?

She approached the desk. The well-groomed clerk raised her hands as if to bless her. "Ah, *Señorita Fielding*. We have a problem with the causeway."

"So I've heard."

"However, no need to worry. A *campesino* by the name of Padrino has arrived by boat. He says you know him. Is this correct?"

"Yes, I know him."

"He informed me he has come to transport you ashore where a taxi awaits to shuttle you to the military airfield."

Jan's first reaction was one of relief. Then she considered the possibility that Padrino was in Ignacio's drug ring. He might not have come to help the American women, rather to get rid of them. But how else could they get to the airport, short of swimming?

"We'll leave in ten minutes," she told the clerk. "Please have our bill ready."

"Certainly, and I'll have your luggage transferred to the boat."

Jan started to say they could handle it themselves, but the clerk lowered her hand on the bell with such decisiveness that she let the game of efficiency proceed. Besides, at the moment she felt too weary to protest.

Although last night's sleep had been longer than the naps on the train, her dreams had run rampant. Twice she woke up scarcely able to breathe, her mind churning with fear and revulsion. In her dreams, Luis crushed her chest against the side of the boat, ragged peasants dragged her through shantytowns, drug dealers, spies, soldiers, terrorists attacked from all sides, their faces interchangeable. Bombs exploded people to pieces.

This morning her head no longer ached, but her body felt fractured. She hurried back to the room, muttering, "I'm okay, Carrie's okay, everything's okay," as if those words were the necessary glue to hold herself together.

CHAPTER 24

Carrie walked out of the hotel ahead of Jan and headed directly for Padrino, who stood at the edge of the submerged causeway. Jan paused on the porch, her eyes, straying to the start of the path that led down to the dock. Forget Luis, she told herself. You'll never see him again. A cloud momentarily blocked the sun. The air alternated between cold and hot, wind and no wind. She rushed after Carrie, determined not to look back.

The boat, built of reeds, was similar to the one she had watched from the window but without a sail, more like the fisherman's boat glimpsed yesterday in the side channel. Padrino wore the same clothes as before, his knit hat pulled over his ears and tied under his chin.

"Where's our luggage?" Jan asked nervously.

"Over there." Padrino waved at the other shore. "Already in taxi."

"What if the driver takes off. He could be a thief."

"He is my cousin," Padrino replied indignantly. "I trust him with my life." For emphasis, he placed his hand over his heart. "See"—he pointed at a battered gray car on the shore—"he waits for you. Bad idea for suitcases and ladies to go in boat together. We sink. So I take suitcases over first."

Jan said, "This boat looks as if it would sink with one of us in it."

Padrino raised his eyes and arms, his red poncho seeming to double in size, brilliant against the gray-brown parking lot. "No time to build better boat. We make do."

Wanting to verify her assumption about Luis, Jan asked, "What happened to your truck?"

"It is gone."

"Is Luis delivering the dynamite and detonators to Cuzco?"

Padrino looked uncomfortable. "Luis is gone," he replied and gestured to the boat. "We go now."

He pushed the craft halfway into the water. From the ground he picked up a pole twice his height. "Come, get in. If we start to sink, I jump out and take you one by one."

Carrie looked around anxiously. "Where are the oars?"

"No oars. I pole the boat over. Pole, pole, pole, very quick. We move fast and no problems. Please, somebody get in my boat."

Carrie stepped in, crouched, and started to walk toward the bow.

"Kneel," he cried. "Crawl. Fast. That is better. Good. Now, you." He gestured to Jan.

With a sigh, Jan climbed in and managed to sit down, her back against Carrie's daypack. The boat smelled like cornhusks. Beneath her, the reeds were wet and slimy. Her jeans would be soaked. When she grasped the sides of the boat, the ropes that tied the reeds together felt like sandpaper. If she and Carrie ever made it to the airfield, they would fly to Cuzco with red hands and wet pants.

"Carrie, are you okay," she yelled over her shoulder.

"I hope so."

Padrino climbed astride, balancing on the heavy-bundled rims. With a great effort, he pushed off and poled like a demon. The craft shot out into the channel.

Charcoal colored water oozed up beneath Jan's legs. "My God, it's sinking," she cried.

He poled faster. "Everything all right," he huffed. "We make it."

In mid channel a gust of wind hit. The boat lurched. Padrino almost lost his balance. Carrie muffled a scream. Jan clutched the rims and started to stand up. The boat rocked.

Padrino yelled, "Sit down." He poled furiously.

Jan didn't dare check on how far it was to land. Another gust sent a spray of water onto her that smelled like fish. Or was it sewage? She tried to keep calm. A moment later she felt a bump beneath her.

Padrino leaned on his pole and yelled triumphantly, "You are here. Now go. Hurry, please."

Carrie clambered out, her denims damp in front and back. Jan nearly fell overboard in her hurry to exit. The seat of her jeans was soaked. When a gust of wind hit, she felt as if a cake of ice was attached to her backside.

"Goodbye," cried Padrino, waving his pole in the air.

"Wait," Jan called. "What do we owe for the boat ride."

"Nothing. Give my cousin an American dollar. It is too much, but he will be happy."

"Thank you," Jan called and Carrie waved.

He waved back, his poncho billowing, his body poised as if for a takeoff. He poled south, easing through the water until he disappeared behind a row of beached boats.

The car was another battered vehicle. The lid to the trunk was missing as well as the rear bumper and a headlight was smashed. Jan noted with relief that their two bags and Carrie's cart were piled in the front seat next to the driver. The cousin, a taller version of Padrino, politely ushered the two ladies into the back seats.

It was a fast, rough drive, brakes squealing like a creature in pain. At 9:45 they arrived at the airfield. The cousin looked pleased with his payment and sped off, exhaust lingering behind in a small gray cloud.

The field was even smaller than the one at Ica. It occupied a shaved-off knoll flanked by steep mountains. On the runway, puddles of water shimmered in the wind like silver disks. The only plane in sight was a military one, tied down on the west side. Near the open doorway of a tin-roofed building, about as large as a tool shed, stood two soldiers wearing green uniforms, black boots and red berets. They held M-16s. The soldiers eyed the women intently. After a brief consultation, they leaned their rifles against the building and sauntered forward.

Carrie spoke to them in Spanish. They knew nothing about a flight today at 10:00. Only military planes were supposed to land here, although occasionally, a private plane was allowed. The soldiers examined their passports and said they were welcome to wait, although they doubted if a plane would come. That's how it was in Peru these days. Since it was getting hot, the *señoritas* might prefer to stay out of the sun. They transported their luggage into the small building.

Inside, one of the soldiers gallantly dusted off two folding metal chairs with his beret and indicated they should sit down while the other soldier produced two Inca Colas from a box. He pried off the metal caps with his back teeth, then, presented the drinks as if they were champagne.

"Watch out for these guys," Jan muttered. She pulled out a tissue and carefully wiped her bottle rim before taking a drink.

Carrie nodded. In haughty Spanish she thanked the soldiers for their kindness, but assured them no more assistance was needed. She said she was surprised that they weren't outside guarding the field. What if terrorists tried to take it over?

The startled looks on the soldiers' faces revealed that leaving the building hadn't entered their minds. However, after a round of laughter, followed by fierce looks from the girls, they bowed curtly and left, retrieving their guns and standing in the shade of the tied-down plane.

Jan looked at her watch: 10:00 and no sign of the flight. They sat down to wait.

10:10. Nothing.

10:30. It was too hot. Using a discarded bottle top, Jan managed to pry open two more Inca Colas and handed one to Carrie. The clear, yellow liquid was warm, but better than nothing. Jan stowed her vest in her duffle bag and rolled up the sleeves of her flannel shirt. The seat of her pants had completely dried.

11:00. The tin roof snapped and crackled as the sun peered in and out of clouds. Two other soldiers arrived to replace the two on duty. The new pair remained aloof, probably having learned about the feisty ladies.

11:30. The clouds were gone, and the wind had died down, the air hotter by the minute. Jan decided to exchange her flannel shirt for the coolest blouse she had, the red, sleeveless one.

Carrie tapped her feet against the rung of the metal chair.

Jan sat down again. Carrie's tapping continued. The sound began to annoy Jan. Suddenly, Carrie popped up like a jack-in-the-box and ran to the door to stare out. "Thought I heard something," she said and resumed her seat, again tapping. For the next ten minutes, she alternated between tapping and leaping up to look outside.

Jan wanted to shout, *Stop jumping up and for God's sake cut out the tapping*. But she said nothing. Yesterday, Carrie had been the calm one, Jan emotional. Maybe only one person at a time was allowed to fall apart around here. This is not a disaster, she decided. If the plane doesn't show up by 12:30, we'll walk back to the causeway and search for someone to pole us over to the hotel. If we can't find anyone, we'll borrow a beached boat and pole it across ourselves. We'll rent another room and wait until either the railroad tracks or the Juliaca runway is clear of water. I'll phone Logan and tell him what's happened. I'll beg him to stay in his room because the man following him is dangerous. I'll strongly suggest he order his food and have it left outside his door, so he can snatch it in when nobody's around.

At 12:04 Carrie ran out through the doorway, crying, "I hear a plane."

Jan was dubious until she, too, heard the distant drone of an engine. Through a cloudless sky, a small plane with no insignia approached from the north. Slowly it circled, reminding her of the condor over Puno. As the plane landed, water splashed fountains on either side of the runway. The soldiers ran forward, guns ready.

A short man in a black leather jacket with goggles too big for his face climbed out of the cockpit. He spoke to the soldiers, showing them a piece of paper. From his jacket he pulled out money and handed it over. The soldiers lowered their guns and stepped aside so the pilot could leave the plane.

"It's Felipe," Carrie said as she ran back inside for her cart.

Jan frowned, "That's the pilot who flew us over the Nazca Lines. What's he doing here? What happened to Luis' friend?"

Through the shed doorway Felipe's smiling face appeared. "*Buenas tardes, señoritas. Venga. Vamos a Cuzco. Rapido.*"

CHAPTER 25

The back of the co-pilot's seat was still broken, the belt missing, so Jan climbed into the rear of the plane. She didn't want to duplicate her scary Nazca experience. Besides, since Carrie seemed excited about a flight with Felipe, let her sit next to him. Jan noted that at least the windshield wasn't taped with newspapers. This helped calm her fears.

A few minutes before take off Felipe opened a leather bag. "*Los alimentos*," he announced, waving at the food inside. Jan took an offered chicken sandwich and ate a few bites to stop her stomach growling. As the plane bounced forward, she wished she had eaten nothing.

The plane ricocheted down the runway, shooting up streams of water. At the last moment before dropping off the cliff, the plane rose. Three times they circled, gradually gaining altitude. The aircraft shook its way north, in and out of fog banks, between close mountain peaks, through narrow, flooded valleys, dropping into air pockets, bouncing on currents. Sometimes Felipe flew so low, Jan saw the eyes of babies strapped to women's backs and the hands of bent-over peasants farming the rocky terraces on steep mountainsides.

She was amazed at the way Carrie sat in the plane, balanced on the edge of her seat, never once falling against its broken back, all the while peering at the scenery and munching on a sandwich with the delicacy of a vicuña. Carrie and Felipe shouted to each other in Spanish over the noise of the engine and the rattles of the plane; every few minutes Carrie swiveled and translated what Felipe had said. Jan tried to act interested but had a hard time concentrating because of the frequent air pockets. She kept telling herself Felipe was used to flying in the mountains, he was in complete control, but when the plane suffered a big drop and he yelled "*Cuidado!*"—look out!—she despaired.

At last the tiled roofs of Cuzco came into view, spreading below like splotches of red paint on white canvas. The plane circled down and landed without a hitch. Breathing a big sigh of relief, Jan climbed out, her knees so weak she nearly collapsed on the tarmac. From among the slew of cab drivers, Felipe chose one and negotiated a ride for Carrie and Jan to the *Hotel Libertador*. Then he blessed them all, waved goodbye and raced back to his aircraft.

The taxi jerked them from the parking lot onto the road. For a while Jan thought the vehicle had lost a cylinder but the driver assured them the only things lost were *los frenos,* the brakes. Continually he shifted gears to compensate. Jan held her breath as they barreled along in yet another contraption verging on collapse.

Arriving at the Spanish colonial hotel, they stepped from the cab onto a narrow cobbled street. Jan's knees still wobbled. The lobby ahead was dim and mysterious. Her panic level rose. Vehicles behind revved their engines impatiently, fumes billowed and the honk of an ancient sedan sounded like a wounded goose. The taxi driver dropped their baggage inside the doorway, shook his fist at the cars, yelled a few expletives and sped away.

When they checked in at the front desk, Logan's note awaited: *I'm in room 203. Call me.* Jan carefully folded the note as if it might otherwise disappear and tucked it into a pocket of her jeans. She peered around the lobby, half expecting to see Brewster or a possible spy. The room was empty except for the bellboy, who, with her duffel hoisted on his shoulder, headed for the elevator, pulling Carrie's squeaking cart behind him.

Jan said, "Carrie, I'm staying down here. I need to see Logan. Figure out what to do. I'll meet you in the dining room at 6:00. Okay?"

"Okay, but be careful what you say to him." Carrie disappeared into the elevator.

Jan grabbed the phone on the counter. She started to dial Logan, stopped and set the phone back on the hook. Wasn't it more important to secure an exit strategy first? Then she could breathe a little easier. She asked the operator to ring *Aero Peru*. No answer. The clerk gave her the airline's street address. She walked the two blocks to *Avenido Sol*. The sign on the door said *Cerrado*, closed. She chewed on her lower lip, her mind a confused jumble of thoughts.

I can't let Logan know what's happening. I won't let Brewster hold him hostage. Got to find a way out of Peru. Brewster will do anything to get the information he wants—kill Logan, kill me. To hell with anyone who gets in his way. Luis, Luis, where are you? Are you safe? I don't want Logan to know about you. What happened to your pilot friend? How did Felipe know where we were? I've got to get us out of this damn country.

Back at the hotel, she rushed up to an agent at a tour desk. "Need a flight tomorrow. Three seats to Lima."

"Sorry, flights full."

"How about trains or buses?"

"Due to floods, other forms of transport have been canceled."

She had a hard time breathing. Trapped. Can't escape. This is all my fault. I've failed.

"Jan?"

She gasped.

Logan, wearing a crew-necked shirt, lounged in the doorway of the hotel foyer. For a moment she didn't recognize him. She'd never seen him outside the office, and her emotional tie with Luis was so strong that somehow the reality of Logan had retreated to a corner of her mind.

Yet here he was, looking good. She didn't know what to do. How should she greet him? This was her boss. Should they shake hands? Hug? After all, he had come a long way to help her. And yet...she felt paralyzed, afraid of doing the wrong thing.

As laid-back as Logan appeared, she knew he was ready to go into action. She was just as determined he shouldn't have to. They had to get away from Brewster. Soon. Soon. "Hey, where's this villain who's 'been following you?" she tried to joke.

Logan didn't appear amused. "Last time I saw him was at lunch, lurking around the buffet table. When I started towards him, he disappeared behind a tour group. I thought *what the hell*, drank another cup of coca tea and went to my room to lie down a minute. Next thing I knew it was 4:30. I'd crashed for two hours. Christ, I never do that." He scanned the lobby and then focused on her face. "How long have you been here?"

"A little while."

"I left a message at the front desk. Didn't you get it?"

She nodded. "I...ah...I thought you might be resting, what with the altitude."

"Didn't come to rest, came to find you. Who's the guy who called me in San Francisco?"

"Don't know." It struck her that Logan was in the same position she had been in with Carrie in *Las Dunas*—worried, feeling something was wrong, getting no answers. She eyed him furtively. He had abandoned the casual look. Standing in the lobby doorway, he was in command mode, analyzing the situation. She felt he could accomplish anything if he set his mind to it. An impulse came to throw her arms around him and hold on.

"How did the temp work out?" she asked quickly. "Any trouble with my computer?"

"No, but once I heard it whisper, *What happened to the lady with the green eyes and the long, dark hair?* I whispered back, *Don't worry. She promised to return.* It replied, *I hope so. This other lady has a lousy touch.*"

His words sent a wave of pleasure through her body.

He moved from the doorway, allowing a bellboy to pass through with a load of baggage. Three couples followed, their bodies drooped with fatigue. Logan eyed them intently.

"Any new P.I. cases?" Jan inquired, trying to make her voice sound matter-of-fact.

"Two. One's an old Italian lady. Claims she got hit by a cable car. Both arms in casts, waved them around like baseball bats. Afraid the true story is she jumped on a moving cable car."

"Sounds like a loser. Did you sign her up?"

"Not yet, but I'm studying Italian." His eyes met hers. "God, I've missed you, Jan. I didn't realize how much you meant to me until you were gone."

Guilt flooded through her. She wanted to hug him, let him know she had missed him, had loved him for a long time. But she couldn't. Now there was Luis, and she cared about him, too. How could her love be so divided? If only Logan had come three days ago, Luis wouldn't be such an emotional part of her life.

"Thanks," she mumbled, realizing the word wasn't the reply either of them wanted to hear.

He rubbed his chin. "Heard the train tracks got flooded. What airline did you fly?"

"No airline. Hitched a ride on a private plane. The pilot lives near here. Convenient for us." She rushed on, afraid he might question the arrangements. "Funny guy, the pilot. His plane's a rattletrap, but he flies it all over Peru. Carrie learned he's a Jesuit priest." She laughed nervously. "Flying with him was pretty scary. Father Felipe, that's his name, lives in the village of Yucay. In the Urubamba Valley. Carrie thinks he's quite intelligent."

"Most Jesuits are."

The look on Logan's face was one she had seen many times: knowing something was wrong and waiting for information to slip out. She must be careful, follow Brewster's instructions: *Say nothing about our business to my new weapon or you risk his life.* Brewster knew she would do anything to protect Logan. From the moment they met at *Las Dunas* he had pegged her. She remembered his words: *Protection might be more up your alley.*

From behind Jan came a banging noise. She spun around. A man pounded his fist on the counter. In a loud voice he demanded another room away from the street, claiming traffic blasted all night.

The woman beside him snipped, "I told you we should've stayed home."

"You're always interrupting," the man snarled at her.

The desk clerk said, "Sorry, sir. No available rooms."

Over the commotion Jan said to Logan, "Father Felipe runs a school for Indian children. Carrie wants to visit. She's a teacher, you know."

He shook his head. "No, I didn't know. Where *is* your friend?"

"Upstairs. She'll meet us for dinner."

He moved closer, touched her collar and whispered in one ear. "I like your blouse."

She didn't dare look at him. Across her mind flashed a picture of herself in the taxi with Luis eying her bare arms. At the airfield she'd changed into the sleeveless red blouse because it was hot. Why hadn't she worn the white blouse instead? She wasn't doing anything right.

A group of tourists poured out of the elevator. They walked across the tiled floor, their feet clacking like castanets, their voices resounding. One of the ladies coughed as if on the verge of pneumonia. At the front desk, the man continued to pound the counter.

Jan broke into a cold sweat. She couldn't seem to swallow. Was it because of the noise, the blouse or Logan's closeness. "I'd like a beer," she shouted above the clamor. "In a quiet place."

"Good idea," he yelled back. "What brand?"

She searched her mind for what she drank in *Las Dunas?* "*Pilsen Callao,*" she shouted.

He nodded. "I'll get it in the bar. Meet you in the courtyard." As he strode away, a small, dark-complexioned man rose from a chair and followed him.

Jan's eyes widened. The seat had been empty when she met Logan, empty when the couple started to argue at the desk, empty when the group clacked out of the elevator. Brushing past a group of tourists, she hurried across the outer lobby to the vacant courtyard.

Questions filled her mind. Who is the man tailing Logan? What does he want? Will more rain come? Is Luis safe? Has he reached Cuzco? Where's Brewster? Did he send Felipe to pick us up? What happened to the pilot Luis sent? Is Logan in danger now? How can we get out of Peru?

The courtyard was square, stone-floored, and surrounded by a narrow, colonnaded porch. At the far end, the back door to the bar stood open. Peruvian music drifted out between muffled spurts of laughter and the periodic whirring of a blender. She sat on a stone bench beside a yellow-flowering vine that wound up a porch column. Bulbous clouds floated in the sky like giant white balloons. The relative peace of the place calmed her mind. Things aren't as bad as I'm imagining, she told herself. Everything will be all right. I'll find a way to get us safely home.

A couple emerged from the bar, followed the walkway, and passed through the double doors to the dining room. Smells of roasted meat, garlic and fried onions wafted out. Jan felt hungry. A good sign, she decided, wanting to be positive about something.

"Here you go," said Logan, coming through the bar doorway with two tall glasses of beer, an inch of foam on each. He handed her a napkin with her glass, then sat down on the stone bench. After a long drink, he said, "I believe you know who called me and why he did. How come you aren't you being honest with me?"

She took a quick gulp of beer and wiped the foam from her lips. She was determined to keep her voice even, sound perfectly under control. "Logan, please don't push me on this. There are things I can't talk about right now. But I'm okay. Really I am. And I'm touched by your concern, glad you came, find it hard to believe you flew all this way to help me." Staring at the flowering vine, she blurted out, "But traveling in a country filled with armed soldiers and police is awful. We should go home on the next available flight."

"Hey, hold on. We can have a great time in Cuzco. I don't see soldiers or police around here. Jarvis is covering my cases. You've just assured me you're okay. My headache's gone. Why hurry back to the grind?" He touched her bare arm. "Evening's warm but you're cold."

She pulled her arm away. For an uncomfortable minute they drank their beers in silence.

Then she recognized the figure in the bar doorway, the same man who rose from the couch when Logan left. "Is that the guy tailing you?" she asked, nodding in his direction.

Logan bounded to his feet. "Yeah! By God, I'll find out what he wants."

She jumped up and grasped Logan's arm. "No, forget it. Let's go in to dinner now."

He looked at her hand on his arm. "Why don't you want a confrontation?"

"I want to see the menu," she replied. "Besides, you're right, I'm cold. I'll feel better in the dining room. And if we go in now, we can get a table near the stage. There's flute music tonight—a great group called *Savia Andina*."

The man in the doorway disappeared. She let go of Logan's arm.

He stared at her. "Something strange going on here—things you won't discuss, people you won't identify. Until I find out what's happening, I have no intention of hopping a plane and flying home."

"I've heard the food at this hotel is good," she said.

His eyes narrowed as though that might help him decipher her thoughts. "I didn't fly to Cuzco to listen to flute music and enjoy the food. I came because I heard you were in trouble. As you know, Jan, I seldom wait around for explanations. Your answers better come pretty soon."

He took her firmly by the elbow and guided her toward the dining room.

CHAPTER 26

They took a table near the stage. Jan watched the way Logan scrutinized each person who came through the doorway, his jaw working up and down the way it did when he prepared for a trial. Aware he was ready to leap into action, she found it difficult to concentrate on the menu. To her relief, Carrie soon appeared in the doorway. "That's my friend," she announced to Logan.

"Who's the tall guy with her?" he asked.

"Don't know," and she really didn't. He wore horn-rimmed glasses and a rumpled tweed jacket over a polo shirt the color of coffee. Clamped between his teeth was an unlit pipe.

As he came closer, Jan recognized the halo of curly blonde hair. Brewster! He didn't look like either of the men he had been before.

Logan rose to assist Carrie into a chair. Carrie smiled and said, "What a pleasure to meet Logan McCloskey, the great San Francisco attorney!"

Reclaiming his seat, Logan said, "As far as lawyers go, I'm a small potato in a big field."

Brewster laughed stodgily and removed the pipe, cradling it in his hand. "That's an apropos image, Mr. McCloskey. Did you know Peru grows 360 varieties of potatoes?"

His voice was different, Jan noted: flat and drier than paper.

Logan looked amused. "A fascinating piece of information, sir. Tell us about yourself, and we might allow you to sit at our table."

"I'm Professor Brewster of Latin American Studies at CCW." He held out his hand.

Logan shook it. "CCW?"

"Cordyne College for Women."

"Where's it located?"

"Upper New York State." Brewster stuffed the pipe into his jacket pocket and took the vacant seat between Jan and Carrie. "We're a small college but we educate our women well."

"I bet you do. What's your first name?"

"Marvin, but I prefer to be called Brewster." He signaled the waiter, who brought additional menus and a pitcher of water.

Brewster continued, "And who is this lovely lady beside you?"

"I'm Janet Fielding," she said coolly, "Mr. McCloskey's secretary."

Another stodgy laugh. "I should've known. It appears you two have an excellent working relationship."

Jan focused on her menu. "Carrie, where'd you meet Professor Brewster?"

"Upstairs," Carrie replied in a small voice.

Brewster said, "I was standing in the hallway, engrossed in a conversation with a tour guide. He was telling me that a friend of mine recently drove a truck from Puno to Cuzco."

Jan looked up.

"A difficult trip," Brewster continued, "what with floods washing out roads and bridges. The guide informed me that my friend had left Cuzco and driven down into the Urubamba Valley. Miss Ross overheard our discussion and asked if the valley contained Inca ruins. I told her about the fortresses of Pisac and Ollantaytambo. She was intrigued." He looked pointedly at Carrie.

"Yes, yes," Carrie said quickly. "Ruins fascinate me."

"When I mentioned my plan of renting a car tomorrow to drive into the valley, Miss Ross expressed a desire to go along. She thought you folks also would be interested, so she suggested we have dinner together and explore the possibilities."

Carrie's broad smile looked ready for a photograph.

"Therefore"—Brewster opened his arms in a magnanimous gesture—"I present the offer of a free car and a free guided tour of the Sacred Valley of the Incas in exchange for your much-needed companionship. I do dislike poring over ruins by myself."

Jan glanced at Logan, who was examining Brewster's face as if studying a map.

Brewster nodded sagely. "Like Cuzco, Ollantaytambo is built on Inca foundations. Everywhere perfectly fitted stone streets and walls. Even the ancient aqueduct is in use." Bracing his hands on the table, he launched into a sonorous lecture. "In the days of the Inca, the fortress of Ollantaytambo guarded the Upper Urubamba River, the natural gateway to Cuzco. Another fortress, Pisac, stood at the other end of the valley. Along with Sacsahuamán, the giant fortress above here, Cuzco was well protected against incursions from jungle tribes."

Jan forced herself to appear relaxed. She sipped water and straightened her silverware.

Logan continued to scrutinize Brewster.

Finally, Carrie spoke up. "I understand there's a Jesuit school in the Urubamba Valley."

"Correct," said Brewster. "It's located in the village of Yucay, adjacent to a church."

"I'd like to visit that school."

"By all means, Carrie, you shall. Nearby is a charming hacienda hotel, the *Alcazár II*. I suggest we stop there for late afternoon tea."

Logan said, "Sounds as if you know the Sacred Valley well."

"I make it a point to go down there whenever I come to Peru, which is often." Brewster pushed the glasses up on his nose. "Is it settled then? You three will join me?"

"No," Jan said, louder than she meant to. "Tomorrow we tour the ruins of Sacsahuamán. I made the arrangements this afternoon."

Brewster pursed his lips. "You can easily change your tour to the following day."

"I'd rather not."

"Goodness," Brewster said, "did you realize your eyes flash like a Spanish gypsy?"

Logan looked perplexed. Carrie shifted in her seat and drank some water. Jan folded her arms and leaned back, glaring at Brewster.

"As further enticement," Brewster said, "there's a colorful market at Pisac on Sundays. Let me remind you that tomorrow is Sunday." He leaned towards Jan in a confidential manner. "At the market, you can buy a pictorial weaving finer than those of the Uros Indians."

Jan felt her face redden. How did he know about the weaving? What else did he know about her boat ride with Luis?

"Why don't you want to go?" Logan asked her.

"No particular reason."

Carrie spoke up, "I'm sure we *all* would enjoy the trip."

"There," cried Brewster, "it's settled." He stood and patted Jan's arm. "Come along, my dear, we'll change your tour date and reserve our car at the same time. Best to get it settled now."

Logan looked at Jan, his face full of questions.

"Okay, well, sure, let's go," Jan said, forcing a smile, "since everybody's eager to visit the valley." She rose. "Logan, please order me that dish *Y Papas con Aji*."

"What's that?"

"Potatoes," Brewster called over his shoulder, "cooked in a yellow chili sauce. It's delicious!" He followed Jan from the table and out the dining room entrance.

They said nothing until they reached a corner of the deserted, shadowy courtyard, the only light shining from scattered lamps attached to porch walls.

"You weren't very cooperative in there," Brewster said to her.

"Why should I be? I gather it was you who phoned Logan in San Francisco."

"A necessary move to facilitate my job."

"Whatever that is," she remarked sarcastically. "I'm sure it won't benefit us."

She sank onto a stone bench. Brewster remained standing. Squinting up at him, forcing an even voice, she asked, "Is Luis safe?"

"He completed the drive, if that's what you mean."

"Where is he?"

"This afternoon he arrived in Cuzco and made a phone call. Then Carlos followed him down the Chinchero Road to the town of Yucay where Luis parked the truck beside the hacienda hotel. Carlos has the place under surveillance. That's all you need to know. Now I need information. To whom did Luis deliver the dynamite and detonators?"

"Don't know," she replied, aware her voice sounded unnatural.

He grasped her arm. "You're lying."

She jerked loose. "What if I scream? What if I said you molested me?"

"I made the terms damned clear."

His eyes were cold, his face like stone. A wave of fear flashed through her.

"Who did Luis plan to meet?" Brewster insisted.

Swallowing hard, she fought back a desire to leap up and run away. She must stay cool, give Brewster just enough information to satisfy him, pretend to cooperate fully.

"A school friend, I think," she said with a set jaw.

"His name?"

"Don't know. We didn't discuss his friends."

"What about Luis' relationship with Ignacio?"

"Ignacio isn't Luis' father."

"Who is?"

"He wouldn't say." She shot him a pained look. "Luis doesn't trust me."

Brewster raised a foot onto the bench.

She jumped away.

"Jesus, you're edgy. What else did you discuss on your boat ride?"

"How did you know about the boat?"

"You were seen," he replied with a smirk.

His hotel spy, she realized, probably the same one who slipped the note under the door, maybe the young waiter who announced the hot breakfast. The spy could have used binoculars from a hotel window, then dashed out and followed her down the path. Thank God he couldn't pursue them into the reed forest. Although maybe another spy....

Brewster said "Come on, tell me more. Surely you learned something while you floated about."

She spoke in a monotone, hollow to her ears. "Luis knows Carrie met the man who spied on him in Arequipa. He thinks Carrie's working against him. He warned me if she didn't stop what she was doing she would get eliminated."

"I was afraid of that," he said quietly.

She glanced at him sideways, surprised at his concern about Carrie's welfare?

"Anything more?" he asked, his voice hard again.

She took a deep breath and decided to offer one more piece of information."Before Luis drove away in the truck, he arranged for a pilot friend to fly us to Cuzco, only his friend never showed up."

"Because his pilot would've flown you to Lima not Cuzco; Luis thought the Andes too dangerous for you. Since I needed you in Cuzco, I cancelled that arrangement and had Felipe pick you up instead. He was late, fixing a damaged landing gear. If you'd tried to leave the airfield, the soldiers would've stopped you."

"How did you know about Luis' plan for us?" she asked, a catch in her voice.

"Bugged his phone line, listened to the call he made to his pilot friend." Brewster chuckled. "Also heard both calls to you— one from Logan and one from the hotel clerk about Luis. Aren't you thrilled to have two men madly in love with you?"

She bit her lips to stop them from trembling. "You pry into everything, don't you? Hover over people. Watch every move. Direct their lives. You even knew about my Uros weaving."

"You were seen fleeing wildly across the parking lot, the weaving clutched to your bosom."

"What a great spy thriller this is!" She felt close to tears. "Buggings. Surveillances. Contacts. Disguises. One day you're an amusing gay who writes romance novels. Next you're a stuffy professor who lectures on ruins."

"In *Las Dunas* I had to be funny and effeminate. Otherwise, you would've sent me packing. If I played that role here, Logan wouldn't go with me to Pisac, which is where I plan to take him after I leave Carrie at the Jesuit school and you at the hacienda."

"Everybody's assignment figured out."

"It doesn't pay to be disorganized," he said. "Also, it's necessary to keep up target practice."

"Is that another one of your characters. Are you also a gunslinger from the Old West?"

His laugh held no amusement. "I played that role once, years ago as an actor. I'm a hell of a lot more successful in what I do these days."

"Which is what?" Her voice rose. "Who pays you? The CIA? The Peruvian Government? The Mafia? A drug lord? A political—"

He clapped a hand over her mouth and hissed, "Quiet!"

A young couple had entered the porch from the lobby. They stopped to peer around the courtyard. Brewster pulled out his pipe and casually walked over, refilling the bowl from a pouch in his pocket. Near them, he stopped and lit his pipe with a match. "*Bonsoir,*" he said as he shook out the flame.

"*Bonsoir,*" they replied.

"*Voulez-vous manger?*" he inquired.

"*Oui,*" replied the young man.

Brewster indicated the direction of the dining room and puffed hard on the pipe.

"*Merci,*" the young man said

"*Il n'y a pas de quoi.*" Brewster watched them enter the dining room.

Although Jan despised Brewster—everything he said made her want to cry or scream—she had to admit he was sharp, the couple's nationality and purpose assessed in an instant.

Brewster again put his foot up on the bench; this time she didn't flinch.

He puffed on his pipe, the coals glowing in the darkness. "I'll leave you and your friends alone after you get two pieces of information for me. In order to do this, you must meet Luis."

She shivered and rubbed her arms. "Luis doesn't want to see me again and I don't want to see him."

"You do and you will. Number one: Who is his father? Number two: Where can I find him? Only you can get this information for me."

"What if I say bug off, Brewster, what then?" She blinked to force back tears. "I don't believe you'd hurt Carrie. I think you're too fond of her."

"Don't force my hand. Besides, now there's Logan to consider."

Tears came. Angrily, she brushed them away. "Who gives you the authority to use force and intimidation? I'll go to the police. I'll call the American Embassy."

In a voice harder than steel, he said, "I'll give you a final warning, Janet. If you go to the police, to the Embassy, to anyone, you'll wish you hadn't. You're in a foreign country at war with itself. Different rules apply here. I know what I'm doing. I have influence. You don't."

She straightened her back. I won't cry, she told herself. I won't fall apart. I'll do what must be done and get us safely home. "All right," she said, her voice controlled. "I'll cancel the tour."

"It's already canceled."

"I suppose the car's ordered, too."

"Naturally." He cradled his pipe in his hand. "We can now return to the dining room."

The wail of a flute cut the air like the cry of an injured animal. The wail moved up the scale, up, up, in a crescendo, joined by another flute and then stringed instruments converging into a haunting melody. It was the musical group *Savia Andina* playing in the dining room.

"That's an eighteenth century folk melody," Brewster said, shifting back into his academic voice. "It's played everywhere in the Andes—*El Condor Pasa,* the condor flies over. As the condor passes, it watches below and waits for death." His smile grew unpleasant. "After all, that's the only way it can live."

The melody climbed again, flutes soaring stronger and higher until they seemed to penetrate her body in clean strokes, like a sharp-edged blade that cuts deep before pain is known.

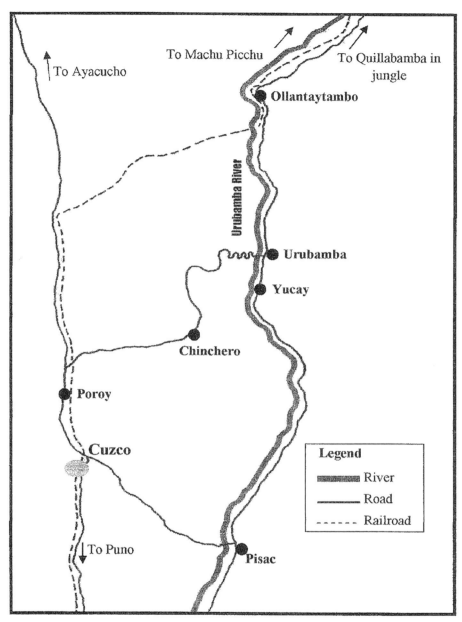

Sacred Valley of the Incas

CHAPTER 27

After a late morning breakfast, Carrie said, "See you at 12:30," and disappeared before Jan could ask where she was going.

The rest of the morning Jan spent with Logan, wandering along the cobblestone streets of Cuzco, examining ancient stone foundations. At one point she impulsively took his arm, surprised at how natural the movement seemed. She wondered what it would be like to meet Logan in Cuzco under different circumstances, at a later time. Would Luis still be rooted in her mind?

At one point Logan said, "I'm thinking Brewster has another reason for this Urubamba trip. Can't believe he only wants to show us ruins. You've made it obvious you don't want to go. Must be a reason for that, too. Incidentally, that little guy is following us."

She held his arm tighter and chattered about the Inca civilization, bits remembered from Carrie's brochures about *quipu* records, swinging bridges, stone quarries—a mishmash of facts with little direction. Logan appeared to listen attentively, now and then adding historical information. He didn't question her about what was happening, didn't again mention the trip to the Urubamba Valley, but she knew it was still on his mind. Behind, at a discreet distance, the little man continued to follow.

At 12:30, as planned, they met Brewster at the the north end of *Plaza de Armas*. An olive green Volkswagen awaited them, engine running, Brewster, wearing dark glasses, in the driver's seat, Carrie beside him. Jan was curious if the two had spent the morning together but didn't inquire. The condition of the car was a relief—clean, no dents, motor sounding good. It was the best vehicle Jan had seen in Peru.

Carrie was exceptionally quiet during the drive and Brewster spoke less than usual. When he did talk, he cranked out sentences as if from memory and when he glanced over his shoulder to assess the scenery behind, his facial muscles looked tight. At first Jan thought he was worried about being followed but after they left Cuzco no other vehicles were on the road.

Beyond the town of Poroy, he announced, "We're taking a secondary road into the Urubamba Valley. The main way is east of here."

"Why go this way?" Logan inquired.

"To visit a ruin above the valley. It's on a hill by the village of Chinchero."

Jan tensed. Luis had driven to the valley on the Chinchero Road.

"It's a pre-Inca ruin," Brewster continued in a dry voice. "Outstanding stone work. Unfortunately, Sunday market's over, but usualy a few vendors stick around." He shifted into lower gear on a small downgrade. "Chinchero is the oldest inhabited town in Peru. It has another claim to fame: its people live longer. Probably a hereditary thing."

He continued driving without commentary. On the outskirts of Chinchero he slowed down and peered about. The ruins on the hill above were massive: immense stone blocks in different sizes and shapes, flat-faced and gray, the color of driftwood, joined together with amazing precision. Rising from a bulwark foundation, the front wall extended the length of a football field. The stones, beveled on their edges, cast slight shadows that emphasized their outlines.

"I remember this place," Carrie cried as she got out of the car. "I came here once with my mother." She hurried ahead and ran up the stone steps.

Brewster walked briskly toward the entry, continually studying the landscape. Jan followed, Logan beside her. On a ledge by the front wall sat three old Peruvian women in black skirts and red blouses. From their shoulders hung black capes edged with strips of multi-colored weaving. Their circular hats looked like roulette wheels, flat on top, slight swelling in the middle.

"In this part of the Andes," Brewster said, turning to squint back at the village, "the hat tells you where a peasant comes from. When we go to Pisac market,"—he stared right and left as he talked—"you'll see all shapes and color, flat hats, bowl hats, one like a fringed lamp shade, tall hats like pilgrims...." His voice trailed off.

"You looking for someone?" Logan asked him.

"What? Oh, no." Brewster ran up the double steps and through the entry, vanishing inside.

The old women on the ledge smiled, faces crinkled, mouths toothless. They held up handfuls of brightly woven belts and broke into cackles that sounded like a flock of crows on a limb. "*Chumpi. Ancha sumaqmi,*" they shouted to Carrie, who had stopped for a look.

Logan guided Jan up the ruin stairs, passing through the wide entry and a second entry, the building double-walled. As they walked about, he slipped an arm around her waist. It seemed as normal as when she took his arm in Cuzco. Jan commented on the huge boulders, wondering how they could have been lifted into place without the help of machines, and Logan remarked on the precision of the perfectly fitted stones, pointing out a five-sided one. They would have stayed longer, but Brewster called through the entry, "Time's up. Got to get going."

When they came out, Brewster, arms crossed, stood on the ledge and Carrie was examining the belts. The women, with darting gestures and explosive sounds, indicated why she should buy this one or that one.

From the direction of the village, an old woman dressed in black like the others, and wearing the same kind of hat, plodded up the hill. Tufts of white wool sprouted like cotton candy around her left arm held against her chest. In her right hand she carried a wooden spindle with a ceramic whorl. Her walk was slow, ponderous. She looked at least a hundred years old, her face deeply lined like a dried plum. She was scarcely winded when she reached the ledge beside the others. Holding her spindle upright in front of her, the wool tucked under her left arm, she spun with lightning motions, pulling the wool into strands between two fingers of her left hand, twirling the spindle with her right. Occasionally she wet her left fingers with her tongue to aid in the process. She grinned at Carrie, a black crescent of gums between her lips, and rasped out a comment to her companions, who cackled at her words.

"What language is that?" Carrie asked Brewster.

"*Quechua*," he replied. "Most *campesinos* in this part of the Andes speak *Quechua*. It's from the Inca days."

"What did she say that was so funny?"

In a surprisingly gentle voice, he replied, "She said your hands are too soft. You couldn't spin half a spindle between sunrise and sunset."

In Jan's mind Brewster's voice triggered the scene of him with neon sleeves billowing, waltzing at *Las Dunas* with Carrie, doll-like in a blue chiffon dress.

Carrie flushed. "The spinner's making fun of me." She raised her chin. "What I can do might surprise her. Think she'll sell me her spindle?"

His voice turned hard. "Anything can be bought. Pay no more than twenty *intis*." He pushed his glasses on firmly and hurried down the hill.

Leaving Logan with the weavers, Jan ran after him. "Brewster, you've been upset the whole trip. What's wrong?"

He leaned against the car and pressed his lips together.

"Look, I'm involved in this," she pushed. "I have a right to know what I'm facing."

"Okay, okay." He straightened up. "Carlos didn't call last night. If he couldn't call then, he would phone this morning at 7:00. If that wasn't possible, he'd meet me at Chinchero. No calls." He gestured widely. "No Carlos."

Jan peered around, trying to think of reasons why Carlos hadn't contacted Brewster. Had he lost his cell phone? Ended up stuck someplace without a cell signal? Maybe he'd gotten sick and passed out. Or was confronted by drug traffickers and taken prisoner. Or infiltrated the Senderistas. Or hid out, unable to make a sound, for fear of being discovered. Or....

"I bought this for you," Logan called to Jan as he strode down the hill toward her. He held out a belt an inch and a half wide and four feet long, tiny geometric designs woven repetitively in red, white, yellow, and black.

"It's pretty," Jan said, flustered, her hands fumbling as she tried it on.

"Thought it might go well with that red blouse you wore yesterday."

"Thanks, Logan." She rolled up the belt, and attempted to fit it into an outer vest pocket with the suntan lotion. Not enough room. She crammed it into the opposite pocket.

"Another weaving," Brewster said.

Jan pretended not to hear.

Brewster called up to Carrie, "Time to go."

The old ladies laughed as Carrie slipped the spindle into her daypack. "*Sumaqllana*," they cried to her and waved. She waved back.

As they all climbed into the car, Brewster announced, "We'll stop off at the hacienda hotel in Yucay."

Logan said, "I thought we were going to Ollantaytambo first."

"I've altered the plan."

"I'd rather go to the hacienda later," Jan said, upset about meeting Luis so soon. "You said we'd have late afternoon tea there. It's only 2:00."

Brewster brought out his pipe and started to fill it, changed his mind and jammed it back in his pocket. "Yucay first," he said in a stern voice, then added more casually, "Need to judge the tea situation. Make sure it's still offered."

"But...." Jan imagined what might happen when Brewster drove up to the hotel. She saw Luis and the rebels charge out, shooting, killing them all. "I don't want tea," she murmured.

Logan gave her a curious look.

As Brewster sped through the village, chickens and pigs scattered. Dust flew. Children stared. Women appeared in doorways. The car narrowly missed a man beside a cart.

"Jesus, slow down," Logan yelled. "What's your hurry?"

Brewster didn't answer nor did he slow down. He careened out of the village and onto the tarmac road that curved steeply down to the valley. Jan grabbed Logan's arm and held on. The VW rocked them from side to side as Brewster navigated the sharp turns, never letting up speed. Far below, the Urubamba River looked like a snake loosely coiled on green velvet.

Near the valley floor, the muddy river took back its shape, tumbling through a corridor of trees and shrubs that lost their green color as the sky grew more and more overcast. When he reached the valley floor, Brewster drove across the river and turned right, skirting a village. He slowed down and continued along the road that paralled the river. Removing his dark glasses, he examined the scenery.

Ahead, on the left side, rose a large boulder. Painted on it in black letters ¡*Viva la lucha armada! ¡Viva Gonzalo!* Out of a fissure protruded a stick, dangling from it a red flag with a hammer-and-sickle emblem, scrawled beneath, *Tawa-nti-n-suyu*. Brewster stopped and examined the rock.

Logan said, "Professor, translate those words for us."

Brewster didn't answer.

Carrie said, "The top says, *Long live the armed struggle. Long live Gonzalo.* Don't know about the words under the flag. They aren't Spanish."

"Who's Gonzalo?" Jan asked.

"Abimeal Guzmán," Logan replied, "the former leader of *Sendero Luminoso*. Gonzalo was his war name."

Brewster tilted the rearview mirror to see Logan's face. "So, you've heard about the Shining Path."

"Read a little," Logan replied and moved from Brewster's vision.

Brewster readjusted the mirror. "What else do you know about *Sendero?*"

Logan met his eyes. "Just historical stuff. What is this—a college quiz?"

"I'm interested in your take on it."

"Okay." Logan folded his arms. "Around 1978 Guzmán formulated his doctrine in Ayacucho, went underground and led his revolution until captured. Still in prison I think. The guy who took over from him didn't last long. After that, the rebel movement died out."

"You know more about the Shining Path than most Americans."

"So do you, Brewster. Where'd you say you taught?"

"CCW in Upper New York State."

"What town's that in?"

"Not in a town," Brewster replied. "In the country, near Glens Falls."

Logan leaned forward. "Mind telling us why you charged down the mountainside like a maniac?"

"A necessary maneuver."

"And what happened to your pipe and glasses?"

"Don't need them anymore."

"Look, Brewster, I'm tired of jockeying around with you. You're evasive about everything." Logan leaned back and narrowed his eyes. "The reason I'm here is because I received a call from a guy who thought I should come. Any idea who that might be?"

"No, but aren't you glad you came?" Brewster eased the car forward, continually examining the terrain. He reinstituted his scholarly tone. "Further down the river, after Ollantaytambo, the jungle starts. Trains go in as far as Quillabamba. En route, they pass Machu Picchu and let tourists off to be bused up to the ruins."

Trying to sound calm, Jan said, "It appears we're the only ones touring the valley today."

"I've noticed that." Brewster's voice was curt. He returned the overhead mirror to its original position and checked the empty road behind. Once again, he became the informative professor. "Coca isn't only grown in the Huallaga Valley." He indicated a field to the left. "See between those protective ridges—new coca plants."

Jan rolled down her window to see better. The fresh air was a relief. She readjusted her cotton skirt and ran her hands over her sweaty neck and forehead.

The coca field was terraced. Recessed between flat-topped ridges of dirt, shaped like chocolate bars, grew short, staggered rows of narrow-leafed seedlings. They appeared vivid green in the metallic light.

Logan leaned across her for a better look. "I thought it was illegal to grow coca."

Brewster opened his window. "It's legal for tea or chewing. Actually, it's not chewed; *coquear* is the word for it. That means "to *coca*," a process of sucking on the leaves adding a little lime powder as the wad is moved about inside the cheek."

"Why the lime?"

Brewster examined an empty side road then looked across the way at a deserted dirt path. "Cuts the bitterness and increases the drug effect. Every coca chewer has his lime gourd or bag with a stick poking out of it. It's only illegal when it's processed into cocaine."

"Therefore," said Logan, leaning back, "until the coca arrives at a processing lab, there's no way of proving intent."

"Correct." Brewster stepped hard on the gas, spurting ahead, jerking his passengers back.

Wind streamed through the open windows. Jan exchanged a guarded look with Logan. She slipped off her denim vest, carefully folding it in half and setting it on the floor next to his sweater. Logan always knew when there was trouble. She remembered his words about Abimeal Guzmán: *He carries the war name of Gonzalo.* Since Guzmán was in prison, and the leader who followed him was gone, somebody new must be in charge of the rebel group. And since in the past *Sendero* caused such havoc in Peru, knowledge of this new leader would be important to the Peruvian Government, or the military, or the police or an extremist, right wing group. U.S. Intelligence and the DEA would be interested, too. Had one of them hired Brewster? Was that why he was here? The possibility that Luis' real father might be the leader of an organization that tortured and killed anyone who failed to believe in its doctrine, horrified her. If true...if Brewster planned to drop her off at the hacienda...if brutal drug traffickers and *Senderistas* were around...beads of sweat multiplied on her neck. She grasped her cotton skirt as though it would help keep her mind and body together.

With renewed determination, she focused on the outside scenery, the antithesis of the rocky, barren plateaus glimpsed on the plane ride between Puno and Cuzco. Here, below the steep slopes, cultivated terraces spilled out like layers of mushrooms.

Shrubs and trees lined the riverbank. On both sides of the valley mountains towered, encased in green and partially shrouded by fog. Not fog, rather clouds, heavy clouds. They hovered on the mountaintops in ghostly forms that faded and then reappeared. They became the shapes of sinister dream figures, carrying rifles and sacks of cocaine.

Clutching her skirt tighter, she glanced at Logan. Even in the cramped seat, he appeared in command, right elbow out the window, left leg extended over the floor hump, sturdy shoe an inch from her sandaled foot. Aware of how silly it was to hold onto her skirt, she let go and smoothed out the crumpled material. The printed pattern startled her. Always before it had been an abstract design of intersecting red lines on a white background. Now the lines looked like veins, bulging with blood. Her hands jerked up from the cloth.

"You okay?" Logan asked.

"Yeah." She had trouble swallowing. A minibus full of tourists whipped past. It was the only vehicle they'd encountered in the valley.

Brewster turned right onto a dirt road and slowed to a crawl. "Yucay," he said quietly, creeping past a cluster of stone houses then crossing another dirt road. A shaft of light shone briefly through the slate-colored sky. Clouds lowered, darkened. She thought it might rain. The streets were empty, doorways shut, cars absent, no sign of activity. Except for the minibus that had passed, the valley appeared deserted.

Jan glanced at her watch: 2:45. She found it difficult to breathe. The sky seemed to press down like a lid to cut off air. Logan reached over and grasped her cold, sweaty hand in his warm one. It made her feel safer but she couldn't look at him.

They approached a plaza the size of a baseball diamond. Grazing on grass stubble were three black and white cows and a hefty black bull with a fierce set of horns. As Brewster eased up to park under a fig tree, the bull lifted its head and snorted. With a bellow, it mounted one of the cows and began a vigorous mating shuffle. On the far side of the plaza stood the two-story, whitewashed hacienda. The roof was red-tiled, the windows iron-barred. Over the door hung a sign, *Alcazár II*. To the right of the building stood a familiar green truck. Bumps rose on Jan's arms.

Brewster slipped out of the car. "Wait here," he said. "I'll check out the hotel."

"Why park so far away?" inquired Logan.

"Cooler for you in the shade." Brewster shut the door with scarcely a sound. He leaned through the open window. "Carrie, move into my seat. There's a breeze on this side of the car." His eyes strayed to the ignition where he had left the keys. Carrie slid behind the wheel. "In the event I get carried away talking to friends, see that tower near the river?"

She nodded.

"That's the Jesuit church. The school is next door. If I don't return in ten minutes, drive there by way of the street we just crossed. Park in the abandoned chicken coop behind the school." He patted her shoulder and then stole toward the hacienda.

Jan leaned out the window and watched him move forward, slowly, passing a line of trees, panning the scene like a TV camera.

"Not the approach of a professor," Logan muttered. "Let's get out of the car."

Jan spoke quickly. "No, the town's too creepy."

"I agree, but I'm getting cramps, and I'm hotter than hell." He opened his door and climbed out, stretching his legs and arms.

Brewster reached the hacienda and crept along the side of the building. He passed the truck and disappeared around the corner.

Wiping sweat from her forehead, Jan looked at the plaza. The bull was gone. No, it grazed on the opposite side. "Please, Logan, come inside," she begged, her eyes on the hacienda.

With a set jaw, he said, "Okay, Jan, I've waited long enough. What's going on here? I don't believe Brewster went in to there to ask about afternoon tea."

"He's coming." Carrie said in a tense voice.

Brewster sprinted toward the car. As he drew closer, Jan noted a grim expression on his face. He motioned in the air, wrist turning, thumb and finger rubbing together.

Carrie started the engine, opened the driver's door and slid back into her seat.

"Logan, get in," Jan demanded.

He climbed into the car and shut the door. "Damnit, tell me what's going on."

"I can't."

Brewster slid behind the wheel, yanked the door closed and whipped a U-turn in the middle of the street. He shot off down the way he had driven.

Jan could stand it no longer. "What about Luis? Is he there?"

"Yeah."

"Do I still have to see him?"

"Not till I brief you."

"What about Carlos?" Jan pressed. "Why didn't he call?"

"He couldn't. He's dead." Brewster whipped around a corner. "*Sendero* hung him on a thorn tree."

"Oh, my God!" Jan gasped.

Carrie hid her face in her hands.

"Who's Luis?" Logan exploded. "Who's Carlos? What the hell's happening? For Christ's sake, somebody tell me."

"Shut up," Brewster bellowed. He swerved around the next corner and speeded up, heading toward the church tower. "*Senderistas* are in the valley. Don't know how many or where they're hiding. We've got to find cover."

CHAPTER 28

Brewster parked the VW behind the chicken coop where it couldn't be seen from the road. Then he hurried across the yard to a massive door at the rear of the Jesuit school and knocked. A peephole opened. An eye appeared then disappeared. Metal grated, the sound of a bolt being drawn, followed by a clanking. The heavy door swung in a few feet, revealing a dark interior and a short figure wearing a black cassock.

After a quick survey of the trees and shrubs along the river, Brewster directed Jan, Carrie and Logan to enter. He darted in after them. The robed figure closed the door and shoved the latch into place. Then he pushed the large bolt across the frame and slipped the chain over an iron hook.

It took a few moments for Jan to adjust her eyes to the dim room. The figure was Felipe, as she had assumed it would be. Without the goggles and frayed leather jacket, he was less of a fanciful creature, more human, although still not completely attached to this world.

The room was thick-walled and large, the ceiling lost in shadows. The only light came from a small, high, iron-barred window that reflected a square of gray onto the opposite wall in a pattern like the grid for a game of tic-tac-toe. The cold, stale air reminded Jan of the cellar her mother once locked her in for three hours. *Never again forget to feed the cat, Janet Fielding*—a terrifying experience she never forgot.

At one end of the room, on a wooden platform raised from the cement floor, stood orderly rows of cardboard boxes and tin containers. She moved closer to read the labels—*harina, café, té, arroz, azúcar*—food supplies. No boxes of dynamite; no bags of coca leaves.

Logan put on his sweater and muttered to Jan, "What a wild ride! You okay? Feels like a morgue in here."

Jan winced at the word *morgue,* trying not to picture Carlos hanging from a tree. Still freaked out, she shivered and buttoned up her vest, glad she had brought it from the car. Beside her stood Carrie wrapped in her blue shawl. "I'm okay," she said to Logan.

Near the entrance, Brewster and Father Felipe conversed in Spanish. Felipe continually moved his head, either shaking it or tilting it heavenward. Several times he pushed air between his teeth with the sound of escaping steam. At last his hands met prayerfully. He nodded and walked over to a small door in the corner of the inside wall. When he opened it, children's voices tumbled out, a unison chant uttered in a staccato language.

"*Quecha?*" questioned Carrie, starting toward the doorway.

Brewster pulled her back. "Correct. Forget them for now."

Felipe closed the door behind him, extinguishing the sounds. Brewster said, "Here's what's been happening. None of it good." He looked at Jan. "Are you listening?"

"Yes, yes." She forced her mind off the bleak surroundings and the reoccurring image of a body hanging from a tree."

"Here's what happened last night. *Sendero Luminoso*"—Brewster barked out the words, his college role abandoned—"stole into the valley. Twelve rebels. They cut communication lines. Barricaded the main road into the valley. For some reason, they left the Chinchero Road open."

His voice took on a deadly tone. "At 4:00 A.M. they executed the mayors of Pisac and Ollantaytambo. Shot them. Splayed their bodies. Nailed them on wooden planks."

Carrie grasped Jan's arm with fingers like splinters of ice.

"At dawn they propped the dead mayors up against the ruins, each body plainly seen above his town."

"Jesus Christ!" exclaimed Logan.

"The mayors represent the government. That's what *Sendero* wishes to destroy. By frightening people, the terrorists eliminate opposition."

Carrie let go of Jan's arm and looked toward the inner door. "Those children should be home with their parents."

"They don't have parents," said Brewster. "Orphans and abandoned children. They live at the school. Other valley kids are holed up with their parents. Education wouldn't improve their lives."

"Knowing how to read and write always helps," Carrie insisted defiantly.

"I doubt it," Brewster shot back.

Logan asked him, "Did you see that minibus pass us in the valley?"

"Yeah. Eight Germans with a Peruvian driver. I met the group at *La Castaña*."

Jan started to ask when he was at the Lima hotel. Then she remembered the man with the goatee. He sat on the couch the night they arrived; he emerged from the breakfast room with the German tourists the next morning. Brewster, of course, master of disguises.

Logan said, "That minibus might be the only non-rebel vehicle in the valley."

"Probably is," said Brewster. "Tours usually come and go by the main road. The group must've arrived yesterday before it closed and stayed last night in a valley inn."

"We ought to let them know they're in danger," Logan insisted.

"That's their problem," Brewster replied. "Also, the train from Cuzco was stopped. Most likely tourists are trapped up in Machu Picchu." He drew his lips into a firm line. "We've got ourselves to worry about. Last night at 9:00, Carlos left a message for Felipe: Luis loaded his chemicals on a train that went into the jungle; the delivery site—a high-tech, cocaine-processing lab ten miles from Quillabamba; the lab owner—Ignacio Acosta."

Again Carrie's icy fingers grasped Jan's arm, the cold penetrating.

"Furthermore, in a later message"—Brewster's eyes shifted between the three faces—"Carlos reported Luis delivered his dynamite and detonators to two *Senderistas*, who distributed them to ten men. Five drove towards Ollantaytambo, five towards Pisac. How and when Carlos was caught and hanged, Felipe has no idea. He didn't know about his death until I told him."

"Who's Carlos?" Logan inquired.

"DEA agent."

"What's your connection with him?"

"None."

"I don't believe that. And this Jesuit priest, what's your relationship there?"

"Not a matter I care to discuss."

Logan barreled on. "I find it peculiar that he was the pilot who brought Jan and Carrie to Cuzco. Somehow you're tied up with him. From the start I figured your professor role was a phony. Why are we here, Brewster? Why don't we drive out of the valley right now? Take the Chinchero Road."

"Janet has business in the valley."

"Who with?" Logan insisted.

"Luis, the Peruvian who accompanied our two ladies on their travels, the same guy who delivered the chemicals and explosives. Claims to be the son of Ignacio Acosta, but I believe his real father is *Sendero's* new leader. I need to find out his name and location."

"What's that have to do with Jan?"

"She's going to go see him. He's at the *Alcazár II*."

Logan shook his head incredulously. "You can't send her there."

"She has to go."

"I don't get your reasoning. Why Jan?"

Jan wrenched her arm from Carrie's grasp and attempted to bring back circulation, rubbing her hands and blowing on them. She couldn't think about what was happening. Her mind was back in the law office. She sat at the computer, producing known quantities while Logan stood in his office doorway, praising her work. The law office, where she felt safe.

Logan moved closer to Brewster. "For Christ's sake give me a direct answer. Why Jan?"

Brewster's eyes narrowed, "Don't breathe on me, Logan. I don't take kindly to it."

"I don't give a damn what you take to." Logan moved even closer. "Why send Jan to do your dirty work."

"It's the only way I can find out," came the steel-edged reply.

Logan's voice rose, "How can she learn what you can't?"

"You won't like the answer," Brewster shouted in his face. "It's because Luis has the hots for Jan. They had a wild affair. She's closer to him than anybody. He'll tell her things I can't discover."

Logan stared a moment at Brewster, as if not sure of what he'd heard. Then, jamming his hands into his pockets, he backed away and met Jan's eyes. "Is this true?" he asked her softly. "Do you love this guy?"

"It's over, Logan." She bit her lip and tasted blood. Her humiliation deepened. "It was a...a physical thing." She closed her eyes and tried again. "I was lonely, and I didn't think that you...." The rest of her words fell back, lost inside. She felt compelled to stand there, wide open, too visible on a stage. Desperately, she wished to be someplace else. "I'll try to explain...."

"For God's sake," Brewster snarled, "don't waste time dishing out explanations for your actions."

"But she needs to tell Logan how she feels," Carrie interjected.

Brewster threw up his arms. "It doesn't matter how she feels. This is survival time. *Sendero* occupies the valley. They're getting ready to set off ten explosions. One likely will be on the Chinchero Road. That's our only way out of here. In less than an hour, I think all hell's going to break loose. We've got to get out of the valley before 4:00."

"Why 4:00?" Carrie asked.

"Four is a symbolic number for this new leader. The mayors were executed at 4:00 A.M. Gonzalo considered himself the fourth sword of Marxism. The *Quechua* words you saw on the boulder, *Tawa-nti-n-suyu,* mean The United Four Parts, the name of the Inca Empire. Janet, are you ready to go?"

Jan swallowed hard. She had difficulty focusing on Brewster's face. The tic-tac-toe square on the wall had darkened, the outside light fading. Soon all lines would disappear. In a shaky voice she said, "What do I do? Run into the hacienda, question Luis and then run out?"

"In the first place you won't run. You'll sneak up to the back door. I'll follow and give you cover. You'll only be in the open for the last few yards. At that point, don't look to your right. Carlos hangs on the thorn tree near the corner of the building. Rap on the back door. It's a blue door." Brewster raised his voice. "Janet!"

"Yes."

"Listen to me. Your life depends on this."

"I'm listening."

"Rap softly. The door leads into the kitchen. Most likely that's where Luis will be. When I looked through the window, he sat at the table. Beyond the kitchen is a central patio. Two side stairways lead up to a balcony and guestrooms. On the ground floor, at the other end of the building, is the front door—directly opposite the kitchen, across the patio, between the stairways. Get the picture?"

She nodded.

"I figure ten *Senderistas* are out laying explosives, but the other two could be someplace within the building. When the door opens, break into tears. Stagger inside. If Luis isn't in the kitchen, call for him. Fall into his arms. You're safest there. Pull him around so he stands between you and anybody else. Tell him you saw his truck parked at the side of the hotel. That's how you knew he was there. Tell him how you longed to be in his arms again."

Jan's mouth was dry. Her body seemed elsewhere. Focus on Brewster's words, she told herself. Don't let your mind wander away.

"Explain that when Carrie wanted to visit the school," Brewster continued, "you seized the opportunity to see him. Make it fast and emotional so he'll forget to relock the door. Meanwhile, look around. Get your bearings."

I mustn't cry, she thought. Listen to directions. Follow them correctly.

Brewster rushed on. "If others are in the room, beg to see Luis alone. Insist on that. He'll want you to go back to Cuzco immediately. Prod him about why. Then, whisper, 'Is your father here?' Tell him you want to meet the great new leader. Find out the name of his father and where he is."

"What if Luis isn't at the hotel?"

"He'll be there. No other place for him to go." Brewster turned to Carrie. "While Janet's gone, tour the school with Felipe. And Logan"—a smile played on his lips, his tone turned sarcastic—"stay here in the dark and contemplate your love life. Janet, precisely what time does your watch say?"

"3:07."

Brewster squinted at his watch. "Logan and Carrie, set your time to ours. Carrie, at 3:40 return here. You and Logan sneak out to the VW. Carrie, sit in the back; Logan, you drive. Proceed to the hotel. At 3:45, back the car in beside the truck. Leave the motor running. Then Logan, switch to the passenger seat."

His eyes took on a flinty look as he turned to address Janet. "At 3:44, find an excuse to dash out of the hotel, back, front, whichever way you can. Jump in the rear with Carrie. By then I'll be in the driver's seat. After that, it's a race to Chinchero before the road is closed or bombed to pieces." He looked from face to face. "Instructions clear?"

"No!" Logan bellowed. "Jan's not going to that rebel hole. Christ, a man's body hangs from a tree. Two mayors are splayed on Inca ruins. The valley's riddled with drug traffickers and *Senderistas*. Any minute everything's going to blow up, and you want her to risk her life for some fucking information. I've listened to enough of your garbage. We're American citizens. We're going to drive out of this valley right now." He lurched forward. "Hand over the car keys."

With a precise movement, Brewster clipped the side of Logan's neck with the edge of his hand. Logan crumpled to the floor. Brewster whipped a revolver from his pocket."Stay back, Janet. You know the consequences of not following my orders."

With difficulty Logan rose and staggered toward Brewster. "She's not going, I tell you."

Brewster aimed his gun.

"Logan, stop!" Jan cried. "This is my business. I'll take care of it."

The inner door opened, revealing the sounds of children singing. Father Felipe, holding a small, wrapped package, came through the doorway and closed off the voices. As he approached the group, he focused on Brewster's gun aimed at Logan.

"*¿Esta cargada?*" Brewster asked him.

"*Sí, con seis balas.*"

"Janet," said Brewster, "you know how to shoot?"

She swallowed. "No."

"Felipe will give you a snub nosed revolver. It shoots six bullets without reloading. The safety catch is on." He indicated the switch on his own gun. "It must be released for the gun to fire. Like this." He clicked his catch off. "Holding the gun with both hands at eye level, you aim directly at your target." He demonstrated, pointing his gun at Logan's heart. "For success, your hands must be steady."

Gingerly, Felipe handed Jan the package wrapped in a piece of white woolen cloth.

"Empty your lower right hand vest pocket," Brewster commanded Jan. "Drop the belt weaving to the floor. That's right. Felipe's gun replaces the belt. No, Janet, unwrap the gun before you put it in your pocket. Point the barrel downward. Keep your pocket unzipped so you can reach the gun quickly."

With trembling fingers, she unwrapped the wool cover and dropped it to the floor beside the belt. She looked down at the belt, then at Logan.

"Don't go," he pleaded.

Logan's voice held an emotion Jan had never heard from him before. Was it fear—caught in a situation he couldn't control? As she slipped the revolver into her pocket, she glanced at the gun in Brewster's hands, marked the coldness in his eyes. He would have no qualms about shooting Logan. He'd kill them all if it helped him do his job.

"Logan, don't try any heroics." Her voice was surprisingly calm. "Please. You mean too much to me."

"But if"—Logan swallowed and tried again—"if anything should happen to you I...."

"Hey, counselor, I'll be okay." She smiled. "Just don't be late with the car." Her hands no longer trembled. She started for the outside door.

Carrie hurried over and hugged her. "Goodbye and good luck."

Felipe unhooked the chain, letting it clank onto the cement, then drew the bolt and the latch. The door cracked open, revealing the schoolyard, capped by a sullen sky. In her pocket, the gun lay heavy and cold. She slipped through the narrow opening and stole out into the humid afternoon.

CHAPTER 29

Looking beyond the schoolyard wall through a thin orchard of stunted apple trees, Jan glimpsed the side and rear of the *Alcazár II*, some 300 yards away. The bright blue door at the back of the hotel stood out, glowing in the strange light that filtered through the overcast sky.

She hunched behind a row of oil drums to consider her options. The quickest way to the hotel would be to scale the wall, about six feet high, and sneak through the orchard. But the ground was too open, only the apple trees to hide behind.

In the south wall, next to the chicken coop, was the double gate through which they had entered the compound. If she took that direction, she would have to pass a line of houses. People hiding inside might think she was an enemy and shoot her.

Another gate, small and narrow, almost hidden by foliage, stood near the point where riverside shrubs met the north end of the wall. It would be easy to reach. On the way there were places to hide: a wooden cart a few feet from where she crouched and a tarp-covered bale of hay further along. Once through the gate, she could follow the river, staying in bush cover until opposite the rear of the hotel. Then, a short orchard crossing would bring her to the blue door.

She darted forward, her feet crunching on the gravel. She ducked behind the wooden cart. Too noisy, she scolded herself. She looked toward the river, searching for movement in the bushes. No sign of anybody.

The weather was oppressive. Any minute it might rain. She wiped her face and dried her hands on her skirt. A rivulet trickled down the back of her neck. She wished she had pinned up her hair.

Turning to see if Brewster was behind her, she was startled to find him a few feet away, gun drawn, barrel pointed upward. He had moved across the gravel without a sound.

"You're headed right," he told her in a low voice. "The gate has an inside latch. Pull it up, slide it off. When you shut the gate, the latch'll drop back down and lock." He raised up slowly to look toward the hotel.

"Stay in the willows," he continued as he squatted closer to her. "Careful where you step. Could be snakes, some deadly. When three apple trees line up with the back door, start your move inward."

He partially raised up for another survey, then came down again. "I'll cover you, ten feet back. If there's trouble, lie flat. I'll do the shooting. Okay, go."

From the cart she slipped over behind the hay bales, this time scarcely a sound under her feet. It was her breathing that made noise now—too fast, too loud. She took a slow, deep breath, softly blowing out a long, steady stream of air. The latch on the gate worked easily but the hinges whined like a cat.

Shrubs grew thick along the river. The air felt even more humid. Her pulse drummed against her temples like rain on a shingled roof. Sweat bathed her body. She heard the gate whine again—Brewster coming through. She looked back. No sign of him.

He's good at this, she thought. Must've had lots of practice.

Along the riverbank, she carefully charted her way, inspecting the knee-high grass before each step. At first, there was a shushing sound with contact. Less noise as she grew experienced. She studied the grass, the willows, the alder trees and all the vegetation by the river. As her concentration grew more acute, she speeded up. Faster steps, no sound.

She froze. From the corners of her eyes she glimpsed a coiled snake. Her heart thumped wildly, her ears rang. It didn't move. Alive? Dead? She blinked. Only a discarded piece of rope. She moved on, slower, even more careful of what lay around her.

There was Padrino's truck, looking like a discarded hulk in a junkyard. Not far from it sat a pile of rusted metal including a broken washing machine. The thorn tree stood at the edge of the building. Don't look at it, she commanded herself. Concentrate on the hotel and what's necessary to get there. The blue door seemed to glow like an illuminated target.

Movement. In the shadows by the truck. She dropped to her knees and cautiously peered out. Vague figures. Clinking bells. A cow appeared, followed by another cow. Another. With a sigh of relief, she watched the three cows from the plaza amble into the orchard, their tails swinging like fly swatters. They lowered their heads and began to graze.

Where was the bull? She craned her neck but saw no sign of it. What if the bull appeared, saw her and charged? Or if she startled the cows and they raised their heads to pinpoint her position? Why kneel here and make up bad situations? Get on with it.

When she reached the spot where three apple trees stood in line with the blue door, she inhaled deeply as if getting ready to go under water. Forcing out her breath, she started the inward move.

At the first tree she paused. The leaves smelled fresh, the apples, tiny. For a moment everything seemed unreal. Was she really hiding behind a tree in Peru?

Again she moved forward, the grass now shorter.

The bull emerged from the truck shadow. She ducked back behind the tree, her heart racing. The bull stood, head down, surveying the orchard. Perspiration dripped down her back. She glanced at her watch, surprised it was only 3:26. It seemed she had been trying forever to reach the blue door. The bull tossed its head. To her relief it sauntered away.

She crept behind the second tree, highly conscious of her surroundings—the bull, the cows, the truck, trees, grass, the blue door glowing in a metallic light. One more tree ahead.

A memory flashed. She played hide-and-go-seek with her sister. *Jan, you always sneak in free.* Beth's lips formed the pout she knew would gain pity. *How come you hide better than me? Because I'm older, silly. Do you always have to be older? Yes, but that's God's fault, not mine.* She arrived at the last tree and rubbed her cheek hard against the rough bark as if it were necessary to feel pain.

Then, in spite of her determination not to look at the thorn tree, she did. A man's body, hands tied in back, dangled from a rope, Slowly, the form rotated right to left, left to right, it's gray, bloated face covered with flies. Except for the tan shirt and the M-shaped mustache that seemed burned into his upper lip, Carlos was unrecognizable. Painted on the front of his shirt was a big, black *S*. The odor of feces floated in the air. She covered her mouth and buried her nose in a cluster of apple leaves. Fool she chided herself and sprinted for the blue door. Eyes closed, she knocked and prayed for Luis to answer.

A familiar male voice inside said, "*Quien?*"

"It's Jan," she called softly. A bit louder, "Luis, it's *Janecita*."

The inside key turned. The door opened. He wore a white shirt, always the white shirt. Was it pity she felt for him now? Or love? She had no idea.

He gasped at the sight of her, his eyes wide and frightened. He peered around outside, glanced over his shoulder, and then whispered, "You should be in Lima."

"Lima?" She faked surprise. "We told the pilot you wanted us to go to Cuzco, so he took us there."

"That was a mistake. How did you get into the valley?"

"By the Chinchero Road. We went to see the ruins. Then we drove down into the valley."

"Why are you here?" Luis insisted.

"Because of our friends. They had the car. We came with them." She realized she sounded stilted, her voice too highly pitched. She tried to relax. "Carrie's visiting the Jesuit school. She was a teacher, you know. I saw Padrino's truck and knew you must be here." She fought back a feeling of panic. "Luis, I had to see you again." Her voice was more like she wanted it to be. "I ran away from you at the dock because I...I was scared about my feeling for you. Please forgive me."

He grasped her shoulders. "Go back to Cuzco. You should not be here." He whipped her around to face the thorn tree. "See, this is what happens now."

Pretending to see the body for the first time, she muffled a scream and pulled Luis with her into the kitchen. She clung to him, her back against the smoothly plastered wall.

The kitchen was empty. Luis' pistol lay on the table. Looking through the doorway to the patio, she located the front door to the hotel. Her body trembled. The gray, misshapen face, branded by the mustache, was printed on her mind

"He had to be killed," Luis said and held her close. "It was necessary."

"No reason is strong enough to kill a man and let him hang."

He brushed a wisp of hair back from her forehead. "You cannot understand these things. For you, life is easy. For *campesinos*, it is hard. Thousands of children, they die each year."

She shuddered.

He held her closer. "*Sí, Janecita.* It is ugly." His voice grew full of contempt. "The government and rich people, they care nothing about peasants who die in the Andes, in the jungles. The poor survive the best they can. For many, only one crop pays for their families to live."

"Coca for cocaine," she said and wished it were all a dream.

"*Sí*, and out there hangs a man who tried to stop the trade."

She leaned her head back and studied his face, the deep eyes, the hawk-like nose, the brown skin that shone like koa wood. "You're not a *campesino,* Luis. You don't need to be a part of this."

"I must help my friends."

"Is Rafael one of them?"

He nodded.

"And your father?"

Again he nodded.

"Your real father? You came here to meet him, didn't you?"

He released her and shut the back door. She grasped his hands before he could lock it. "Who is your real father, Luis?"

"Why must you know?"

"I want to understand why you do these dangerous things."

He looked through the doorway into the patio.

"Is someone else here?" she asked quickly, still holding onto his hands..

"Rafael. He rests upstairs. Soon a man comes to take us into the jungle."

"Your father?"

"He would not want you here."

"Why not?"

"Questions. Questions."

"I need to know how you feel."

"This much I tell you. My mother was a poor Indian girl from Ayacucho. When I was born, she died. Ignacio and my father, they were good friends. Once, Ignacio almost died from a fever. My father nursed him back to health. In gratitude, Ignacio took me as his son. I owe them both my life." He kissed her hands. "I tell you this so you understand why I must help them. Do not repeat my story."

She nodded. This much she could do for him. She let go of his hands.

He walked to the patio doorway and looked up at the left stairway then across the balcony. Turning back to Jan, he said, "Find your friends with the car. Return to Cuzco by the same road. It is the only one open for my father will drive in that way. Leave before 4:00."

"What happens then?"

"No more questions. Soon a jeep comes to the back of the hacienda. Pedro Mendino must not see you here."

"That's your father's name?"

He frowned. "This is a bad time, especially not good for you and me together. Come. Be quiet." He led her across the tiled patio to the front door. Without a sound, he unbolted it. "I wish for another time, another place," he said, taking her in his arms

"So do I," she whispered.

She wanted to show him she cared, even if it was all wrong and she didn't understand her feelings for him. Even though Brewster was using them. Even though she loved Logan.

Abruptly she pulled away and backed off into the patio. This wasn't right. No longer could she play the spy game, even if Luis hated her when he learned the truth.

"What is it?" he asked. "Why do you look so frightened?"

"I can't keep up the lie." She swallowed hard. "I must tell you. I know *Sendero* controls the valley."

His eyes grew big, his lips parted. "You know?"

"And I know the chemicals you bought in Arequipa were shipped to Ignacio's cocaine-processing lab. And I know you delivered dynamite to *Sendero* so they can blow things up. I know all these things."

He grabbed her shoulders. "How?"

"I could make up a story, but there have been too many lies, too much hidden for too long. Brewster forced me to come here. He forced me to meet you at Lake Titicaca."

"Brewster? You did not want to meet me there?"

"More than anything I wanted to be with you. But not his way. He threatened to kill Carrie if I didn't meet you at the lake. He's been forcing me to get information."

His fingers tightened on her shoulders. "What information?"

"The name of your real father and where he can find him."

Anger distorted Luis' face, turning his lips into thin, gray lines. He shook her shoulders. "Is this Brewster man from the government? The military? The National Police?"

"I don't know where he's from. I know nothing about him." She was close to tears.

Luis let her go. "*¡Madre de Dios!*"

She glanced at her watch. "Brewster's outside now." Her voice trembled. "He has a gun, and he gave me one, too. Here." She pulled it from her pocket and held it out. "I don't want it. I doubt if I could use it anyway." She watched him examine the revolver. "Soon a car will come for me." She tried to keep her voice steady. "In the car will be Carrie and Logan."

He looked up at her. "Your friend Logan, he is here?"

"He flew into Cuzco yesterday." She looked at her watch. "In four minutes I'm supposed get out of here. Brewster hopes to drive us out of the valley before your dynamite explodes."

"I see," he said contemptuously. "This Brewster man has everything planned."

"Look, Luis, I won't tell him Pedro Mendino is your father. I'll say I couldn't discover anything about *Sendero*'s new leader. Come with us. I can't believe you want to stay mixed up with drug smugglers and fanatics who torture and kill people."

He backed away from her, a steely look in his eyes. "The government, the military, the police, they are full of corruption and evil. Oppressors. They kill and torture more people than *Sendero*.

We must get rid of them. Give power to our people. The revolution is everything. One day Pedro Mendino will be *El Presidente*."

"Then what will happen? Will life for the poor get better or will it be the same old thing? Once, on a Moche jar, you showed me a jaguar, draining blood from captives and celebrating with it. Your *Senderistas*, the Peruvian government—all of them are jaguars. They bleed the people."

From behind her a male voice said, "The world is full of jaguars, *señorita*. Only the most cunning survive."

She whirled to see a thin-faced young man with Indian features. He wore jungle camouflage and black boots, a rifle slung over one shoulder.

"You must be Rafael," she said.

He gave Luis a sharp look. "She knows my name. Unfortunate."

Luis rushed between them and spoke to Rafael in Spanish. Their words flew faster and louder. She understood enough to know that Luis kept telling Rafael the lady presented no problem. She would leave and say nothing. He could vouch for her. Rafael kept saying she knew too much, not only his name, but the identity of their leader and what *Sendero* was doing in the valley. He had heard her say this and more. She must not leave here alive.

"*No, no*," Luis cried, standing in front of her.

"*¡Traidor!*" Rafael shouted. He started to pull the rifle off his shoulder.

"*¡No se mueva!*" Luis shouted. He pointed Jan's revolver at Rafael, who froze, a look of disbelief on his face.

"*Janecita*," Luis cried, "go."

"Come with us," she shouted. "I'll help you. Don't be part of this."

"I must stay," he cried. "Run! Now!"

In despair, Jan rushed toward the front door.

Two shots rang out.

Instinctively, she knew Luis had been hit. She turned and saw him stagger forward onto the patio. The revolver fell from his hand and clattered across the tile like a harmless toy.

"Oh, my God," she moaned.

The rifle still hung over Rafael's shoulder. At the center of the patio stood a middle-aged man with a somber face, heavy eyebrows and a thick grizzled beard. He, too, wore green combat fatigues and black boots. In his hands, he held an automatic rifle.

With a groan, Luis slowly collapsed to the patio floor.

The man lifted Luis' hand with the toe of his boot, then let the hand fall limply. He heaved a sign and slung the rifle back over his shoulder.

From the steps, Rafael said in a hoarse whisper, "*¿Esta muerto?*"

"*Muerto*," the man replied, his voice without emotion.

"Murderer!" Jan screamed. She ran into the patio and knelt beside Luis, gathered him into her arms, cradled his head against her chest, blood spreading across her vest. She rocked him back and forth. "He risked his life for you, Pedro Mendino," she cried. "What a great leader you are. You even murder your own son. And you," she shouted back to Rafael, "his best friend, the only one he trusted. Why didn't you save him?"

Rafael shook his head as if to rid his mind of the scene. He ran into the kitchen and disappeared out the back door.

Mendino continued to gaze at her as if she were an apparition. "Luis revealed secrets," he said in a tight, mechanical voice, his face like a mask. "He was a traitor. I will not allow anyone to interfere with our plans. Our cause is moral and just."

"Damn all bloody causes!" she hissed at him. "They're nothing but a license to kill."

"As if seeing her for the first time, Mendino unslung his rifle and pointed it at her.

She glared at him without a trace of fear. "Are you brave enough to shoot a woman?"

From behind him, another shot blasted out. Mendino crumpled, falling forward, a glazed look on his face. With a cry, Jan pulled Luis away from the path of the falling body, as if, somehow, she could protect him from contamination.

Brewster knelt, flipped Medino over, whipped a cell phone from his shirt pocket and clicked a picture of the dead man's face.

"How can you live with yourself?" Jan spit out, still holding Luis close.

"I don't," Brewster replied. He retrieved Felipe's snub-nosed revolver, pushing on the safety catch before slipping the weapon into his back pocket.

She heard an engine start up. A jeep sped past the kitchen doorway. Rafael, she thought.

"You've got a minute to get out of here," Brewster yelled over his shoulder as he started for the back door.

In a daze, she set Luis down as if he were an offering. She managed to get to her feet, tottering at first. Somehow she walked through the kitchen and out into the orchard. It was raining. Hard. A deluge. She stood there, face upturned, blood running off, turning pink, washing away. At first she didn't realize she was crying. Her tears joined the water that poured from the sky. Her face, arms, hair, blood-soaked clothes, all heavy, blending, fading. "Luis, Luis, Luis," she cried.

In the distance rose the church tower, a blurred backdrop for a few apple trees, an arrogant bull and three cows. The force of the rain twisted the grotesque body of Carlos this way and that. In Jan's mind rose an even more terrifying vision: Pedro Mendino and Luis hung in the air, their lifeless bodies joined together. She screamed and staggered forward.

"Jan!" It was Logan. He ran towards her. "What happened?"

"Luis is dead," she sobbed. "Killed by his father and by me."

CHAPTER 30

When Jan came to, she was lying down, knees bent, hands over her face. After a moment of panic, not daring to move, she realized she was in the back seat of the speeding VW. She remembered getting in under her own power, scarcely aware of who she was. Then, either she had passed out or fallen asleep. Her clothes felt clammy. Both combs were missing from her hair. Something warm lay across her shoulder—a sweater, Logan's. Her watch read 3:53.

The scene at the hacienda burst into her mind. She threw off the sweater and bolted upright, feet braced against the floorboards, hands flat on the seat, body rocking as the vehicle bounced along the road. She blinked at her surroundings, afraid to move again.

Brewster drove through heavy mist, gas pedal floored, hurtling the VW forward, plunging blindly, windshield wipers clicking like metronomes. Beside him Logan sat courtroom-straight. The warm wind, forcing through Brewster's partly opened window, swept across her face. The steam that rose shroud-like from the earth resonated deep in her bones.

She clutched the back of Logan's seat and shouted over the sound of the wind, "Where's Carrie"

Logan turned and seemed to appraise her condition. "At the school."

"How come?"

He reached over and pried up her icy hands, rubbing them vigorously between his warm fingers. "She stayed behind to teach the orphans."

"Stayed?" Startled at the revelation, Jan swayed on the edge of her seat, holding on to Logan as if he were her lifeline. What might happen to Carrie raced through her mind—living among strangers who spoke *Quechua,* a language she didn't know; staying in a valley taken over by terrorists and drug dealers, where people were tortured and hung, where bombs exploded.

Safety isn't my concern, Carrie had said in Puno. The words had meant nothing to Jan then. Now she realized how desperately Carrie needed a cause, something to give her life meaning. The plight of the orphans must have touched her deeply. More so since she had lost a child. Perhaps she felt if she helped these children it would atone for the damage her father had done. *Goodbye and good luck,* Carrie said as Jan left the Jesuit school, and it really had been goodbye.

Brewster dimmed the bright lights that glared against the fog. He hunched forward to see better. Logan let go of Jan's hands and opened the lighted glove compartment. Jan recognized Filipe's revolver. The sight triggered a picture of Luis falling from the gunshot, of him dead in her arms, of standing in the rain, his blood spattered over her. Her eyes filled with tears.

"Here's a note from Carrie," Logan said. He shut the compartment and handed back a folded paper. "Your hands are still cold from shock. Better put my sweater back on."

She nodded and draped it around her shoulders.

Brewster sped past the boulder with *Sendero* graffiti. The car tires squealed as he turned left, meeting the Chinchero Road. Shifting down, he started the zigzag up, the car groaning with the climb. The fog thinned. Patches of sky appeared. Soon the mist lay below them, the sky turning bluer by the minute. Brewster turned off the lights and windshield wipers. The climb steepened. He shifted into first gear and put on his dark glasses.

Jan sat back, bracing herself on the curves, the unopened letter in her hands. She tried to stop trembling. "Thanks for your sweater," she said to Logan. He nodded.

The steaming valley lay far below, the river hidden, Luis gone, and now Carrie. Jan wiped her hands and face on her skirt and opened the letter.

Dear Jan,

To stay here and teach isn't a sudden decision. Since I talked with Felipe on our flight to Cuzco, I've been turning the idea over in my mind. There's no reason for me to return to the States. I don't want to see my father again, nor will I accept any more of his money. Except for you, I have no strong ties. I want to help these children and believe I can be useful here. It's a second chance. Father Felipe promised to teach me Quechua and my Spanish is good. For a while it may be difficult but I'm determined to make a go of it. When you read this, you will have made it through your ordeal.

Logan is a fine man, worth your risk. I wish Luis and Brewster could have taken another direction, but life is full of wishes that cannot come true. What seems more important is to follow up on those that can.

Please ask the Cuzco hotel manager to store my suitcase until I return to pick it up. Thanks for all your help. I'll write more later. You'll be my best friend always.

Love, Carrie

Carefully, Jan folded the letter, creasing it again and again until it was a tiny square. She tucked it into her right vest pocket. The belt weaving was there. Logan must have slipped it back where the gun had been. Closing her eyes, Jan offered a prayer for Carrie's safety, realizing it was the only time she had ever prayed. "I want my life to have meaning too," she murmured.

They were half way up to Chinchero when the dynamite exploded. It came in a series of bursts that sounded like underwater detonations. The car vibrated. Immediately, Brewster pulled to the side of the road and leaped out. Standing at the edge of the cliff, he focused binoculars on the scene below. "Can't see the valley floor, " he shouted. "Too much fog. All I can see is the top of the church and a number of rising smoke clouds."

"The Jesuit school?" Jan cried, pushing her way out before Logan could help her.

"No explosions in that area," Brewster replied.

Jan came up beside him. "But if *Sendero* controls the valley, won't Carrie be in danger?"

"She's safe for a while. Right now the group's aim isn't to control, it's to disrupt—strike, destroy and run. Most likely the terrorists melted back into the jungle before the blasts occurred."

Jan peered at the white-domed church tower, barely visible above a patch of fog. Over the valley hung small clouds, the green covered mountains rising tall behind them.

"They hit the train tracks," Brewster said, his binoculars still aimed, "and the power stations and the roads leading into the valley. There was an explosion west of Yucay—don't know the target. Might have been the bus of German tourists."

Jan stared at the place where she judged the *Alcazár II* would be, lying under the white blanket. In her mind she saw Luis lying on the patio floor, the body of his father beside him. A voice in her head said, *It's your fault, Jan. It's your fault they're both dead.*

Brewster pulled out a handkerchief to clean his binocular lenses. "Well, that's that."

"Is it?" growled Logan. "In your warped mind, is it okay to threaten people, force them to your dictates and commit murder? Do only results count and to hell with how you get them?"

"That's a peculiar statement from an attorney. You know the importance of results."

"I don't lie or kill people," Logan snapped, his eyes narrowed to slits. "Christ, Brewster, you murdered a man. Now you quip, 'That's that,' as if you'd just concluded one of your phony lectures. You told us you only wanted to discover the leader's name and location. But when you found him, you shot him."

"Janet's life was in danger."

"You didn't care about her. You went there with the intention of killing the leader. You even had the gall to tell me you snapped a picture of his face for verification. You're nothing but an assassin. Pay you enough and you'll get rid of anybody."

"You'll never know who contracted me," Brewster snarled, "or why I did this job."

"I don't need to know. Nothing justifies what you do."

Abruptly Brewster started back to the car. "One more thing," he said, turning back, "Mention to anyone about Felipe's involvement in activities outside the school, and you'll not only harm Felipe but a network of people including Carrie." He paused, as if to let his message sink in, before climbing back into the car.

During the rest of the ride to Cuzco, Jan sat in the middle of the back seat, her body erect and stiff, fists wedged into the plastic upholstery, ankles locked against the floor hump. Again and again tears filled her eyes as she relived the violence of the last week.

If only she hadn't come to Peru. Yet Carrie had begged her to come. Should she have refused? If Carrie had come alone, would she have had an affair with Luis? Would Brewster have sent Carrie to the hacienda? Would Luis have died?

Forget scenarios, she commanded herself. Fact one: you came to Peru with Carrie. Fact two: you made choices—stuck your nose into other people's business, fell for Luis, didn't follow Brewster's orders, blurted out the truth at the wrong time. If, after you found out about Luis' father, you had slipped out of the *hacienda* and followed Brewster's instructions like a goddamned zombie, Luis would still be alive. The ifs rose around her like vengeful ghosts. It's done, she shouted to herself. Done. Irreversible. Face it.

She pressed her fingers hard on her cheeks as though that might force out answers. Her eyes burned; a fire smoldered in her head. The engine droned on and on as they wound past stone huts, expressionless people in doorways and crossed bleak, rocky plateaus that looked like the surface of the moon.

Brewster drew up in front of Hotel Libertador. Logan leapt from the car and threw back the front seat so Jan could get out. As she started to leave, Brewster said quietly, "When you write to Carrie, tell her"—he grasped the wheel tightly as if it would help with his words—"tell her I admire what she's doing." His mouth hardened. "Nice knowing you folks."

The little man who had followed Logan opened the passenger door and slid inside. Brewster executed a military cutoff salute to Logan, gunned the car up the street toward the plaza, whipped around the corner and disappeared.

Jan ran into the hotel.

Flocks of candles in clear-glass balls illuminated the interior. It came back to her that the streets had been dark when they drove through Cuzco. At the time, she had been too upset to consider why. A sign on the front desk read, *Excuse our power failure. Candles have been lit in the rooms and on the stairway. Soon the emergency generator will be in full operation.*

She hurried for the stairway.

Logan called after her, "I'll try to get plane reservations for tomorrow. Afterwards, I'll stop by to see how you're feeling."

"All right," she called back. Forcing her legs to be strong, she walked up the stairs, stumbling now and then in her haste to reach the imagined safety of her room.

When she finally opened the door, the first thing she saw was Carrie's cart, silhouetted by flickering candlelight. Suitcase attached, it stood in the middle of the room like a lonely sentinel. Carrie's plan to stay must have been made before they drove into the valley. Obviously, she had come back to the room this morning and packed her case before meeting them at the plaza.

Never an inkling about her plan, Jan thought, never a hint. Did she keep her secret because she considered me too negative, too weighed down with problems? Or did she feel the need to make the decision by herself? In Arequipa she had said, *Maybe you don't know me as well as you think you do.* Maybe nobody knew anybody except at a particular moment.

Jan's eyes rested on the bungee cords, haphazardly pulled around the frame. She took the cords off and realigned them so the cart would be balanced. A few things hadn't changed.

The bed looked inviting. She longed to climb between its sheets and go to sleep. But Logan was coming by. She glanced at her watch. Enough time for a shower. Removing her clothes, she neatly folded each piece; order was still important, especially when her life felt fractured.

The warm water pelting against her neck and back soothed the aches and invigorated her body. She stepped away from the stream and soaped herself. Reaching for the shampoo, she lathered her hair. Then she scrubbed hard all over. Moving back under the spray, she rinsed and rinsed and rinsed as if by doing so she was eliminating the hurt.

She pulled on the hotel's terry-cloth robe, wrapped her hair in a towel and wandered to the window, gazing down on the procession of headlights that crawled up the dark street like night animals. Candles and flashlights floated along the sidewalks like giant fireflies. From a distance, reality can't be identified, she thought. Must get close to understand.

A few minutes later Logan arrived. "We're confirmed for the morning flight. Tourists caught at Machu Picchu had to cancel. We may be the only passengers."

"Good news for us but bad for them."

"Yeah. The desk clerk says plans for rescue are under way."

She nodded and rewound the towel into a turban. Her knees felt weak. She sank down in a chair at the nearby table.

He sat down opposite her. "The generator's operating for the kitchen only. I'm told hotel lights'll be on soon." He picked up the candle holder on the table as if to study it. "Are you all right?" he asked, running a finger through the flame.

"I think so."

But she knew she wasn't. She unwound the towel from her head, tried to fold it, gave up and dropped it on the floor. Her hair was tangled. Order no longer seemed possible.

He said, "I asked for soup, sandwiches and tea to be sent up. Not much else available."

"Soup sounds good."

He set the candle holder back on the table and they looked at each other as if to assess thoughts. Not knowing what to say, she closed her eyes and waited for him to speak but he didn't. Somehow the silence didn't seem strange to her. Rather, it was a comforting lull, a respected timeout.

Supper arrived. She ate a quarter of a clubhouse sandwich and all of the chicken soup. He devoured his sandwich and the rest of hers. "I'm starved," he said with a laugh.

She laughed, too, not sure why, but the act of doing it relaxed her a bit. She said, "Did you know the first day I worked for you I was scared?"

"No, you never showed it. Right away you impressed me with your thoroughness. After you went home, I discovered you'd even boxed the loose paper clips on top of the filing cabinet."

"You noticed that?" she said with a grin.

He gave the nod of one who had noticed much.

"I wanted to prove I could do the job. Hard to believe that was four years ago."

"Seems longer." He smoothed his thumb across the palm of his other hand. "You came a month after Sandy left."

"Your wife?"

He nodded.

"You said you were in the middle of a divorce but I didn't know when she left. I only knew you were unhappy."

He looked up. "I thought I kept that under cover. How'd you see through it?"

"You worked weekends. All files would be off your desk by Monday, a slew of letters and complaints waiting for me. Mondays were tough."

"Why didn't you say something?"

"I figured if weekend work helped you through your crisis, then I wouldn't mind handling the extra load." Her gesture to sweep away his concern flickered the candlelight. She waited for the flame to stabilize. "What happened to your marriage?"

He cleared his throat and shifted in his seat. "Sandy fell for another guy." He stretched out his legs. "I'm making it sound simple but it wasn't. I can't identify all the miscues, wrong things said, problems handled badly. Little things added up over time—three years, two months, eight days, three hours and ten minutes. The length of our marriage." He snorted. "In my private life, I find it easier to calculate time than know how to deal with it."

Impulsively, she leaned forward and grasped his hands.

"For a while," he said quietly, "I blamed the guy. Then I blamed her. Then myself, the longest blame." He shook his head. "I had to attach fault."

"That's how lawyers make money."

"Yeah, but I'm sick of it. What bothers me most is when it becomes the focus of life, when every problem has to be pinned down as someone's fault."

In a small voice she said, "My mother blames me for my sister's death."

"How did she die?"

"She...drowned."

He slipped his fingers outside hers and squeezed reassuringly.

Closing her eyes, she went on. "I was twelve years old. We were out in the ocean, swimming, laughing, pretending to be mermaids. We splashed water at each other and laughed and laughed. Until the undertow caught us." She swallowed hard. "Then disaster. All at once. I tried to reach her. I couldn't."

Opening her eyes, she said, "I really tried. Mother said I didn't but I did. Beth disappeared. I looked and looked. Then I fought for my life. Barely reached shore. I wanted so much to be forgiven. So much." Her voice broke, her fingers tightened on his hands. "And now, Luis. He died trying to protect me. Because he cared about me, he's dead. I wasn't the cause of my sister's death but I *am* the cause of his."

"It was Luis' decision to protect you."

"But if I hadn't been there...."

"You were there."

She pulled her hands away. "I made a wrong decision, at least I think I did. At the time, it seemed important to tell him the truth. Perhaps I should have told him in Puno. Or maybe not at all."

Slumped in her chair, she let the tears flow. "Lately I've breached a dam inside of me."

"It's good to let it go."

She wiped her tears on the sleeve of her robe. "I'm not sure what's good. Or what I should've done. In your office I felt safe because I operated under set rules and followed every one. I came down here and the world was different. No rules to follow. I made decisions but some of them came disastrously late."

They were quiet for a while. She was aware of his eyes examining her face. Finally, she bolstered up courage and found her voice. "Logan, I know one thing. I can't go back to the office computer and grind out documents, even for you. I need to find a job that in some way helps people, especially those trapped in poverty. I have to figure out the best direction, the right path to take."

She met his eyes, pleading to be understood.

He nodded. "You're a great secretary, Jan, but I realize that's not enough for you. You need to accomplish something significant, and I'm sure you can do it." He shifted in the chair. "As for me, although I enjoy the challenges a lawyer faces, I'd like to carry them to a more meaningful level. Not sure how or where."

"Could we help each other find what we're looking for?"

Logan smiled. "I was hoping you'd say that,"

She reached for her teacup. Somehow she couldn't locate it. "I'm not functioning well right now," she said wearily. "I doubt if I can even make it to my bed."

Before her words were finished, he was there, lifting her to her feet, guiding her over. He eased her under the covers and raised them up under her chin. "Everyone has problems, Jan. All any of us can do is give it our best shot." Leaning over, he kissed her forehead.

She grasped his hands and brought them to her lips. "I'm so glad you came to Peru."

His chin worked up and down in his thoughtful way. "I came because I love you, Jan." He paused and met her eyes. "But I feel it would be a mistake right now if I tried to show you how much."

"You've shown me," she said, a tremor in her voice.

"Want the candles blown out?" he asked as he started for the door.

"No," she replied. "Leave them lit. They'll burn out on their own."

THE END

Made in the USA
Charleston, SC
28 October 2010